I0760896

BLOOD WITCH CURSE

BOOK THREE OF AURA HEALERS HALL

THOMAS K. CARPENTER

Blood Witch Curse

Book Three of Aura Healers Hall

Hardback Version

by Thomas K. Carpenter

Published by Black Moon Books

Cover design by
G&S Cover Designs

Opening Chapter Image by Grand Design
Chapter Header by Andy Vinnikov

Discover other titles by this author on:
www.thomaskcarpenter.com

ISBN-13: 978-1-958498-25-5

The Hundred Halls Universe

Season One

THE HUNDRED HALLS
Trials of Magic
Web of Lies
Alchemy of Souls
Gathering of Shadows
City of Sorcery

THE RELUCTANT ASSASSIN
The Reluctant Assassin
The Sorcerous Spy
The Veiled Diplomat
Agent Unraveled
The Webs That Bind

GAMEMAKERS ONLINE
The Warped Forest
Gladiators of Warsong
Citadel of Broken Dreams
Enter the Daemonpits
Plane of Twilight

ANIMALIANS HALL
Wild Magic
Bane of the Hunter
Mark of the Phoenix
Arcane Mutations
Untamed Destiny

STONE SINGERS HALL
Song of Siren and Blood
House of Snake and Tome
Storm of Dragon and Stone
Sonata of Shadow and Thorn
Well of Demon and Bone

THE ORDER OF MERLIN
The Order of Merlin
Infernal Alliances
Tower of Horn and Blood

The Hundred Halls Universe

Season Two

THE CRYSTAL HALLS

Shadows in Amber

The Emerald Eclipse

The Sapphire Strategem

Chains of Obsidian

The Bloodstone Rebellion

AURA HEALERS HALL

Half-Pint Hex

Full Moon Demon

Blood Witch Curse

Twilight Horn

The Deathless King

Other Works

ALEXANDRIAN SAGA

Fires of Alexandria

Heirs of Alexandria

Legacy of Alexandria

Warmachines of Alexandria

Empire of Alexandria

Voyage of Alexandria

Goddess of Alexandria

KINGMAKERS SAGA

The Stone Tree

The Crystal Bard

The Ghost Tower

The Champion's Prophecy

The Shadow Labyrinth

The Autumn Empire

OTHER SERIES

The Dashkova Memoirs

Gamers

Mirror Shards

BLOOD WITCH CURSE

Arcanium loves books
Coterie adores power
Assassins will kill you
Stone Singers has a stone flower

Animalians is a zoo
Alchemists, you'll devour
Tinkers loves gadgets
Protectors makes you cower

Aura Healers wants to fix you
Blue Flame has a tower
Dramatics loves the spectacle
Oculus has grown sour

One Hundred Halls
Each with their own magic
The Patrons protect
Because faez madness is tragic

In the city of sorcery
Invictus is the Head
His students are many
But the foolish end up dead

- A Children's Rhyme

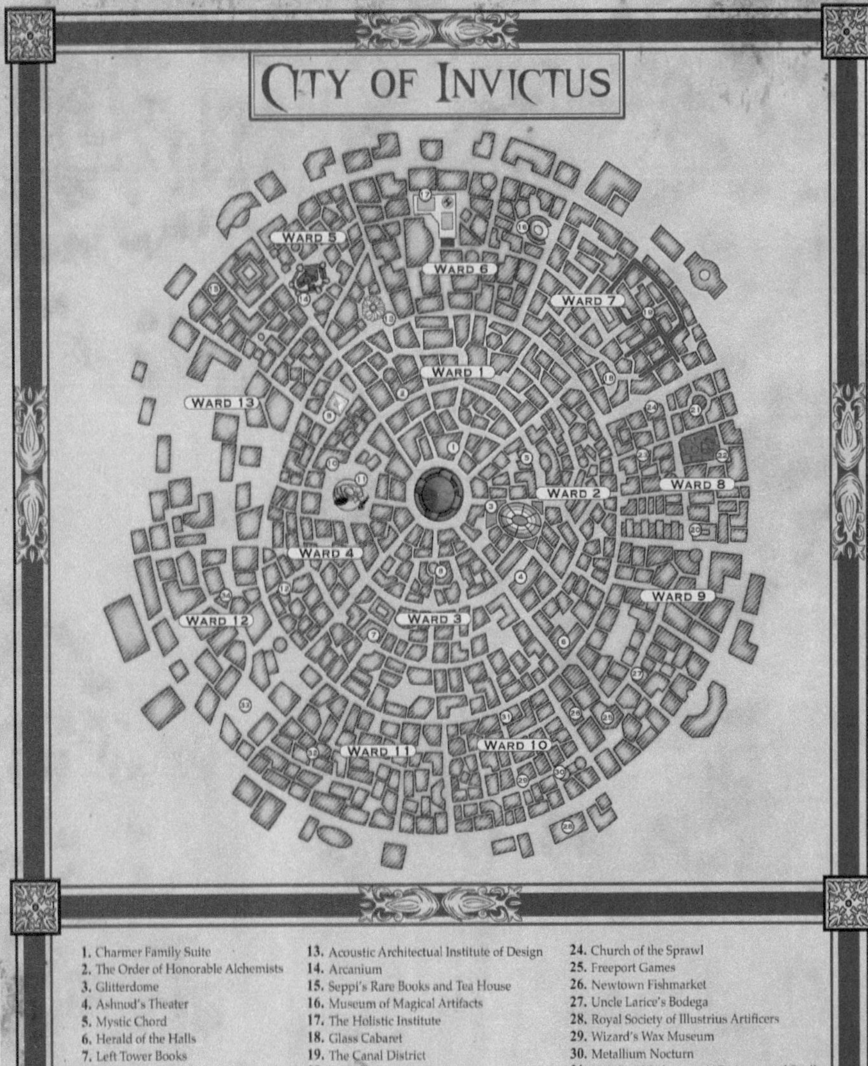

City of Invictus
Ward 5
Ward 6
Ward 7
Ward 1
Ward 13
Ward 2
Ward 8
Ward 4
Ward 9
Ward 3
Ward 12
Ward 11
Ward 10
1. Charmer Family Suite
2. The Order of Honorable Alchemists
3. Glitterdome
4. Ashnod's Theater
5. Mystic Chord
6. Herald of the Halls
7. Left Tower Books
8. Protectors
9. Coterie of Mages
10. City Library
11. Statue of Invictus
12. Amber & Smoke
13. Acoustic Architectual Institute of Design
14. Arcanium
15. Seppi's Rare Books and Tea House
16. Museum of Magical Artifacts
17. The Holistic Institute
18. Glass Cabaret
19. The Canal District
20. Oestomancium
21. Animalians
22. Invictus Menagerie and Cryptozoo
23. Goblin's Romp
24. Church of the Sprawl
25. Freeport Games
26. Newtown Fishmarket
27. Uncle Larice's Bodega
28. Royal Society of Illustrius Artificers
29. Wizard's Wax Museum
30. Metallium Nocturn
31. Howling Madwoman's Fortunes and Spells
32. Enoichian District
33. Oba's Autumnal Garden
34. Gamemakers Hall

ONE

The lights flickered above the patient, bringing Lily's head up as she examined the fixture. The scent of wires burning followed by rich, loamy soil had her confused. The patient, a burly electrician with an arm that looked like a gorilla's, followed her gaze.

"Electrical problems? You'd think a big fancy place like this would be up to snuff on their wiring," said the man in a thick Boston accent. "Or is that why they have a bunch of children as doctors? I swear you're younger than my daughter, but twice as pretty."

Lily inhaled through her nose. The only thing she smelled was the man's body odor and the antiseptic wipes she'd just used on the bite wound on his shoulder. The other scents were no longer present. She looked him straight in the eye and he flinched away.

"Your shoulder should be fine in a few hours. Try not to move and let the ointment work its magic. I'll be back later to check on it."

"A few hours? I got to get back to the job site, or the boss will dock my pay. Do we need to get a second opinion? No offense, but you look like one of those weirdos in the entertainment ward that make their arms grow long, not a doctor."

Lily clucked her tongue. "I'm not a doctor. I'm a healer. It's your choice, but unless you'd like your arm to rot off by the end of the week, I suggest you stay here. Necromites are serious business."

"I've had worse," said the big man, puffing up his chest. "You kids in your fancy coats don't know how good you got it. Last year I nearly had my leg taken off by a speckled locanath in the sewers."

Lily seriously doubted it was a speckled locanath but she wasn't about to get into a pointless argument with a self-important blowhard.

Boon stuck his head through the door, saving her from further interaction. His silver earrings jangled.

"Meeting in the blue room with Dr. Fairlight in five."

Lily pulled the plastic gloves off her hands and tossed them in the bin.

"Fairlight? What's it about?"

Boon shrugged. "Maybe we're getting an award for best Aura Healer class ever."

Lily rolled her eyes.

"Hey, Doc," said the patient.

The earlier confidence seemed watery thin in his eyes.

"I said I'll be back later to check on you."

"I'm gonna be alright, aren't I?"

Lily frowned.

"Make sure you don't touch yourself with that arm. Either arm to be safe. Don't want it to make any other appendages fall off."

Lily marched out of the room as the patient called after. She caught up to Boon. He raised an eyebrow towards the open door.

"A real winner?"

She shook her head. "They found a nest of necromites and he told his co-workers he wasn't afraid of a few measly insects."

Boon whistled. "He's lucky to be alive."

The rest of the third years were waiting when they arrived. Technically, it was still their second year, but the new semester was only a few weeks away. Dr. Decker was standing in back with his arms crossed, looking like someone had pissed in his cereal.

"What's bloody wrong with him?" whispered Lily.

Boon shrugged. "He's been like that all day. I asked him a simple question on rounds earlier and he stared at the wall and never answered. Then he walked out of the patient's room. I had to finish the wound enchantment on my own even though it was my first time using the spell."

The whiteboard had a numbered list scrawled in Dr. Decker's handwriting, but he was making no move to explain it. Lily read the new rules in her head: seven, you can't save everyone, eight, sometimes the best medicine is doing nothing, and nine, magic can do a lot of things but it can't heal the soul. She didn't understand the rules like she had in the previous years.

They seemed more like excuses than rules.

Lily checked back to Dr. Decker, seeing the darkness in his eyes. She couldn't understand the reason for his pain, or the cynicism of his new rules—even more than past years.

The Chief of Staff, Dr. Fairlight, came in a minute later. Her dirty blonde hair had touches of gray around the crown. She gave Dr. Decker a long look before checking her watch twice. The lines around her mouth deepened.

"Thank you for coming on short notice. I'll get started since we're all extremely busy."

She looked over the room as if she expected questions.

"The first order of business is that you'll be starting your rotation in the Curses and Supernatural Virology Ward tonight rather than your normally scheduled time in a few weeks."

The class murmured amongst themselves as Damon raised his hand.

"But I have patients, and the next class won't be replacing us until then."

Dr. Fairlight sighed heavily. "We'll be rearranging the shifts to cover. I'm afraid we have no choice."

"Is there an emergency?" asked Sasha in her posh London accent.

"You could call it that, though it's been going on for some time. The Curses Ward happens to be the oldest part of the hospital complex. Most of it was built in the '60s and half the equipment's probably not much newer. So I'm sure you've heard about the state of the facilities. The good news is that we've found a wealthy donor to upgrade the ward. He's making his first visit later this week and since you'll be the class interacting with him, we pulled your schedule ahead."

Lily checked back to Dr. Decker, who looked like he either hadn't heard or didn't care. He was staring at the floor in a daze while her classmates seemed excited by the news, which was more than unusual. By this time, she would have expected at least one quip from their instructor.

"I bet Dr. Nansoon will be pleased," said Damon, cheerfully nodding.

The head of the Curses Ward was well liked in the hospital and Lily had heard Damon talk more than once during the summer about how excited he was to be working under the head of the department.

Dr. Fairlight's lips flattened. "About Dr. Nansoon. In exchange for a considerable amount of money for the hospital, our donor requested a change in leadership of the department. He wanted the top minds in the discipline to have the best equipment in the world."

A fervor grew like the flapping of wings. Dr. Fairlight held out her hands to quell the rebellion.

"Don't worry. This was agreed upon by all parties. Dr. Nansoon was nearing retirement and looking for less responsibility anyway, and his replacement is the top doctor, probably in the world, when it comes to curses. She spent the last four years in Paris at the head of the Hopital Malediction improving outcomes for the Seine Seven when no one thought they'd live past a month, and before that, she was a member of this very hospital, so I'm pleased to offer her a warm return."

Dr. Fairlight cleared her throat as she looked to the back as if she expected Dr. Decker to say something, but he looked completely unaware of his surroundings.

"With no further ado, I present to you Dr. Christina Martinez!"

A round of tepid applause preceded the entrance of an attractive woman with wavy brown hair, a white coat, and a clipboard under her arm.

Lily caught a whiff of burning wires again, but this time with a hint of rot. She checked the lighting fixtures but there was no flicker. She was about to ask Boon if he smelled it when Dr. Decker marched out of the back of the room, slamming the door behind him.

The entire class went silent. Dr. Fairlight and Dr. Martinez stared after his unusual exit with trepidation.

"Thank you for your warm welcome," said Dr. Martinez, opening her arms and continuing with a clearly prepared speech about how excited she was to be back and how much she would need their support in working with the donor to improve the ward. Lily only barely heard because she was reviewing what had happened with Dr. Decker, trying to figure out why he'd acted like a petulant child.

When Dr. Martinez's speech was finished, the rest of the class surged forward to introduce themselves. Everyone had collectively decided to ignore their eccentric instructor's actions, and the uncomfortable mood washed away as they chatted with the new head of the ward, offering congratulations and their help.

Lily waited until everyone had finished talking to Dr. Martinez before approaching. She offered her hand.

"You must be Lilith de Meath," said Dr. Martinez with a pleasant smile and brown eyes twinkling with intelligence. "I've heard so much about you."

"I prefer Lily, and I ain't heard of you before today, which makes me curious why Decker would be so rude on your first day. Clearly you knew each other from before he went on his walkabout. I hope this won't affect our instruction, as this was the year I was most looking forward to."

Dr. Fairlight held out her hand. "Lily..."

"No," said Dr. Martinez. "I appreciate her directness. It's a fine quality in a doctor as long as they know when to use it. Yes, Oren and I know each other from before. Very well, in fact."

Her gaze flickered towards the door where Dr. Decker had stormed out.

"We were married for ten years."

TWO

The metal tool looked like a cheese grater, or a medieval torture device, Remi hadn't decided. She dragged it across the leg of a woman who seemed oblivious to the painful procedure as she read from the *Herald of the Halls*. Tiny scintillating scales popped loose from her leg, scattering across the cracked, faded tiles.

"How's the ointment coming?" asked Remi, over her shoulder.

The mixer spun in fits and starts. Lily smacked it with her hand and it gave a few seconds of uninterrupted spinning before finally giving out.

"Bloody hell," said Lily, growling at the equipment. "This rich new donor better have deep pockets with the state this ward is in. Would get more done using a bone cauldron."

Remi chuckled under her breath as she shifted the descaler to another portion of the woman's calf.

"Doing okay?"

"Oh, yeah, no worries, love," said the woman with a bright smile. "I have to do this once a month."

Remi checked over her shoulder at Lily's progress. "You really want to work in the Curses Ward after this?"

Lily had jammed a wooden spatula into the ointment and was using her leverage to mix the pasty material.

"Aye, even if there wasn't a rich well-to-do throwing his green about, I'd be asking to work here."

The little bits Lily had revealed to her about the state of her family helped Remi understand the desperation.

"Any ideas which ward you want to specialize in for your final two years?"

Remi shook her head as she exhaled. "I can't believe that time is here. And no. Not a clue."

"You've got an entire year to figure it out."

"You and I both know that it'll be over before we know it. It's already weighing on me."

The grater bit deeper, cutting the woman's leg. Remi grimaced.

"Sorry."

The patient looked over her paper and shrugged. At the same time, the lights flickered.

Remi didn't think anything of it until Lily asked, "Do you smell that?"

After a long inhale through her nose, she said, "Electrical fire?"

"You don't smell the sulfur?"

Remi sniffed again.

"A bit. Smells like rotten eggs if they were being sold by a boutique in the first ward, if that makes sense."

"Aye, it does," said Lily with her head tilted and brow knitted.

"Remind you of something?"

"Those kinds of smells, sulfur and brimstone, like standing in the mouth of a volcano, they're associated with the Fomorians."

"Irish legends?"

"Not legends, real folk from the realm of nightmares. Mara. My people and the Fomorians were at war in the olden days. Probably Damon's clan too."

"Mara?"

"Aye, the realm they hail from," said Lily as she jabbed the wooden spatula into the thick ointment as if she were stabbing someone repeatedly. After a dozen thrusts, the utensil snapped in half, which brought a round of cursing in Gaelic from the Irish witch.

"That was impressive," said Remi with a grin.

Lily pulled a wooden spoon out of a drawer.

"Do the Fomorians still exist?" asked Remi as she continued scraping.

"Of course. After they destroyed their realm they tried to invade the Fae, but got nowhere because they were outmatched, so then they tried this one."

"And then?"

Lily paused with the new spoon in the mixing bowl, rainbow-colored hair more unruly than normal.

"They disappeared. Some of their names show up now and then in myths, but they've learned to hide their devious ways. The Balgae, the druidess Biróg, Balor of the Evil Eye. The last one could open his eye and spew flame and destruction."

Remi snorted. "Watch out for anyone who smells like sulfur and could use a bottle of Visine."

"Visine?" asked Lily.

"Never mind."

Remi used her fingernail to break loose a knot of scales that had gotten stuck in the descaler.

"What do you think of Dr. Martinez?"

"I don't care who she is as long as she can help Medb," said Lily.

"What about Decker's—"

Remi froze when Dr. Decker entered with a datapad under his arm. His flat stare told her that he'd heard.

"How's the descaling?"

The leg barely looked like it'd been worked over despite the pile of shiny scales all over the table and floor.

"Progressing?"

The wrinkles around his mouth creased with shadows.

"Switch to the smaller-grade holes. You should have had all the scales removed already."

"Aye, aye, captain," said Remi, holding up the descaler in a salute. "Not to pry, but are you okay?"

"That sounds suspiciously like prying."

"You're not exactly acting yourself."

Dr. Decker narrowed his gaze. "And how would you know who I really am?"

Remi shared a worried glance with Lily.

"I guess I don't."

"Dr. Decker," began Lily, "were you and Dr. Martinez really married?"

A bell sounding on his datapad had him frowning into its face. He stabbed his finger into the screen before finally looking up.

"We were."

"What's she like?" asked the Irish witch.

Dr. Decker ground his teeth. "Rule number nine."

"Nine? Magic can do a lot of things but it can't heal the soul. What's that have to do with her?"

He jabbed his finger at the datapad. "You'll get your answers in an hour."

Dr. Decker uncharacteristically rushed out of the room, leaving Remi in stunned silence.

"He's as shook as a beggar's cup," said Lily.

The phone in Remi's pocket buzzed. She checked her messages at the same time as Lily.

"Get the same one?" asked Remi.

"Yep. Blue room in an hour."

"What do you think it's about?"

Lily looked after where Dr. Decker had left in a rush.

"I guess we'll find out."

THREE

The AC unit wheezed out mist and warm air as Damon kicked it again, rattling the window. The front had a foot-sized dent from his boot. He gave it another shot, following up with a flat fist on the control panel.

"Sorry, Missus Jacobs. I'll see if I can get maintenance up here to fix it. It's too hot not to have air-conditioning."

The older woman was sitting in bed looking like she was on her way to a party with her hair perfectly curled and wearing ample jewelry around her neck and on her fingers. The only thing missing was that she was wearing the light blue throwaway patient gown rather than something shiny and expensive.

"I would appreciate it, young man," she said, using a folded magazine to cool herself.

A stack of High Arcane magazines sat on a table next to her bed. She'd been reading them when he came in. The front of each cover was a rich former Hall mage who'd gone on to fortune and fame. Damon guessed there weren't many Aura Healers in those pages.

His pocket buzzed, announcing a meeting in the blue room.

"Sorry, Missus Jacobs. I'll swing by maintenance on my way back from this meeting I have to attend."

"If I've melted into a pool of old flesh, you'll know why," she said with a wry grin.

Damon marched across the hospital at a good pace. He'd only been in the Curses Ward for a short time, but he already saw the need for the upgrades. Everything was either outdated, in a state of disrepair, or not working at all.

When he reached the blue room, he found a tall broad-shouldered gentleman in the kind of suit Damon had seen on Missus Jacob's magazines speaking with Dr. Martinez. Half the class had already arrived and were seated on the chairs.

Damon was about to take a spot next to Boon when the gentleman turned and held out his hand.

"You must be Damon Wolfhard."

Damon froze. "I am? I mean, I am."

"Brennan Boleros. I'm going to be your fairy godmother."

Dr. Martinez rolled her eyes. "What Brennan means to say is that he's the donor that's going to fund the ward upgrades."

"That's great, I was just trying—"

Brennan put his hand on Damon's shoulder and gave it a healthy squeeze. Not only was the donor an equally big man, but he was unusually strong. Damon wondered what Hall he was an alumnus of.

"I'd like to chat with you afterwards," said Brennan, gesturing towards the seats.

Damon took a seat next to Remi, who was studying a thin tome in her lap and mumbling under her breath.

"Look at you now."

"Huh?"

"Nothing."

Remi glanced up. "Are the twins in town yet?"

"Two days ago. They stopped by the hospital last night. Trials start tomorrow."

Remi looked him directly in the eyes. "You've nothing to worry about. They're going to crush the trials."

Damon remembered how precarious his own trials had gone. It was hard to be confident in the face of so much uncertainty. He worried just as much about them passing safely as them getting into the Hall of their choice.

A chair crashed into another in the back of the room, startling the class to find Dr. Decker moving through the gaps. He was wearing a fresh white coat over his green scrubs, and his hair was combed in the front.

When he reached Dr. Martinez he tried to give her a hug, but she leaned back and he was forced to maneuver to the side awkwardly. At the same time, Brennan offered a hand but Decker ignored it.

"Ouch," said Boon from behind.

Dr. Decker didn't look himself. He stared at his shoes then out the door with a pinched grimace.

"I think we're all here, so we can get started," said Dr. Martinez with her hands clasped comfortably behind her back. "I'd like to start by introducing our honored guest, Brennan Boleros. I'm sure you've all heard that he's given the hospital a tentative agreement about funding the ward's modernization. But I wanted to talk about the man behind the money—"

She paused, glancing back at him with a warm smile, which Brennan returned with a wink.

"Oh shit," muttered Remi, looking up from her book.

"What?" whispered Damon, leaning over.

Remi gestured back towards the front with mirth in her eyes.

Dr. Martinez turned back to the class. "Brennan has been a supporter of the healing arts for many years. When I was in San Francisco, he came to the rescue of the hospital when a poltergeist outbreak damaged a lot of the equipment and then again in Paris when the Seine Seven needed experimental and very expensive treatments. He's always been there for our patients—"

"Or maybe it's not about the patients," muttered Dr. Decker as he leaned against the wall.

Crimson bloomed on Dr. Martinez's cheeks as she jawed at empty air and squeezed her hands into fists before forcibly relaxing them.

Brennan held up his hand as he stepped forward. "I appreciate the kind words, Christina, but I don't want to make this about me. And that's why I'm here talking to you. The first thing I want to be clear about is how big a challenge this upgrade is going to be. Everything from the building to the equipment to the infrastructure will need to be replaced. And while I have a healthy fortune at my disposal, I cannot do it alone, nor do I want to.

"Fifty-eight percent of first-time donors give similar or increased amounts to the same organization in the following three years. While Golden Willow has a great charity outreach team, I want to get into the pockets of those wealthy families who haven't previously given and who could help this hospital and this city even more."

The class gave Brennan a thunderous round of applause. Everyone except Remi, who was staring with slitted eyes. Damon elbowed her.

"Sorry, I instinctively distrust rich people," she said, taking up the clapping with the rest of her classmates with a throwaway shrug.

When the noise died down, Dr. Decker said in a low voice that carried across the room, "Those rich bastards shouldn't need encouragement."

The mood started to stiffen until Brennan broke into melodic laughter.

"Oren is quite right. Those rich bastards shouldn't need encouragement."

"It's *Doctor* Decker."

Brennan bent at the waist in Decker's direction. "My apologies. I've been hanging around Christina too long."

He turned back to the class.

"Dr. Decker is right. They shouldn't need encouragement, but unfortunately they do. That's where the class comes in. Old rich people love to see the fresh faces that will change the future. They want to know who's going to be using the equipment that their hard-earned money—"

Dr. Decker snorted with derision, receiving a glaring look from Dr. Martinez.

"—that their hard-earned money is paying for. And while the unfortunate stories of your patients might sway some folks, the families that we're going after are more squeamish about the sick, so it's best if they associate our healthy brilliant students with the ward upgrades."

"I guess we're not all as honorable as you," said Dr. Decker with flat lips.

"Oren," said Dr. Martinez quietly.

"It's okay, Christina," said Brennan. "Dr. Decker is free to speak his mind. But what I am going to need from all of you is your help wooing these reluctant benefactors. During the course of the year, we'll be holding a number of events, in the hope of getting them to give us large and very obscene amounts of money. I hope I'll have your support on this important endeavor."

Damon rose with the rest of the class to give Brennan a standing ovation. The applause was briefly marred by Dr. Decker slamming the door on the way out, but the mood wasn't dampened too much, because everyone had spent the last week in the Curses Ward, so they knew how badly the department needed upgrades.

The class circled around Brennan, who charmed everyone with handshakes and jokes, everyone except Remi, who stayed in the back with her arms crossed.

When there was no one else left, Damon approached Brennan as he chatted with Dr. Martinez.

"Damon Wolfhard. Thank you for staying after. What Christina and I wanted to talk to you about was your role in this charity campaign."

"My role?"

He felt an airiness in his chest.

"Look, I'm going to be blunt. This fundraising business is a real shit show. There's lots of palm pressing and forced smiles while eating tiny portions on even tinier plates. I've done enough of these things to know that you have to rely on a few superstars to bring home the bacon."

Damon checked around the empty room. "I'm not a superstar. Nor am I that great with people. You should get Boon or Sasha."

Brennan reached out and squeezed his shoulder. "They're both great, but after reviewing everyone's history, I know you're the man for the job. Between your family's tragic history, the fact that your twin sisters are joining the Halls this year, and your personal story, you're gonna knock 'em dead. Not only that, but the rich love a good therianthrope. Especially a werewolf."

Damon fought to keep his hackles from rising.

"I know, Damon. I know. It's ugly business, this fundraising thing, but I know these people. It takes a certain kind of story to get them to give up their money."

Dr. Martinez put a comforting hand on his forearm. Her floral perfume was soothing.

"Brennan knows what he's talking about. I've seen him work a room. His presence alone at a charity event usually triples the take."

"I want to help, I just worry that I won't be good at it," said Damon.

"You've nothing to worry about," said Brennan. "Christina and I will be there by your side to guide you through these events, and after the first one, I bet you'll find you like them. Trust me, there are benefits to having wealthy donors as friends."

He winked at Dr. Martinez, eliciting another eye roll from her.

"You're such a child, Brennan," she said with a dimpled smile.

"Don't worry about it right now," said Brennan. "We won't be having our first event for a little while."

Damon thought about the AC unit in Missus Jacob's room. "If you want to help right now, I have a patient who's sweltering in a room without AC."

Brennan hesitated then reached into his wallet. He handed over a wad of bills.

"Pick up a unit at the local hardware store. Are you in?"

"Of course. I'll do anything to help the patients of Golden Willow."

"Great. And I would tell you good luck on your sisters' behalf but I'm sure they'll have no problem getting into Dramatics and Protectors," said Brennan as he gave Dr. Martinez a hug and left the room.

"How did he know what Halls they want to get into?" asked Damon after Brennan was gone.

"That's why he's so good at raising money. He makes sure he knows people, what makes them tick, what motivates them."

Damon frowned. "He wasn't, like, going to interfere with their admission process, was he?"

Dr. Martinez lifted a shoulder. "He'll probably give the selection committee a kind word about your sisters. Don't worry, Damon. He's a real straight shooter. Nothing will be out of bounds."

The weight of the bills in his hand was heavy. "I should go do something about the AC unit. Could probably buy a half dozen with this."

Damon headed back the other way, looking to find the head of maintenance. He was headed to the offices when he felt a worrying prickle on the back of his neck and half-turned to find a black cat strutting down the tiles after him.

The black cat froze when spotted and turned its head in an almost human manner before sprinting the opposite direction and disappearing around the corner. He shook his head and by the time he'd reached the maintenance offices, he'd completely forgotten about the cat.

FOUR

They're coming to get me! I need protection!"

The patient stood on the bed with his arms above his head, cheeks crimson from shouting. The blue gown was only half tied, so half his hip was peeking out. Lily checked behind her to see if Dr. Decker had returned, but he'd chased Dr. Martinez down the hall a short time ago and it appeared he wasn't coming back.

"Don't worry, Mr. Rohas. We won't let anything happen to you. You're safer than a lamb in a manger at Golden Willow," said Lily.

"Or a lamb to the slaughter," said Mr. Rohas. "He looked at me with those bloodred eyes. He's out to murder me, Doctor."

"For the third time, I'm a healer not a doctor, Mr. Rohas, and would you please return to your bed before you hurt yourself."

"I… I—"

Lily checked the hallway to make sure no one was in listening range.

"The other options is I can put a Body Bind Lock on you and you won't be moving for the next three hours, which means you'll probably mess yourself if you have to use the jacks."

Mr. Rohas screwed up his face. "Jacks?"

Lily growled under her breath. "The pisser. The bathroom."

The patient lowered himself into a sitting position and finally noticed that he was exposing himself. He pulled the covers over his hips while he kept his gaze firmly locked on the open door.

"I swear to you, nothing will happen."

"But my curse."

"Twasn't a proper country curse, but a good ol' hex found in any local spell shop. We'll get it unraveled in a few days max, but we can't do a thing until you sit still."

"I can't believe she did that to me," said Mr. Rohas, running his hands through his lush black hair.

"Maybe you shouldn't have cheated on Jenny."

The patient scowled and crossed his arms. She knew she wasn't supposed to moralize with the patients but he'd admitted to sleeping around on numerous occasions, sometimes two or three times in a week. The fact that his Jenny hadn't done worse was a miracle.

"It wasn't my fault," said Mr. Rohas. "Jenny's sister hit on me. I didn't know how to say no."

"With her sister?"

The words tumbled out of Lily's mouth.

"Right? See, you get it. It wasn't my fault."

The shock wasn't that he'd slept with his girlfriend's sister, but that the sister had initiated it, or even participated. Lily couldn't believe that siblings would do that to each other. None of her sisters would ever hurt one another like that, and if they had, the rest of the family would make sure they knew how badly they'd screwed up.

"Doctor?"

Lily found herself staring out the window.

"Woolgathering."

"Is this another sheep thing?"

"Thinking about how much I miss my sisters."

Mr. Rohas stared into his lap. "Oh." He paused. "They live in England?"

Lily put her hands on the bed. "I will pretend, Mr. Rohas, that you did not say that. They live in Ireland. It's an entirely different place."

The patient cocked a smile that she assumed he thought was endearing.

"Are any of them as cute as you?"

If she wasn't working at Golden Willow, she would have taught him a lesson using a spell, just like his ex-girlfriend Jenny, but she didn't want to get in trouble.

Again.

Lily offered a derisive smile.

"My sister Evangel has been known to make men go mad due to her beauty, and Nyx has been confused for being Fae on more than one occasion."

"Two sisters? Nice."

Lily ignored him.

"Those are my sisters who men talk about the most, but all my sisters are beautiful in their own way. Zella is as fit as a footballer, Alice is cute but far too young for you, Kerensa has a wicked tongue that drives men to do stupid things, and even Biddy, the oldest, could turn a man's head if she decided to put aside the matronly schoolmarm look. But even if my sisters were in the city of sorcery, I would advise them to stay as far away from you as possible, Mr. Rohas."

"Oh."

"Like I said, we'll get you fixed up in no time. But this event should be a warning that one day you'll piss off the wrong woman who knows more than a five-dollar hex she found at a discount spell shop. Next time, you might find yourself turned into a sweet and delicious little lamb, or banished to another realm entirely."

Lily had meant to scare him, but the way he was staring in abject horror with his jaw dropped and his eyes wide with fright made her wonder if she'd overdone it. Then she realized he wasn't staring at her, but over her shoulder.

She turned slowly, not wanting to spook whatever was behind her.

The glimpse was brief.

The only thing she saw was the eyes. Baleful, menacing eyes. Floating near the ceiling.

Then it fled.

"Bollocks."

Lily ran into the hallway, checking both ways. She spotted a haze in the air to her right and followed the apparition at a full sprint.

She nearly lost it at the nurses station. The two women and one man working stopped their conversation when she stumbled to a stop.

"What's wrong?"

Lily closed her eyes for a moment, feeling the presence of the ghost. She sensed the dislocation to her left and ran after it. The being had a head start and it flew like a wind spear. She was running full out when she came around the corner, nearly slamming into two familiar women.

The ghost chase fled from Lily's mind as she stared in surprise at two of her sisters.

"Biddy. Alice. What are you doing here?"

FIVE

Nurse Mandy caught Remi in the hallway on the way to the cafeteria. It'd been a long day. She'd been leeching the blood from a cursed pustule that kept refilling itself despite the gallons already removed. The leeches, glistening black creatures as big as her thumb, had been acquired from Arcane Phytology Hall's botany dome because they'd been modified by magic to remove cursed blood.

"They're scaring the patients," said Nurse Mandy, then she gave Remi a once-over, screwing up her face. "Did you get in a fight with a blood bag?"

The front of Remi's scrubs had crimson splatters all over the front.

"Who?"

Nurse Mandy startled out of her thoughts. "The witches."

"The witches."

"You know, Lily and her sisters. They're arguing near the faez imaging machine, scaring the patients waiting for their scan."

"Lily's sisters?"

Remi wasn't sure why but a sense of cold dread filled her stomach.

"Yeah. One of them's cute as a button, but barely looks old enough to be out of high school while the other looks like she breaks rulers over students' rears for fun."

"Alice," said Remi. "And Biddy."

She'd heard Lily talk about her sisters enough to know them from a brief description.

"What are they doing here?"

"I don't know, but everyone's afraid to talk to them," said Nurse Mandy. "But when I saw you, I knew you'd be able to get them to calm down."

"I'll take care of it."

"Thanks, Remi. And don't be a stranger. I miss our little breaks in the parking lot."

"I'll make time," said Remi as she hurried the other way.

She heard the de Meath sisters long before she saw them. Three women, angrily speaking in a mix of heavily accented English and Irish Gaelic made it impossible to understand what was being said. Most of the yelling was coming from Lily and Biddy, while Alice was standing to the side in an emerald peasant dress, her big green eyes observing the argument with a sense of sadness.

"...you've no bloody right!" yelled Lily uncharacteristically.

Except for the time she'd gotten in an argument with Dr. Decker, Remi had never seen Lily get angry, but her cheeks were blotched from shouting.

The older de Meath sister answered in Gaelic until the end, which Remi caught as she came up to the three women.

"...lack of progress forced Medb to send us across this bloody and cursed ocean."

"Hey—"

The word was barely out of Remi's mouth before Biddy de Meath turned on her. Lily's sister was barely in her late twenties, but looked like she'd been born in the 1800s on the prairie, wearing a drab gray smock over a beige dress. Auburn hair was pulled back into a severe bun at the back of her head that pulled the flesh of her forehead tight.

"Whoever you are, this doesn't concern you," said Biddy. "Please remove yourself from this conversation while I converse with my absent sister."

"I know who you are, but that doesn't mean you have the right to scream like a lunatic in the middle of the hospital."

Remi extended her arm towards the open door across the hallway where a roomful of scared patients were staring out with concern.

"Then where do you suggest?" asked Biddy with her chin raised.

"Come with me."

Remi led the three sisters to a nearby waiting room. The single gentleman reading a golfing magazine in his sport jacket immediately scurried out when they arrived. Remi put a privacy enchantment on the door before spinning around.

"Okay, now you can yell and scream like a bunch of banshees."

Three sets of widened eyes followed her comment. Lily started to open her mouth, but Biddy turned on her.

"I'll take care of this, just as I have to for the entire family."

Remi expected a retort from Lily, but her roommate looked like she'd been hit in the forehead with a two-by-four.

"Don't you dare use that slur," said Biddy, shaking her finger in Remi's face.

"Slur? Sorry, I thought it was just a term for a ghost."

"Biddy. Bridget. Please. She'd have no way of knowing," said Lily, appearing reduced by the encounter. "This is my roommate, Remi. Remi, these are my sisters, Biddy and Alice."

The younger de Meath curtseyed, holding the flared portion of her dress wide.

"Lovely to meet you," said Alice with a glance of embarrassment directed at her sisters.

Biddy stared down at Remi, who felt like she was about to be run over by a drab semi with green headlamps.

"You've said your piece, now let me speak to my troublesome sister. Alone."

Remi never thought she'd see the day Lily was called troublesome.

"I don't like the way you're speaking to my friend," said Remi, crossing her arms.

"This doesn't concern you."

"Maybe you don't understand the point of friends. Stuff like this *does* concern me, because it concerns Lily."

"Remi..."

Remi ignored her friend's pleading tone.

"You want it to concern you?" asked Biddy. "Did you beg your sisters to let you join the Halls so you could save our Medb? And then after we let you, you squandered this opportunity playing nursemaid to foolish sick people who probably deserved their fate rather than fix our patron?"

Remi got back into Biddy's face. "These aren't foolish sick people at Golden Willow." She paused. "Most of them anyway. But even the worst of them deserve their care, and your sister, Lilith, is really bloody good at helping them."

Biddy spoke low and mean. "I don't think you understand that if Medb dies, an entire generation of witches die, and then all the people and creatures we protect will follow. Medb is the first domino of many."

"Well you don't understand that Lily has saved this city from numerous threats that would hurt or even kill a lot of people," said Remi, putting her hands on her hips.

"Remi...please..."

"Hush, Lil," said Biddy, holding out a dismissive hand.

"Don't call me Lil," said Lily in a whisper.

"There is no one more important than Medb. That's why we agreed Lil could come to the Halls, but it appears we were wrong to grant this selfish endeavor."

"Biddy," said Alice, putting her hand on her older sister's arm. She had a soft voice that matched her doe eyes. "You shouldn't be so hard on Lily. She gave up a lot to come here."

The corners of Biddy's lips curled towards the floor. "Sometimes I think that's *why* she came here."

Remi caught the resentment of the eldest sister, but there was little time to ponder when Lily stepped forward.

"Remi. I just remembered, I was boiling water for tea in the room when I ran into my sisters. Would you go back and turn it off for me?"

The sweetness in her roommate's voice confused Remi more than the request to turn off a teapot that had been broken for a week.

"Why are you even here?" asked Remi.

Biddy crossed her arms. "To speed our dear sister's efforts up, and if this ill-conceived attempt cannot be salvaged, to bring her back home."

"I don't want us to get in trouble for having the teapot in our room," said Lily quietly. "We need to hide it, or they'll make us *change* roommates."

The heavy emphasis on the word *change* made Remi realize she wasn't talking about the broken teapot, but it was a code for something else. Change? Changeling. Neko.

"Right," said Remi, shaking her head. "Sorry. I'll go right away. You can continue your argument. I'm sure I'll see you around."

She moved towards the door while Biddy watched with suspicion.

"Biddy," said Lily. "If you have something to say, now is the time, or

I need to get back to rounds."

Once Remi was in the hallway, she hurried towards their room in haste. She wasn't sure why she needed to hide Neko, but it was clear that was Lily's intent.

Or so she hoped.

When Remi burst into the room, the white rat was asleep on her bed, curled on a pile of dirty laundry. Little whiskers shifted with questions as the rat squeaked softly.

"Lily's sisters are here. You have to hide yourself."

Remi ran over to the window and opened it.

"Go hunt. Anything but stay here."

Neko stood and stretched with his pointed nose facing downward.

"Please, hurry. I don't know why, but Lily clearly has a reason. You need to hide."

The sound of heavy footsteps approaching had Remi quickly locking the door. A second later, the handle rattled.

"I demand entry," said Biddy from outside.

Remi grabbed Neko and set him on the windowsill as she opened it up.

"Please," she whispered. "Go hunt. Get out of here."

"Who are you whispering to?" asked Biddy.

A low murmuring outside told Remi that an unlocking spell was incoming.

Remi pushed on the white rat's little round butt. Neko shimmered like a mirage for a few seconds and then expanded into a larger form that looked like a raccoon with monkey paws. He scurried out the window, heading up the brick wall towards the roof.

As the door started to swing open, Remi grabbed the broken teapot from under the bed and put it on the table.

Biddy marched into the room with Lily and Alice standing outside.

The eldest de Meath sister ignored Remi and the teapot, heading straight to the open window. She looked out in all directions before scanning the room.

"What are you hiding from me, *sister*?"

"Nothing, *sister*," said Lily.

Biddy approached the teapot. "It's not even on."

"It's broken," said Remi. "I threw the water out before you got here, but I think it finally died after two years of regular use. A bummer, but I'm sure we can afford a better one now."

Remi smiled sweetly at Biddy, who sensed the deception by her pinched expression. After a few seconds of locked eyes, Biddy made a disappointed grunt under her breath and marched out of the room.

"Come, Alice. We need to acquire lodging."

Biddy paused, checking over her shoulder.

"We'll be back to discuss your ineptitude later, Lil."

After the sound of footsteps retreated to silence, Lily spoke under her breath.

"It's Lily."

SIX

Damon was reviewing the faez analysis for a patient of his in the Curse Ward who had had a spell backfire, binding him with golden chains that they'd so far been unable to break, when Boon came running up out of breath.

"We need you right away."

Damon tucked the clipboard under his arm.

"Lead the way."

They ran down two hallways, narrowly avoiding a food cart and two separate gurneys. Damon reviewed procedures from their first year in the ER, expecting an emergency, though he wondered why it wasn't something Boon could fix.

When they burst into the fourth floor break room, he found not a life-or-death emergency but a group of his fellow Aura Healers standing around a long table filled with alchemy implements, two plates of hot dogs, some cups, a spell-test dummy, and other equipment from their over two years of work in Golden Willow.

"Oh, thank Merlin," said Ethan. "You're the only one that can beat her."

"Beat her?"

All eyes shifted to Sasha. A wrestling championship belt hung on her shoulder. She wore a white coat over her Union Jack shirt with her arms up high in victory position.

"I thought there was an emergency."

Boon put a hand on his shoulder. "There is. If we let Sasha stay champion we'll never hear the end of it. Think about it, mate. Do you really want to suffer this all year?"

As if prompted, Sasha turned and fired finger guns at them, each shot sparking with faez.

"Aces, baby! You think you can mess with London, baby, I'll give you the raw end of my boot."

Sasha rode up on Ethan's hip, humping him like an ill-behaved canine in heat.

"I fucked you up last round. Can't be beaten, 'cause you know I'm the Princess of Power, baby! The Duchess of Kickin' Your Dick In! The Baroness of Badassery! The Queen of—"

"Sasha! Enough!" said Boon. "See?"

"I don't have the slightest clue what's going on," said Damon, rubbing his forehead.

"It's the Initiate Olympics," said Sasha, continuing to fire finger guns and hump an exasperated Ethan, who stared out the doorway with a blank expression.

"It's the Idiot Olympics, is what it looks like," said Damon.

"Doesn't matter what it looks like. What matters is popping this annoying balloon with questionable teeth."

"That's rude," said Sasha, squeezing her lips tight.

"Come on, Damon. Please," said Boon.

Damon sighed heavily, seeing the need in his friend's face.

"Fine. What do I have to do?"

Boon exhaled. "Oh, thank Merlin. Look, it's very simple. First you have to titrate this potion, removing the nightshade extract. Then you use the five elements to heat up this beaker until it hits one ninety-eight. Next is the divining rod, which you'll use on this test dummy. You have to make the aura purple before you can move on. Then you eat these half dozen hot dogs."

"Hot dogs? What the hell does that have to do with being an Aura Healer?" asked Damon.

"Duh, we never get time for a full meal, so we have to scarf it down," said Boon.

Damon frowned. "Right. Makes sense. Go on."

"Then you cast Nystul's Illuminating Aura until you can see your hand bones. Last is a cup of Jeb's special energy potion and then you have to put this suture in your own arm one-handed. Five stitches."

"After the energy potion? Blood and bone, you guys are sadistic."

Boon held up his left arm, which had a jagged line of stitches along his wristbone.

"Tell me about it."

"Let's get this over with. I don't want Dr. Decker to freak out on us because we're not doing our work."

"Oh, Decker's already been here. Sasha wiped the floor with him. He blamed his failure on not being as practiced as we are at these tasks."

Bryan spoke up from the corner. "And he nearly choked on the hot dogs."

Damon gathered near the front of the long table. He reviewed the steps in his head as Sasha bounced on her heels.

"Contestants! Are you ready?" asked Boon with his arms up, drag race style.

Damon nodded.

"Three. Two. One. Go!"

Right away, Damon was behind.

Sasha was a wiz in the alchemy lab. She titrated the nightshade in half the time. He moved on to the beaker heating by the time she was halfway done with hers. He poured as much faez as possible into the flames, which singed the hairs on the back of his hand, but the way the others were cheering for him made him not want to disappoint.

He started to catch up with the diving rod on the test dummy. Sasha looked like she was flagging after multiple rounds.

When he got to the hot dogs, she already had two down, but looked like she was struggling. Damon dipped into his therianthrope nature, which helped his jaw extend so he could engulf each hot dog in two bites.

Nystul's Illuminating Aura was simple, but when he reached the sutures, he realized why they'd had to drink the energy potion. Right away his hands were shaking from the sudden burst of power. He'd been ahead, but Damon looked up to see Sasha on the third stitch while he was struggling with the second.

"Go Damon! Come on!" yelled Boon.

Not wanting to disappoint his friends, he didn't bother with neat lines or being careful puncturing his flesh and rammed the needle through his arm, completing five jagged stitches to win the match.

"Winner!"

He held up his hands as Sasha slumped against the table. Boon was patting him on the back around the time he heard soft clapping from the entrance.

As Sasha placed the championship wrestling belt on his shoulder, he found himself face-to-face with Brennan.

Heat rose to Damon's cheeks.

"This probably looks—"

"You don't have to apologize," said Brennan with a smirk. "I've been around hospitals long enough to know that residents, and especially trainees, blow off steam in a variety of unusual ways."

He tilted his head.

"Though this one has to be the strangest."

Damon belched behind a closed fist, hating the smell of the hot dogs that came back up.

"Can I speak to you outside?"

Damon followed Brennan into the hallway. Damon was used to being the tallest, so it felt strange to be looking up at the wealthy donor.

"Again, I'm really sorry—"

"You don't have to be. I totally understand. You work long hours on rude and unappreciative patients. Blowing off steam is natural."

Damon nodded as he looked at his shoes. His nerves were still firing from Jeb's elixir and his arm was bleeding from the rough stitches.

"Remember when I told you I'd be needing you soon? The first charity event of the season is next week, a swanky place in the fourth ward near the Coterie Obelisk."

"I don't know. I'll have to check the schedule."

Brennan smirked. "I already checked with Christina. She cleared you that night."

"Then I guess I'm in."

"Fabulous." He looked him up and down. "I'll have a suit sent to your room. If there are any problems, I'll send my tailor over to make adjustments."

"Your tailor..."

Brennan cocked a smile. "The advantages of being fabulously wealthy." He checked his expensive watch. "I have to meet Dr. Fairlight for some discussions about vendors, but I wanted to stop by first and let you know. Thanks for doing this. I know it's not what you thought you'd be doing when you joined Aura Healers."

"Happy to help my patients in whatever way possible."

Brennan was halfway down the hallway when he turned and snapped his fingers.

"Oh, and bring a plus one. Whoever it is, let Christina know. I have an account at a boutique she can use for a dress." His forehead bunched up. "Or he. Whoever you'd like."

"See you around?" replied Damon after the wealthy businessman left. He didn't know what to think about the charity event, except that it was like a difficult procedure that had to be done to save the patient. Which in this case was the entire Curse Ward. As if to prove why he needed to attend the event, the lights flickered momentarily, buzzing with energy clicking to darkness.

SEVEN

A light rain pattered against the metal on the HVAC as Lily looked out upon the city from the roof picnic table while Neko lounged on her lap. Half the Spire was hidden by the blanket of gray clouds, which made the city seem almost normal, except for the hazy illusions she could see in the second ward reflecting on the fog bank.

"I thought I'd find you here," said Remi, coming up from behind. "Your sisters are in the building."

Lily stroked Neko's back as the white rat shuddered at the mention of her sisters. The world outside the hospital was peaceful, even with the whirl of an incoming helicopter. She could stay on the roof all day if circumstances were otherwise.

"I know."

Remi plopped onto the picnic table and stroked Neko's back, which prompted Lily to lean into her friend's shoulder.

"Is that why you're up here?"

Lily sighed. "The weather reminds me of home."

Remi craned her neck at the sky. "Dreary."

"Sunshine always follows rain."

"What's the deal? We haven't had a chance to talk since then, but clearly you don't want Biddy finding Neko."

"I—"

The words barely left her mouth when she heard the heavy footsteps of Biddy's wooden shoes clapping on pebbles on the tar roof.

"Neko, behind!"

The white rat leapt onto the ground, while Lily spun and held her arms out protectively.

"You fecking eejit!"

A single strand of dark brown hair had escaped Biddy's severe bun, giving her an unhinged appearance.

"What the fook are you doing with that *agathrú*?"

Biddy had her hands up. The smell of sorcery was in the air, but Lily kept her arms wide and made no motion for spells. She didn't want it to escalate.

"Biddy. Stop. Neko isn't dangerous."

"You're a bloody fool if you think that," said Biddy.

Alice came running up from behind. She'd changed out of the peasant dress and was wearing jeans and a Halls sweatshirt. Her hand went to her mouth when she saw what was going on.

"What's going…? Oh no, Lily."

Clued in by Remi's wide-eyed stare, Lily checked behind her to see Neko had transformed into a tiger-like being with three-inch claws.

"Why are they so concerned? What haven't you told me about Neko?" asked Remi, face scrunched up.

"Do you trust me?"

"Of course."

Electricity crackled off Biddy's fingertips. "You can't trust a bloody changeling, Lil. You should know that. Move aside so I can take care of it. If you don't, I can't promise you won't get hurt."

"Wait a fucking second," said Remi, turning on Biddy. "Before anyone is casting a single spell, I want to know what's going on. You too, Lily. You told me Neko was safe, but their reactions tell me that's not the whole story."

The rain picked up its pace, tinking off the metal and coating everyone in a light sheen. Lily's stomach twisted as she saw the disappointment in Remi's eyes.

"Agathrú are the worst kind of tricksters," said Biddy with a snarl. "They lure children into the forest, then after they get lost, take their place in the family, sucking life energy from the parents until their deception is revealed. By then, the child is long dead and the changeling moves on to another family."

"That's not Neko."

Remi turned towards her sisters. "I agree with Lily. We wouldn't be alive without his help." Then back to Lily. "But I need to know the whole story. Neko's living in my room, after all."

"Changelings are Fae creatures, but not bound to it like a Green Man or the faerie folk. They're unaffected by the corruption."

"That doesn't tell me a damn thing you haven't already said."

Lily closed her eyes.

She'd missed her sisters so much, but why did it have to be Biddy? Why couldn't it have been Nyx, or even Kerensa? They could have had a lovely time catching up and laughing about all the men they'd twisted into knots with their looks and sharp-tongued wit. There'd been a time when Biddy had been fun to be around, but that had been when Lily was young and the eldest de Meath hadn't drained the joy out of her own heart in an attempt to be like their mother.

"The original changelings were bred to sniff out Fomorians when the two peoples were at war. They would even sneak into Mara as spies to learn their plans, but once the Oak Father beat back those devils, the agathrú were allowed to go wild. More wild than they already were. It's true, some snuck through the barrier between realms, especially in the years when it was thin, and caused pain and misery in the Emerald lands. But that's not Neko."

"If this isn't proof enough that I should drag you back home to face a tribunal from the sisterhood, I don't know what is," said Biddy.

The electricity no longer danced across her fingertips, but her arms were still half-raised.

"I'm not going back. I came here for a reason, Bridget."

"You've had two years to find a solution. It appears to me you just used this as an excuse to get away from your sisters. They'll be so hurt when I tell them the truth," said Biddy.

"That's not bloody fair, and you know it," said Lily, wiping her cheek with the back of her hand. "I gave up everything, my connection to Medb, the Eó Ruis tree, my home, my *sisters*. Everything."

She looked to Remi.

"And I don't regret a moment. No. I haven't found the solution to the corruption yet. Or how to fix Medb. But I haven't stopped trying. We won't find a solution back home, no matter how nice it is. I know in my heart the city of sorcery is where we'll find the truth. Our truth. And save our family from the kalkatai. Please, Biddy. You have to understand. You have to give me more time."

Lily was so overflowing with emotion, she almost missed the curling of Biddy's fingers. When the limb-lock spell came flying from her lips at Neko, Lily threw herself in the way.

Her limbs stiffened until she was a board, slamming onto the hard roof, giving Neko a chance to leap away, bounding over the HVAC unit and disappearing onto other parts of the hospital roof.

Remi knelt by her side, holding her up as her body convulsed with the impacts of the magic.

"You bitch. That's your sister."

Remi rose up and started to go after Biddy, but she knocked her away with a simple push spell. The limb lock hadn't hit Lily directly, so she was able to sit up slightly.

"Remi, don't. She outclasses you."

The warning didn't dissuade her friend, who threw herself at Biddy with fists swinging. Lily's older sister casually shaped a ball of golden light covered in leaves and vines and threw it at Remi. The cage captured her. Remi pounded her fists against the spherical barrier, shouts lost to the magic and the increasingly heavy rain.

"I've got you," said Alice, helping Lily into a sitting position.

"You're too sweet," said Lily.

Biddy snarled at them. "Don't let your sister fool you, Alice. She's abandoned the family. She only cares for herself now."

Before Lily could muster a retort, Biddy stormed away. A few seconds after she left, the golden vine cage that held Remi collapsed, letting her fall to the ground.

"What in the Merlin was that?"

Alice helped Lily sit at the picnic table.

"Our eldest sister is the strongest witch of her generation," said Alice softly.

"I thought Lily was powerful."

Lily hung her head. "No. Biddy has more raw power than any of the rest of us. But she's bloody stubborn and thinks she knows better than everyone else, which makes her the worst of us."

"She's said the same thing about you," said Alice with a frown.

Lily looked up into her kind sister's face. "Why did you come, Alice?"

"I wanted to make sure Biddy wasn't too hard on you. I know how you two fight, and I hate it."

"I know that's not the whole truth."

Alice placed a flat hand under her chin and offered a weak smile.

"I wanted to see the city of sorcery. As you said, it's the most important place in the world. Why wouldn't a witch want to visit it?"

It was the truth, but Lily also saw the fear of what would happen if Medb died, which would destroy the sisterhood. Alice had come to Invictus to see the sights before she might die, which made what was at stake all the more real.

EIGHT

The VIM, or Veil Imaging Machine, looked like it'd been designed in a torture facility. A spikey crown hung over the patient's head while the arms of the equipment looked like pincers about to rip them apart. It'd been made in the '70s when designs were purely functional.

"I know," said Remi to Jasmine, a young woman around her age with umber skin and wide, fearful eyes. "It looks like it comes from the Oestomancer's Carnival, but I assure you, looks are deceiving."

"How does it know if there are ghosts attached to me?" asked Jasmine, staring suspiciously at the machine.

"I don't have the slightest idea how it works. The normal technician is out sick today. There's been a rash of illnesses, but there's not much to it and it really isn't dangerous," said Remi.

It wasn't the whole truth. There were ways in which it could fail, but she wasn't about to frighten the patient, who looked ready to run out of the room.

"Lean back," Remi told her.

Jasmine rested her shoulders against the body-shaped catch. Remi pulled the spiked crown atop her head, the soft points gently resting against her tight Afro. The pincers wrapped around the patient, mostly to keep her from moving too much.

The control panel had a power dial, an overload meter, and three buttons. Start. Stop. Emergency Shutdown. The last one was under a plastic case so no one accidentally pressed it.

"Alright, Miss Crockett. Remember, there's nothing to worry about. The VIM just gives us a peek into the Veil to see if anything is hanging on you, causing those weird things to keep happening."

"I just want to know why," said Jasmine tepidly. "I haven't been able to have a date in months. Ghosts keep scaring 'em off."

"We'll get you sorted out," said Remi.

Before she'd joined Aura Healers, she never would have imagined using that phrase, or operating equipment like the VIM machine, but here she was. Remi clucked her tongue in amusement.

After she pressed the start button, the machine slowly wound up, wheezing like an old man running a marathon. The whine hurt her ears for the first few seconds before shifting into a more pleasing hum.

Soft, greenish light came out of the thorns on the crown, illuminating the patient's head. Remi had witnessed the machine's use before, but it still left her with lingering dread in her stomach.

The Veil was the place between the living and the dead. Most of what she'd read in her studies strongly suggested that it was to be left alone. Living creatures were not tolerated in that realm for long and those that did dare to explore sometimes brought things back with them that they would later regret. The VIM machine was only illuminating things from the Veil, not actually opening a portal, but the connection was still worrisome.

"What's happening?" asked Jasmine.

Remi stared at the machine as if it would tell her something. "Try not to move your head."

"I don't like this."

"It's just machine noise," said Remi.

"Not that. The other noise."

Remi turned her head. "What noise?"

Jasmine grimaced.

"It's hard to hear."

"Maybe it's part of the machine," said Remi, elevating her voice to be heard over the high hum.

"No. I've heard it before."

"What does it sound like? Just tell me, don't move your arms."

Jasmine paused with thought. "Like light clapping. As if someone was applauding me from a distance."

Remi screwed up her face as she tried to imagine the sound Jasmine had described.

"I'm not hearing it. Let me turn up the VIM."

The dial went from zero to one hundred, with the safe range ending at seventy-five percent. She turned it until it was around sixty, which was the beginning of the yellow range. The hum increased in frequency, making Remi's teeth ache slightly.

"Can you hear it now?"

"Oh, yeah," said Jasmine, nodding. "Real good. The clapping is getting faster."

Remi was supposed to stay behind the control panel, but she wanted to hear the noise that Jasmine was describing, so she moved near the patient. At first, she didn't hear anything, then she could pick out the soft applause, which rose and fell in tempo.

"Maybe this isn't a ghost," said Remi, shaking her head. "But what it is, I don't know."

"Are we done yet?" pleaded Jasmine.

"A little bit longer. I feel like we should figure this out while you're in the VIM."

After returning to the control panel, Remi set the machine at the limit. The overload meter was well below the red range, so she felt comfortable in its operation.

When Remi looked up, she saw an apparition near the VIM. He was hazy and hard to see, as if through a fog cloud.

"Oh, I hear it for sure now," said Jasmine, nodding.

Remi crept back around, examining the ghostly image that was to the patient's left. Details came into focus as she neared.

"He looks like someone your age, messy dirty blond hair, wearing a thin necktie. Is that familiar?" asked Remi.

"I don't think so. A necktie?"

Remi took a few steps forward. The apparition seemed to be bouncing slightly. She could only see his upper half, from his chest to the top of his head.

"He's wearing a floral shirt."

The ghost seemed to be in a state of pain or rapture, she couldn't tell. His eyes were in the back of his head and he was rocking back and forth.

"I think I remember..."

When Remi was only a few feet from the ghost, she could hear the noise that Jasmine had been describing.

"Oh."

"Oh, what?" asked Jasmine from the machine.

"I know what that noise is."

"What?"

"And he's not wearing a necktie. It's a cord around his throat. He looks like a surfer."

"A surfer? Oh, I remember him. I dated him last year. We went out twice, but he was too spacy. No job, living on people's couches. Jacob or something like that. Does this mean he's dead? What's he doing?"

Remi swallowed. She didn't know how to explain.

"You're still hearing the sound?" asked Remi.

"Yeah."

"It's the sound guys make when they're alone in the bathroom."

"Oh, shit," said Jasmine. "Is he…?"

"Jerking the tube snake? Yeah. I think he might have died from autoasphyxiation. That cord is tight around his throat. Was probably thinking about you when the lights went out."

"Oh, Merlin," said Jasmine. "Now that I know what the noise is, I can't ever unhear it. Gross. Am I going to have to listen to Jacob greasing his pole for all eternity? I have the worst luck with dating, I swear."

"The good thing is there are spells to send him through the Veil. Now that we know—"

The lights dimmed and the machine made a heavy clunk, startling them both into silence. Remi checked to see if the power might go out. The ward was constantly having electrical issues.

"Doctor..."

The machine's whine increased in frequency and volume.

"I'm not a doctor," said Remi as she hurried back to the control panel.

She slammed the meat of her fist on the stop button. Nothing happened.

Jasmine banged on the pincers holding her in. "Let me out."

"Just a second," said Remi, staring at the equipment, trying to understand what was going on. She turned down the dial, then hit the stop button, but that didn't keep the power meter from creeping towards the red line.

"Not good, not good," Remi mumbled under her breath.

A high-pitched scream had Remi checking to make sure the VIM hadn't caught fire. It hadn't, but Jasmine was staring towards the doorway, her jaw dropped, a wailing sound leaving her mouth at a high rate.

When Remi checked to see what Jasmine saw, all she could see were two red, baleful eyes floating near the ceiling. Cold dread shivered down her spine. Remi had never believed that evil could have a feeling, but standing in the presence of the malevolent apparition changed her mind.

"Stay back," said Remi, raising her hands, preparing a five elements spell that she knew would probably not work. She'd only assisted in two banishings, never done one herself, so she had no idea how to get rid of a ghost that clearly had no interest in leaving.

The glowing red eyes floated into the room. She felt them bore into her. It was like being shot with a dread cannon, or being held under water, or buried alive in a wooden coffin. Her mental fingernails scraped against the fresh pine as the presence grew near.

Then a voice echoed from the eyes.

It came from far away and right in Remi's ear. The words sounded like they'd been dipped in gravel and dumped in a bucket of blood.

"Lilith..."

Hearing her friend's name snapped Remi out of her trance. She raised her hands and shot a weak force bolt through the gap between the red eyes. They glowed more intensely for a moment, then the apparition fled the other way.

The VIM machine, which sounded like it was two shakes from falling apart, returned to the regular smooth operation. The grinding reduced to humming and then it started powering down, the pincers opening, releasing Jasmine from the cage in a slow wheeze.

As the machine went through its final stages before turning off, the sound of Jacob's fapping drifted away until it could no longer be heard.

After thirty seconds of silence, Jasmine asked, "What was that?"

"Don't worry," said Remi, thinking of what the ghost said. "It wasn't looking for you."

"Yeah...I think I'm okay with Jacob slapping the beef compared to whatever nightmare that was."

Remi was busy thinking about what she was going to tell Lily, but she reminded herself the patient came first. She gave Jasmine an off-smile.

"Let me grab one of the others and let's make sure you don't have to hear Jacob anymore. Let you get back to dating without interruptions."

"Thanks, Doc." Jasmine tilted her head. "Can I get out of the machine?"

Remi hit the off button with the meat of her fist just to be certain.

"Yeah, now follow me. Let's take care of your ghost."

NINE

A late September wind whistled past the side entrance of Aura Healers Hall, briefly drowning out the sirens of the incoming ambulances. Damon relished the air across his face and tousling his hair. He'd been dreading the charity event since Brennan had asked him to attend, but now that he was outside the hospital, getting ready for a night out, he wondered if it would be more pleasant than he initially thought.

The steady clicking of heels on concrete alerted him to Remi's arrival. He turned and let out a soft whistle.

"Hey, no making fun," she said, frowning and holding her arms to her chest.

The slinky black dress hung on her small frame like a whisper. Her trademark messy mullet turned the outfit into something both elegant and punk.

"I barely recognize you."

Remi hit him with her black, sparkly clutch purse. "I said no making fun."

"I'm not. You look all fancy and grown up, yet it's still you. It's perfect."

Remi eyed him suspiciously, but then the taxi pulled up. She stumbled slightly getting into the back. The driver shook his head when Damon gave him the address.

"I don't know if I'll be allowed to drop you off in this, but it's your dime."

"You look pretty good yourself," said Remi as the taxi pulled away. "Sorry, I should have said that earlier, but I've never worn anything like this."

She tugged on the strap of her dress.

"That's right. You never did Homecoming, or Prom, or any of that."

"I hope I don't embarrass us," said Remi, forehead hunched.

Damon grabbed her hand, which triggered a heavy sigh.

"If you're not having fun anymore, let me know and we'll leave."

"Can we leave?"

He smiled wistfully. "We have to at least go for a little bit. Let's try to have fun. But if you're not, just give me a signal and we'll get the hell out."

The taxi driver was right about his concerns. When they arrived at the address, which was a skyscraper in the fourth ward near the statue of Invictus, the cop directing traffic didn't want to allow the taxi into the drop-off lane.

"We'll get out here," said Damon, handing over a wad of bills that included a healthy tip.

Damon clutched Remi's hand as they walked past the line of black limousines, two ghost-drawn carriages, and a small boat on wheels made to look like a pirate ship.

He had them duck under the velvet ropes to cross the red carpet and reach the double doors at the top of the marble steps.

"Sir, you can't be here, this is a private event," said the bearded guard in runed armor standing near the doors.

"I have an invitation," said Damon, pulling out the card.

The guard didn't give it a second look. "I saw you walk up the sidewalk. If you were really part of the event, you would have been let out like the rest of them. I don't know who you two are, but you're clearly not supposed to be here. Turn around, before I have a couple of my guys waiting inside make an example of you in front of all these nice people and cameras."

Damon checked back to the sidewalk where the people were being let off. Paparazzi snapped pictures as couples climbed out of their fancy vehicles.

"Please. We work at Golden Willow," said Damon. "We're here by personal invitation of Brennan Boleros."

"I don't care if you think Head Patron Pythia invited you," said the guard. "You don't belong. Now move along before I get in trouble for allowing the trash to stink up the place."

Remi stepped forward, putting her finger in his face. "How would you like—"

"Marcus, what's the problem?"

Damon turned to see Brennan striding up the red carpet. The older man was the paragon of the handsome wealthy donor.

"These two kids were trying to sneak in," said Marcus.

Brennan put his hands on their shoulders. "You mean my guests?"

Marcus blinked. "They're really with you? They got dropped off in a taxi. I thought they were trying to crash the party."

"What happened, Damon? I sent a limo."

Damon stretched his eyebrows upward. "A limo? I didn't know."

"I sent an email yesterday."

"Sorry," said Damon. "I worked a double shift. Haven't slept in thirty hours."

"You gonna be okay?"

"Of course. Got one of Jeb's elixirs coursing through my veins."

"Wonderful," said Brennan. "Come with me. I was just heading up."

The elevator car was big enough to fit two dozen people, with a marble floor and mirrors on the ceiling. Three other couples joined them for the journey up, including an astonishingly beautiful woman with smoky brown skin, jet-black hair, and an intensity to her gaze that made Damon feel completely exposed. She radiated danger.

"Priyanka," said Brennan. "I'm pleased you were able to squeeze us into your busy schedule."

She arched an elegant eyebrow. "I'm in town for a few days."

The elevator doors opened and Priyanka was first out, striding into the entry hall. Damon led Remi out last. She elbowed him in the ribs once the rest of the group had gone forward.

"What was that for?"

"I'm surprised drool wasn't coming out."

He turned on Remi. "You don't know who that was?"

She checked down the hall. "Should I?"

"Priyanka Sai, Patron of the Assassins Hall."

"Oh shit," said Remi, swallowing. "And to think I was going to kick her in the shins."

"I don't think that would have worked out so well." He held out his arm, which she hooked around. "Let's check this out."

"I wasn't excited about being here, but what was her name again?"

"Priyanka Sai."

"In another life, I would have joined her hall," said Remi, smirking.

"And then we would have never met."

Remi shrugged. "Never know."

The conversation died in their throats when they stepped through the double doors. The enormous ballroom was filled with hundreds of wealthy potential donors milling about while waitstaff brought them bubbly golden drinks and tiny bites to eat.

But that wasn't what had swallowed their words.

Rather than tastefully decorated walls, the outer portion was all glass.

And it was daytime.

Damon led Remi over to the edge. The scene below wasn't the city, but a vast, rolling landscape with rushing rivers crisscrossing between its hills. Angled birds winged through the sky.

"What is this?" gasped Remi.

A tall man with high cheekbones, piercing eyes, and Scandinavian good looks next to them said, "Abhainn. Realm of Rivers. It's more beautiful up close."

"But how?" asked Damon at the same time he realized they were talking to Aleksander Grimm, the Patron of Arcane Phytology. He was holding a tumbler of thick golden liquid.

"There's a more technical arcane term, but most people call it looking glass. That's the actual realm we're looking into."

"Fuck me running," said Remi, bringing a gasp from a couple of older ladies behind them. They gave an angry glare before storming the opposite direction.

Aleksander burst into melodic laughter. "You must be students. Aura Healers, I presume?"

He held out his hand. They took turns shaking it and introducing themselves. Aleksander lingered longer than prudent when he had Remi's hand. Damon started to get angry, but then Aleksander released his grip.

"Brennan invited us."

"Parading you around for donations?" asked Aleksander.

"I suppose, but I'm not sure what to do to get them to give," said

Damon.

Aleksander smirked. "Just let them talk. The more rich people ramble the bigger the donation." He checked across the room. "I'll see you around."

As he left, he winked at Remi, which brought heat to Damon's cheeks.

"What was that about?" he asked, trying not to sound accusatory.

Remi looked mystified as she shook her head. "I don't know. When our palms touched, there was a weird spark and it felt like he was looking right through me. It was like standing near an active volcano, or a massive power transformer."

"He *is* a Hall Patron."

"I feel weird being here."

A heartbeat later, the screens shifted to a different view. Another realm entirely, Damon assumed, by the darkness lit with volcanic eruptions. The land was covered in a thick smoke that crackled with sparks. Damon heard someone nearby call it the land of nightmares and he didn't disagree.

"Let's grab a drink and try to talk to some rich people."

"Can I steal their watches?" asked Remi with a sly grin.

"Seems a little—"

"I was kidding. These people have enchantments and other protections on them. No way would I risk it."

Damon exhaled. "Good. I didn't know."

The next hour they milled about the floor with drinks as the looking glass changed realms every twenty minutes, chatting with the wealthy potential donors, most of whom were significantly older. Due to the availability of sorcery-aided appearances, it was hard to tell true ages, but they made a game of guessing to help pass the time when they weren't trying to convince donors to give generously. Damon found that Remi was quite adroit at getting them to talk, which he assumed came from her years of running cons.

Around the time they were getting new drinks, they ran into Brennan with Dr. Martinez on his arm. The head of the Curse Ward looked transcendent in a silvery dress that accentuated her brown skin. Even Remi whistled softly upon their approach.

"My, my," said Dr. Martinez with a smirk. "The pair of you clean up quite nicely. I see you've been chatting up the donors. Nicely done. Septa Foss, the owner of the Museum of Magical Artifacts, says she was quite impressed with the pair of you and plans on giving generously to the campaign."

Remi held up her glass. "You look pretty amazing too, but standing around the three of you makes me feel like a child."

Dr. Martinez froze mid-word when a familiar voice rose above the light chatter.

"—not whiskey, that's swill!"

The four of them turned to see Dr. Decker in an ill-fitting suit with a busty girl on his arm. She was practically falling out of her hot pink dress as she stumbled by his side with a heavy purse on her arm.

"The gang's all here," said Dr. Decker with a slight slur.

Dr. Martinez stiffened as he joined the group.

"Oh," said Dr. Decker, turning towards his date. "This is… What was your name again?"

"Amber."

"Christina, Damon, Remi. This is Amber. She's my date tonight."

The glassiness of his eyes told Damon how snookered their Aura Healer's instructor was.

"This place is so fancy," said Amber, craning her neck at the surroundings.

"Oren," said Dr. Martinez tightly. "We're here on the hospital's behalf."

"I'm fine."

His bloodshot eyes said otherwise. He downed his drink in one gulp, and as he put his hand back down, the tumbler slipped out of his grip, crashing to the ground. Glass shattered over their shoes.

"Whoopsie," said Dr. Decker.

Damon crouched down to pick up glass, but Brennan said, "I'll send the staff over to clean it up. Don't worry. These things happen."

As Damon returned to standing, he saw all eyes upon them, many glaring in Dr. Decker's direction. Heat rose to Damon's cheeks by association.

"Oh, balls," said Dr. Decker.

Blood poured out of a cut on his hand, caused by a chunk of glass. Dr. Martinez quickly pulled a handkerchief from a clutch purse and shoved it into Dr. Decker's hand to staunch the bleeding.

"Help me get him out of here," said Dr. Martinez with a pulsing jaw.

Brennan headed the other direction while Damon, Remi, and Amber followed Dr. Martinez into a side room. An enormous stuffed manticore dominated the space from the corner, while leather couches circled around a giant unlit fireplace. The walls were wood paneled and the window looked out at the Spire.

"I can do it on my own," said Dr. Decker, yanking his hand away from Dr. Martinez.

As soon as the handkerchief came away, blood dripped onto the expensive rug. Damon snatched the cloth from the ground and jammed it back into his instructor's fist.

"I've got you, Dr. Decker," said Damon.

Dr. Martinez mouthed a thank you. "Let me go see how Brennan's coming with the cleanup."

After she left, Damon made Dr. Decker sit on one of the couches. Remi slid an old newspaper under his arm to catch the blood. Their instructor stared at the empty fireplace like a limp doll.

"I'm going to put a quick binding on the wound when I pull the cloth away."

Dr. Decker made no move to answer as his chin dipped slightly.

"Hey, Amber," said Remi. "What else has Dr. Decker taken?"

His busty date was looking through a desk in the corner. She glanced up with a shrug.

"Not sure. The latest party supplement, if you know what I mean. We were having a good time on the dance floor when he told me we were coming to a rich people's party. I thought he was kidding, but here I am."

With Remi's help, they closed up the wound with two short spells. As they started cleaning up the dried blood on his arm, he was snoring with his head on the back of the couch.

Remi glanced up at Damon. "He's a mess."

"Hopefully his scene didn't impact the charity event too much."

Remi punched him in the arm.

"What was that for?"

She checked back to Amber. "I bet he wasn't even planning on attending until he got snookered up."

"What should we do now?"

"Keep an eye on him until he wakes," said Remi.

"What's this?" asked Amber.

They turned to see her holding up a curved dagger from the desk.

"Looks expensive."

"I'd put that away," said Damon.

"Check out the crest over the fireplace. Society of the White Stag," said Remi without moving her head.

Damon approached Amber as she tried to shove the blade into her enormous purse. He gently pried the weapon away. The hilt had strange runes that he didn't recognize from his studies. The unusual markings faintly glowed crimson.

"This would cause you more harm than good," said Damon.

Amber pouted.

"This is lame. Tell Oren he knows where to find me," she said as she headed out, snatching a small glass bauble from a shelf as she left and shoving it into her oversized purse.

As if to answer, Dr. Decker snored sharply before returning to an unaware mumbling.

"Is this what happens to us when we work in the hospital too long?" asked Remi.

The unconscious Dr. Decker smelled like alcohol and glitter. Damon couldn't smell any other unusual pathogens.

"Not all the other doctors are like him. But it's a risk, for sure."

"Dr. Martinez seems to have her shit together."

Damon shook his head. "Which is part of his problem."

"Yeah. He's got it bad."

A deep voice carried through the walls, startling them both to turn their heads. It sounded like an argument.

Damon followed Remi towards the source, which seemed to be right beyond the stuffed manticore. He put his ear to the wall.

"That sounds like Brennan," he said.

Remi frowned. "I can't hear who he's talking to."

The second voice was scrambled as if it were being modified by magic.

"…I need you to kill Mark."

The words were unmistakable. He checked back to Remi, who appeared to have heard the same thing by the look on her face. He shoved his ear back to the wall in time for the next part of the conversation.

"It's gotten out of hand. We can't allow this to continue. It'll bring the whole thing down. I'm not paying for half-assed results. Mark has to die."

The voices, which had been perfectly clear a moment before, turned to mumbles as Brennan and his guest moved away. After a period of silence, Damon heard a door close.

"Did you hear that too?"

Remi crossed her arms. "He just put a hit out on Mark, whoever that is." Her eyes widened. "I wonder if that's why Priyanka is here? Maybe that's who the other person was. She is an assassin after all."

"Somehow I doubt he's contracting with the head of a Hall."

"Not her, but one of her many knives," said Remi. "I'm going in there to see what they were talking about."

"What? No. You can't. They'll see you head into the room."

Remi tilted her head as she walked over to a panel and after a quick inspection, pressed a section of the wall. The panel slid into the wall, revealing the room on the opposite side.

"How did you know how to do that?"

"I know a lot about people trying to hide things," she said, strolling through the opening.

The office on the opposite side was much smaller than the one they'd come from. Glass cases filled with ancient weapons were displayed along the walls.

Remi started digging through the desk, opening drawers and looking through papers.

"You shouldn't do that."

"You really want to work with someone who hires contract murderers?" asked Remi.

Damon sighed and joined her at the desk. He saw numerous documents addressed to Brennan.

"Whoa, check this out," said Remi.

She lifted a large bottle of hot sauce from a drawer. "I guess he likes his spice. This is made with enchanted lava peppers. This stuff makes that little game last year look pedestrian. I'd probably make me go blind."

"I don't think he's going to kill anyone with a bottle of hot sauce, except maybe his taste buds."

Damon was checking a folder which appeared to be a guest list for the party when Remi shoved a paper into his face. It looked like an invoice.

"What am I looking at?" he asked.

She jabbed her finger at a line next to a large dollar figure with the name "MARC" listed beside it.

"Marc? Who's that?"

"Not who, but what," said Remi. "Magically Aided Repelling Curses. It's not a person, but a project. Look at these documents. I don't understand most of it, but it's part of the ward refurbishment. Looks like Brennan's not happy about results and wants the project killed."

"That's a relief."

The sound of voices outside the door startled them. The door cracked, but stayed only slightly ajar. Damon helped Remi shove the documents back into the desk and they hurried through the secret door before they were discovered.

A heartbeat after they returned to the room with Dr. Decker, the study door opened, revealing Dr. Martinez with the guard Marcus from the front door. She raised an eyebrow at their location.

"Thought I saw a mouse," said Remi, joining them at the unconscious Dr. Decker.

"This him?" asked Marcus.

"Can you get him out without making a scene?" asked Dr. Martinez.

The bearded guard shifted his mouth to the side. "I'll take him through the kitchen elevator, but I can't get him all the way back to the hospital."

"We'll go," said Remi.

"Are you sure? The party is only half over. There's going to be speeches and, oh, never mind." Dr. Martinez smiled wistfully. "I'd probably go too."

While the party was distracted by a recent change in the looking glass, revealing a misty jungle over rolling hills, Damon helped Marcus carry the unconscious Dr. Decker through the kitchen and into the elevator. A black limo was waiting below. Remi climbed in behind them.

Around the time they pulled up to Golden Willow, Dr. Decker stopped snoring and sat upright.

"Party over?"

"Yep. Thought it best if we all get some rest."

Dr. Decker blinked before nodding and climbing out the door, right as they pulled up to the sidewalk. He marched inside, leaving them in the back of the limo.

Damon started to follow, but Remi tugged him back. She pressed a button, pulling the privacy window down.

"How long does Mr. Boleros have this vehicle?"

The driver spoke over his shoulder. "As long as you want. Billing is by the hour."

"Thanks." She turned back to Damon with a sly grin. "Where do you want to go?"

"Not the Invictus Zoo."

A curt laugh slipped out. "Yeah. Not there." She leaned forward. "Take us to the second ward, entertainment district. The long way."

Remi hit the button and climbed onto the seat next to Damon. She smelled like floral perfume. He thought about leaning over to kiss her but she dug into the central compartment, pulling out a bottle of champagne. After uncorking it, she poured two glasses and leaned back next to him.

"Is this what prom was like?" she asked, leaning on his shoulder and sipping from her drink as the lights of the city drifted past.

"In a weird way, yeah. Minus the secret doors, Hall Patrons, and obscene wealth. But otherwise, pretty similar."

"That's nice."

Damon smirked. "There is one more thing we should do to complete your prom experience."

Before she could ask a question, he leaned over and gently removed the glass from her hand, setting both of them in a door panel. Then he cupped her jaw with his hand, pulling her in for a kiss.

"Oh," she said softly before biting his lower lip.

TEN

The patient's arm was covered in a translucent green slime. Lily watched as Dr. Martinez scraped a sample using a metal spatula, depositing the goo into a vial for later investigation.

"I'm not going to die or anything?" asked Leslie, forehead knitted. Her arm was being held in a velvet vice with a protective barrier to keep her from accidently brushing against the slime.

The patient worked in the Invictus Sewer Department, which was notoriously dangerous, as magical critters often escaped from pet cages or Hall experiments, disappearing into the tunnels beneath the streets. She had short hair on top with the sides shaved and tattoos covering neck and arms.

Dr. Martinez gave the patient a confident smile. "I won't lie to you. We don't know anything about this goo that's infected your arm, but I can assure you, this is the best possible place to get you fixed up and back to work."

Leslie's mouth hung half open. "I just got a new tat. That little glowy butterfly near my elbow. It's gonna be okay, right?"

"I can't say until we have results."

"I can run it down," said Lily, holding out her hand.

"There's no need," said Dr. Martinez. "I have a meeting with Dr. Fairlight in ten, so I can swing by on my way to her office. In the meantime, I'll need you to cast—"

"Blaze's Blood Attunement and a Growth Inhibitor," finished Lily.

A smile grew on Dr. Martinez's lips as she winked at the patient. "I'm leaving you in good hands. I'll be back in an hour to check on you. We should have results by then."

After Dr. Martinez left, Lily dug into the spell supply closet, pulling out four runed cubes, a faez extinguisher, and medically enhanced chalk.

The patient stared at Lily with apprehension when she set the cubes on the edge of the bed.

"What's that going to do? I don't really like anything to do with magic," said Leslie.

Lily raised an eyebrow. "Yet, you work a hazardous job that puts you in regular contact with it."

"The pay and benefits can't be beat. And I'm helping my mom with her bills. Her flat got destroyed in the Event when some idiot mages knocked over an apartment building near the Glitterdome. Nearly killed her and destroyed everything she owned."

"What a bunch of eejits, but it's good she has you," said Lily as she prepared the cubes for the spell. Most magical biologicals needed faez to grow, so dampening them would usually help delay adverse effects for a time. Eventually, they'd have to deal with the root cause, but it would help in the short term.

"Were you in the city when it happened?"

Lily glanced up as she adjusted the cubes. "I was a wee lass at home, but we watched it on the telly. Was very frightening, even from across the pond."

"Will this hurt?" asked Leslie as she scratched the side of her neck.

"Not a bit. And once we get results, we should be able to identify the biological and give you the correct elixirs. You shouldn't need to be here any more than a few days."

"A few days… My boss is going to kill me."

"If you prefer, you can return right away and then you'll most likely die," said Lily.

Leslie swallowed. "I know, I know."

"Alright," said Lily. "Once I start this spell, you have to remain as still as possible. No noise, or distractions."

"Can I breathe?"

Lily smiled. "Only through your ears."

"What? Oh, a joke." Leslie's cheeks burned crimson. "I'm such a dope. Is this going to be dangerous?"

"I won't lie to you. It can be, but the spell is simple and as long as we don't have any distractions, there shouldn't be an issue. Okay now, hold still. It'll only take a minute or two."

The cubes were situated on either side of her slimy arm. One pair near the wrist and the other near the elbow. Lily started by weaving threads of faez between the cubes. Golden light was barely visible, but she could sense the raw magic with her hands as well as her eyes.

With the faez matrix in place, it was time to attach the dampener, which would complete the magical circuit. Lily was coaxing the golden threads through the miniature machine when she felt a presence at her back.

"What the…?"

"Don't move," said Lily through gritted teeth as the patient's arm shifted in the matrix, threatening to destroy the carefully constructed spell.

Leslie stared over Lily's shoulder with mouth slightly agape. The fear reflected in her eyes was tangible.

"Doctor..."

"Don't move, but tell me what you see," said Lily as she continued working the threads.

"Red eyes filled with hate."

A chill washed against Lily's back. The apparition was powerful enough to crack open a portal to the Veil—the place between the living and the dead. If she wasn't in the middle of the procedure, she'd banish it, but that wasn't an option now.

"Tell me if it does anything unusual. I need to finish this."

Leslie nodded tightly while Lily focused on the threads. She had three more maneuvers to complete, each requiring a medium amount of finger dexterity before she could release the faez inhibitors to work on their own. If she was interrupted, the magical construct could blow back on both of them, supercharging the slime and possibly killing the patient.

One down, two to go.

Lily was working the second when Leslie said, "It's moving closer. It's, like, right over your shoulder."

The presence felt like ice knives being shoved into her back. Lily concentrated on the spell as the malevolent eyes shifted into the edge of her vision. She sensed a familiarity, but couldn't focus on it as she tried to finish the job.

As Lily worked the third and final connection, a ghostly arm appeared from the gloom. She could do nothing as the apparition hooked corporeal fingers into the golden threads and ripped them from the cubes.

The blowback slammed into Lily's chest as if she were being whipped by structural cables, throwing her across the room.

The patient screamed as the translucent green goo on her arm bubbled and expanded.

With the wind knocked out of her, Lily struggled to regain her feet. She sensed the baleful glee from the glowing red eyes, but before they could interfere again, Lily blasted it with an eviscerating spell.

The ghost screamed and the red eyes fled from the room.

Lily scrambled to her feet. The patient was trying to yank her arm out of the protective barrier.

Green slime bubbled and exploded, sending gooey particles across the room. Lily felt splatters against her face and neck.

"Please, help," said Leslie in horror. "It burns."

The slime was rapidly transforming her limb, which suggested the goo had been a mage's project. Sometimes she wanted to slap all the students in the Hundred Halls for their hubris, not understanding how their magics could affect other people.

Because she'd been exposed, the protocol was to hit the emergency alarm and head to an alchemical shower to wash off the slime, but that would certainly doom Leslie to a horrible and early death.

"Prepare yourself. This is going to hurt."

Lily grabbed Leslie's forearm, fingers sinking into the green slime. It was like having a really bad sunburn and pouring whiskey on it, but Lily fought through the pain. There was no way to quickly eliminate the slime, but she thought she might be able to halt its growth long enough that other techniques could save her.

"Get ready. Hold still."

Leslie tensed as she locked her body into position.

Drawing on her well of faez, Lily poured elemental magics into the slime. Water and spirit would probably feed the goo rather than suppress it, but of the other three, she was mostly gambling.

Fire could be purifying under the right circumstances, and air could pulverize it, but she chose earth in hopes that it would slow the reaction.

Lily poured raw elemental earth into the green slime. At first, she thought it wasn't working as the goo continued to bubble.

But the longer she fed it, the slower the boiling. The slime seemed to be thickening even as it burned her hands.

When Lily could no longer keep her hands in the green goo because it was hardening into a thick covering, she yanked them out, and as black dots swam into her vision, she hit the emergency call button with her elbow.

Lily took two steps back towards the patient before the tile floor rose up to meet her.

§

Lily woke in another part of the hospital. Her hands burned, but she couldn't move them. They were being held in glass tubes filled with bubbling pink liquid.

Wires and other medical devices were attached to her legs since they couldn't use the veins in her arms. She ached across her entire body.

Lily studied the sky outside the room, but it was dark, so she had no way of knowing how long she'd been out, and without use of her hands, she couldn't call a nurse.

The door swung open revealing Dr. Martinez. Her look of concern was unmistakable. Lily could tell how close it'd been, because doctors with as much experience as Dr. Martinez never let their true emotions slip out.

"How are you feeling?"

Lily cleared her throat. "Rubbed thin. Like someone took steel wool to my skin."

Dr. Martinez checked the bubbling pink tubes. "The mixture seems to be working well."

"How is Leslie?"

"She'll lose the arm, but you saved her life with that, whatever it was you did. But it almost cost you."

"I'd do it again if I had to," said Lily.

The curl of smile hooked to Dr. Martinez's lips. "I know you would." She paused. "Leslie told us about red eyes?"

"An apparition of some kind. It interfered with the faez-dampening field, which blew back on the both of us. It was almost like it knew how to create the maximum havoc. I thought the hospital was warded."

"It is. We even did a cleansing last week, which makes this very curious. Any lingering ghosts shouldn't be able to become corporeal, nor stay on the hospital grounds unless they're tied to someone or something, or they're that powerful."

"Or both."

Dr. Martinez grimaced. "An unsettling prospect. But that's not for you to worry about. I've passed this information along to the arcane maintenance group. They'll take care of it."

Lily wasn't too sure about that, but she wasn't about to argue, feeling as washed out as she was.

"Do my sisters know?"

"They've already demanded to see you. Twice. I told them you weren't ready for visitors. Would you like me to notify them?" asked Dr. Martinez.

Lily shook her head.

"Family squabbles?"

"Not everyone agreed with my decision to come to the Halls," said Lily.

Dr. Martinez rapped her knuckles against the glass tubes. "I for one am glad you made that choice. I'm sure Leslie is as well."

"But she lost her arm."

"Leslie is very aware that you chose to help her, putting your own life at risk, when you could have easily fled and hit the emergency call button.

There are very few doctors who would have made that choice."

"I'm not a doctor."

Dr. Martinez smirked. "A couple of letters in front of a name don't make one a doctor."

Her phone buzzed. After checking it, she let out a big sigh.

"I have to go, but one of the ward nurses will be along shortly to change the solution and feed you, if you're feeling up to it."

"I'm starved." Lily paused. "How long will I be here?"

"A day, or two. You'll have to keep your arms bandaged and covered in an alchemical cream, but you'll be one hundred percent within the week. This is, after all, the best place to have an emergency."

After Dr. Martinez left, Lily leaned her head against the stiff pillow and closed her eyes. She tried to imagine the feeling when she'd stared directly at the malevolent eyes. Her focus had been on saving the patient, but part her felt like she'd recognized the presence. In the heat of the moment, that feeling could have been mistaken. They were taught as healers not to put too much stock in their emotions during an emergency but she couldn't help but think that she was right about her assumptions.

And even if she was wrong, there was still the mystery of how an apparition could make itself corporal despite the hospital wards. When Lily had the use of her arms back, her first visit would be to the library. She wanted to know if there were any old ghosts who were bent on vengeance against the hospital.

ELEVEN

The door to Dr. Martinez's office had pictures of the doctor with her patients. Remi studied them, finding so many smiling faces. In addition to her brilliance, the head of the ward had a real gift for making people feel at home. It was an unusual combination. She only had to look to Dr. Decker's eccentric ways to know how giftedness usually turned out.

"Come in, Remi," said Dr. Martinez after she knocked.

"How did you know it was me?" asked Remi.

"Because I sent for you."

Remi tilted her head. "I'm twenty minutes late."

"I recognized the squeak of your sneakers," said Dr. Martinez.

Remi lifted a shoe, examining it for damage. "Squeak? I enchanted them specifically not to make noise."

"Exactly," said Dr. Martinez.

"Oh."

"A good doctor has to be observant, much like a detective, which is why I'm worried about you."

"You are?"

"I don't see your name on the ward interviews," said Dr. Martinez, folding her hands on the desk. "You have to pick a specialty by the end of the year. I know you think you have time, but the months will fly by and it's not always easy to meet with the heads of departments."

A pit formed in Remi's stomach. "It's not that I'm not planning on staying."

"Then?"

Remi rubbed the back of her neck. "I don't know. Deciding is hard."

"Not just any decision, but the one that will set you on a path for years, probably decades, to come. Which means you have to weigh all those parts of yourself, your history, your parents, your friends. Add to that the question of if you want to stay in Golden Willow afterwards, or head out to other hospitals, or something else entirely."

"Dr. Martinez," said Remi, exasperated.

A grin broke across her face. "I know. I'm not making it any easier. But here's the thing. You don't have to decide today. But what you need to do is gather more information. Just like a good detective. Or a thief."

"I don't do that anymore."

"I'm not saying you do. But I think those skills are part of what make you a good healer. You have a good knack for people and you know how to analyze a patient. Far too many healers and doctors are throwing spaghetti at the wall."

"I don't know about having a knack for people. I know how to manipulate them, that's all."

"What's the difference?"

Remi frowned.

"I don't know. Intentions?"

"Exactly. Do you know why I have all those pictures on my door?"

Remi turned slightly, thinking about the reasons. "Because you want to signal to your patients that you're friendly and that you have the patient's best interests at heart."

"Not just the patients. Nurses see that too and it changes how they work with me."

Remi smirked. "You'd make a good con artist."

"I'd make a good lot of things, but this is what I chose. But now it's your turn. You have to start your investigation. Plan your con. However you want to frame it in your mind."

Remi nodded enthusiastically.

"I'll get right on it. I swear. Signing up tomorrow once I check my schedule."

"Good," said Dr. Martinez.

"Doctor, since I'm here, can I ask you a personal question?"

Dr. Martinez lifted her chin and raised an eyebrow. "I won't know until you ask. Go ahead, but I can't promise anything."

"What happened to Dr. Decker? The older staff calls him Dr. O.D. and everyone knows he had a major breakdown and left the hospital for many years, but no one has ever told us why."

"Are you curious because you like gossip, or you're worried that it might happen to you?"

Remi lifted a shoulder. "Both."

Dr. Martinez gestured towards the chair. "Sit. I'll tell you a story, but under no circumstances should you ever bring it up with Oren."

Remi mimed zipping her lips closed as she glided into the chair.

"A decade ago. I don't know, time has slipped by so fast, but before, when we were still married and young arrogant residents, we thought we could fix anyone, no matter the problem."

Dr. Martinez smiled wistfully as she looked out the window.

"Oren especially thought that the normal rules of death and illness didn't count for his patients, and in many cases, he was right. He cured or fixed people that no one thought had a chance for survival.

"He'd come to feel so confident about his abilities he started promising families positive outcomes despite Dr. Paddock warning him not to."

"Dr. Paddock was his teacher?"

"A mentor. He was a kinder person back then," said Dr. Martinez with rounded eyes.

"This is the part where you tell me everything fell apart."

Dr. Martinez squeezed her lips white. "You know your tragedies well. The deaths started seemingly at random. Unexpected passings that bruised Dr. Decker's ego, but did not dissuade his focus. It was ones and twos here and there, but before long, the pattern was unmistakable.

"There were investigations. They found trace amounts of nightshade and other poisons in their blood, or significantly higher doses of their medications. People accused him of murder, over three dozen counts, and some thought the number higher as not all deaths could be attributed to an alchemical death."

Dr. Martinez kneaded her hands together as her expression broke with anguish. Remi could see the pain of those years reflected in her eyes.

"Oren was the one to catch him. He was too brilliant not to see the patterns himself and unravel the threads. It was an orderly. Martin Freely. His wife had been bitten by a couple of supernatural spiders during the Portland zoo disaster. Martin joined the staff to be by his wife's side while they tried to fix her, but it'd taken so long to get her out and fly her to Golden Willow that there was almost nothing Oren could do."

"Martin blamed Oren."

"He didn't show it. Martin continued to work in the hospital long after Maria passed. Then he started poisoning Oren's patients. Once Oren figured it out, Martin confessed to everything in a long letter, but they still investigated Oren as if he'd been part of it. He was exonerated, but the suspicion and the deaths broke him. He went into a funk, disappearing for days at a time, coming back covered in glow-in-the-dark paint and glitter, smelling like an elixir laboratory."

Her nostrils flared as her face screwed up in pain. Remi could see how Oren's recent behavior was only bringing back those old wounds. For both of them.

"I still loved him, but there was nothing I could do. I fear even coming back now was a mistake. But I couldn't let our history determine the fate of the hospital. I hoped his multi-realm walkabout had healed him enough that we could coexist, but I don't know."

"Rule number seven, you can't save everyone; rule number eight, sometimes the best medicine is doing nothing; rule number nine, magic can fix a lot of things, but it can't heal the soul," said Remi breathlessly. "Those weren't rules for us, they were a reminder for himself."

"Now this business with Brennan is bringing all that back."

"What happened to Martin?"

Dr. Martinez gripped the edge of the table. "He hung himself in the room where Maria died before they could take him into custody."

"There's no chance the apparition I saw and that nearly killed Lily could be this Martin, could it?"

Dr. Martinez's jaw pulsed with thought. "We have specific procedures for cleansings, especially after a suicide. If we didn't the hospital would be overrun with apparitions. Besides, the Veil wards are active and working as intended. Even if we hadn't made sure he passed over, the wards could keep him at bay."

"Yet, the apparition with the red eyes nearly killed Lily."

"If something seems like it can't be true, then another cause is likely."

Remi shifted her mouth to the side. "Is this one of your rules?"

"It's not Martin."

Remi didn't agree, but she wasn't going to argue with Dr. Martinez after bringing up old wounds.

"Thank you," said Remi.

"My pleasure," said Dr. Martinez. "Just make sure you sign up for your ward interviews."

Remi saluted and closed the door on her way out. She had rounds in ten minutes, but once her shift was over, she planned on heading to the library to read the files on Martin Freely. Maybe there'd be something familiar in the text that would help them identify the ghost as Dr. Decker's serial killer orderly.

TWELVE

"Are you sure you haven't seen the Enochian Stone?" asked Damon as he leaned on the nurses station counter.

Nurse Mandy glanced up from her paperwork. "Do I look like the keeper of your ward's equipment? Shouldn't you be looking on your floor, or wag your fingers to find it? You're a Hall mage. Do something arcane."

His cheeks burned as the cluster of nurses smirked between themselves. Nothing was worse than a group of nurses at the end of their double shift. Not that he blamed them. He'd said some pretty atrocious things in the throes of being sleep deprived.

"Dr. Paddock said someone from the Supernatural Ward borrowed it from the ER yesterday."

Damon knew he'd made a mistake as soon as four sets of eyes burrowed into him at Dr. Paddock's name.

"Don't tell me you're taking his word over mine," said Nurse Mandy, crossing her arms.

Damon held up his hands in a gesture of peace. “That’s not what I’m implying. Please. We’ve got a patient on the fifth floor that got caught in the faez blowback when a couple of Coterie mages got drunk and started a fight with some Protectors at a bar in the fourth. This kid had nothing to do with it, but he’s paying the price. He’s in a lot of pain and Dr. Martinez thinks the Enochian Stone is our fastest way to fix him.”

The glare could have split concrete.

“Half the world’s problems could be solved if we didn’t have mages,” said Nurse Mandy, receiving head nods from the other nurses in support.

“Have you seen it?”

Nurse Mandy returned to her paperwork, nostrils flaring as she exhaled.

“I’m just going to act like you didn’t ask again.”

Damon started to go around the counter with the intent of searching the station himself, but decided the impact to his career wasn’t worth it. He would just have to assume that the Enochian Stone wasn’t where Dr. Paddock said it was. He did like to blame nurses for mistakes he’d made.

“Who else would need it?” he asked himself in the hallway, scratching the back of his neck.

He hadn’t transformed in a while, which was making his skin crack. The switch to his werewolf form was good for his pores. Maybe he’d invite Remi to his room to watch as she’d said she was curious to observe up close. He’d thought she was joking the first time she’d said it, as most people treated his therianthrope as a burden, but she seemed delighted by the prospect.

Damon headed to the Supernatural Children’s Ward in hopes of finding the Enochian Stone. He was halfway to the elevators when he spotted a black cat in the middle of the cross-hallway.

He remembered that he’d seen the same cat a month before.

"Shoo. You shouldn't be here," said Damon, waving his hands forward like an invisible brush.

"*Mrrroew.*"

The intonation felt like a rebuke.

"Seriously, cat. Shoo."

He took two steps forward and the black cat leapt off its haunches and sauntered away, checking over its shoulder as if it were expecting him to follow.

"I don't have time for this, whatever games you're playing."

The black cat paused at the stairwell door, looking back at him with a sereneness that bordered on annoying.

"I'm not going to—"

Before he could finish, the door surged open and the cat slipped past an orderly carrying a warding cable on his shoulder. The smell of brimstone wafted into the hallway.

"Hey, keep that open," said Damon, hurrying after the cat.

He wasn't sure which way the feline had gone, but heard a faint meow as if the cat was leading him on. He crept up the stairs expecting an ambush and keeping his hands at the ready to use five elements.

"If this is a prank, I suggest you take it elsewhere. I need to find the Enochian Stone, not chase a dumb cat."

At the last part, the feline stuck its black head over the stairs and gave him a forceful *mrrrow*!

Damon raced up the stairs and by the time he'd reached the rooftop exit, he was certain there was something supernatural about the black cat. Especially when he found the door closed, but no sign of the creature.

Sticking his head out the opening, he found the cat a dozen steps away, waiting for him to follow. With his senses on high alert, Damon followed at a careful pace, keeping the black cat in his sight the entire time.

"What does it want?" he asked aloud.

He sniffed the air and after a moment's thought spoke again.

"What does *she* want?"

When the black cat came to the midpoint, he thought she would lead him to the place where he hung out with his fellow Aura Healers, which would have been suspicious. But the cat trotted behind an HCAV unit on the way to the helicopter pad.

Coming around the corner, he found the black cat sitting about thirty feet away next to a lump of jet-black stone and a sprig of something green.

Damon hesitated until he realized what the first lump was.

"Hey, you stole the stone!"

Before he could take a single step, the black cat burst away, running at speed. He would have chased her, but the Enochian Stone was more important.

He crouched and examined the stone before daring to touch it. Old runes had been carved into the obsidian, which glowed under the presence of faez. He drew the raw stuff of magic from his mind and breathed it over the object, relaxing when the strange markings illuminated, proving that it was real.

With the Enochian Stone in his possession, he examined the greenery, finding a handful of small leafy sprouts. Using the divining rod in his back pocket, he poked around the bundle until he realized what he was looking at.

He grabbed a single tiny sprout, holding it before his eyes, and counted the round leaves. One, two, three, four.

"Blood and bone."

Four-leaf clovers. A whole bundle of them. At least thirty or forty. Maybe more.

He couldn't imagine anyone had collected them by hand. They were too rare. The only place he knew you could find an abundance of them was in the Fae.

But that wasn't the important part.

Four-leaf clovers could make a potent elixir that along with the Enochian Stone would help counter the binding that afflicted his patient.

"Thank you?" he called after the black cat as he headed back towards the stairwell.

Damon paused at the door, hoping for the creature to reveal itself, but eventually he realized he needed to get back to his patient. The mystery of the black cat would have to wait.

THIRTEEN

Lily was sitting in the break room reading old newspaper articles about Martin Freely when a nurse stuck her head in the door. After Remi had told her about the history of Golden Willow's serial killer, Lily agreed that the red-eyed apparition could be related, despite assurances from Dr. Martinez.

Psychic stress could sometimes make the barrier thin between their realm and the Veil, especially when it was related to an original cause. Dr. Decker's mental state was barely above a frayed hangman's noose.

"Healer Lily?"

"Yes, Nurse Tishanti?"

A smile formed on her broad lips. "I know you're on break, honey, but we're having trouble with the patient that was just admitted and the doctors are all in a meeting with Dr. Martinez."

Lily glanced at the readings on her phone, before swiping it away.

"Ar scáth a chéile a mhaireann na daoine." She followed the nurse towards the patient's room. "What's the problem?"

A hunched forehead was followed by hesitation. "This one is... strange."

"Nurse Tishanti. Just last week, a woman was belching bubbles that we couldn't pop and they filled the hallway, causing a major traffic jam."

The nurse wrestled with her words. "Yeah, that was odd alright, but you know there is strange and then there is *strange*."

No more explanation was forthcoming, so Lily kept her mouth shut, wishing she had Neko with her. With her eldest sister in the building, she couldn't risk her companion getting caught and sent back to Ireland. While she only saw Biddy every few days—who knows what she was doing in between—she always showed up at the worst possible moments.

The nurse stopped outside the closed door.

Lily raised an eyebrow.

"No way. I'm not going back in there. But I know you'll do just fine."

Nurse Tishanti went the other way, leaving Lily perplexed as to what she was about to encounter.

Lily stuck her head through the open door, seeing a woman in the bed with her knees up and staring at something behind the blankets with concern. She had frizzy, dirty blonde hair in the shape of puffy clouds and a long equine face.

"Miss Andrika Karlov?" asked Lily after she grabbed the chart. "How can I help you today?"

"Are you a doctor?" asked Miss Karlov in a thick Eastern European accent.

Lily rotated towards the head of the bed so she could see what the woman was staring at. A heavy stone formed in her gut, making each step ponderous.

"I'm a healer. A mage trained in the healing arts. Is there something wrong with your leg?"

The last word trailed away as Lily saw what the woman was afraid of. Next to her bent knee was a small wooden man with dark, swooping hair and eyes like dense, coal-smashed hate.

"Crow have mercy," she muttered.

The curse slipped out without warning. The little wooden man turned his head with an odd grin on his lips. Lily couldn't explain it to herself, but she felt an unrepentant fear that shook her spine.

"You're a bolgchainteoir." Lily shook her head. "A ventriloquist."

She dared to move next to the bed, close enough that she could see the woman's right arm was underneath the puppet.

"I perform at the Cracked Theater, which is in the ninth ward. You can call me Andrika, and this is Beis."

"What seems to be the problem?"

Lily could have checked the chart, but she didn't want to take her eyes off the puppet, which was staring at her as if she'd killed its entire family. She felt a keening hate emanating from the wooden construct.

"I came to hospital because I have cramps. I was in your ER with great pain, which sometimes happens for me. It is a misfortune of my family's women."

Lily furrowed her forehead. "This is the Curse Ward. We don't deal with cramps, unless there is a supernatural origin of your pain?"

"No, not that I am aware of."

Her gaze shifted to the puppet, which was regarding them both with malicious glee.

"Then what's the problem?"

Andrika slowly removed her hand from beneath the puppet, which was still slowly moving its head back and forth.

"It started doing this right after we arrived."

"Has this ever happened before?" asked Lily, keeping her hands at the ready.

Andrika shook her head vehemently. "It's just a puppet."

The lights flickered, distracting Lily to look away. When she turned back, the puppet's eyes glowed with a faint crimson hue.

"This place will burn for what it's done."

The voice coming out of the wooden puppet sounded like broken glass and hate. Lily wished she was closer to the emergency call button, but didn't want to take her eyes off the puppet to move in that direction.

"Who are you?" asked Lily.

The puppet's eyes lit up like tiny infernos. "Vengeance!"

The tiny construct scurried up Andrika's leg, leaping at Lily before she could move. The possessed puppet moved faster than she thought possible. Before she knew it, stiff wooden hands were strangling her and she fell back against the steel cart, landing heavily on the tiles.

"You're gonna die, haegtesse!"

The possessed puppet weighed more than its little body suggested, holding her down. The apparition inside the construct was using its spirit powers to affect the world. She tried to throw it off but it was too strong.

Andrika shrieked from the bed, cowering atop the covers. Lily tried to tell her to hit the emergency call button, but she couldn't speak, and darting her gaze at the red disc wasn't cluing in her patient either.

Lily punched the puppet twice in the head, but the construct cackled with glee. She followed it up with a gust of flame, which washed over the wooden man, but the fire didn't seem to burn the hair or clothes, except for a little candle of flame on its arm. When the puppet moved to put it out, Lily launched the construct across the room, slamming it into a nurse's cart in the corner.

With the puppet off her, she scrambled to the supply closet, pulling out drawers until she found a handful of paint markers. By the time she turned back, the puppet had pulled out a scalpel from the cart.

"You won't be much of a haegtesse without eyes," said the puppet, demonstrating its alacrity with a few quick swipes of the blade.

The puppet bounded towards her like a marionette on speed. She blasted it with a wind spear knocking it momentarily off course, but then it leapt like a high diver. She caught it mid-air. The blade slashed through her scrubs, finding home in her forearm.

"Begone, Daemhan!"

The warding sent the puppet spinning out of her hands to land on the tile floor. She quickly drew a runic barrier. The puppet ran into the warding and after climbing back to its feet, raised its hands and started casting a spell.

Lily was almost too shocked by the sudden display of magic to defend herself when all the cabinets opened up and the dozens of metal utensils and other equipment came flinging out at her. She was caught in a maelstrom of steel.

Calling to her primal magics, she exploded force outward, sending the blades and other equipment flying into the walls. The puppet seemed surprised by the reversal, giving her a chance to complete the circle around the puppet.

It was trapped before it realized it. She completed the incantation as the puppet raged against the invisible walls, only a few inches from her face.

When it was complete, the lights blew out and pieces of tile fell from the ceiling.

Emergency lights flickered on, revealing a limp puppet in the middle of the banishing circle. Lily leaned back against the desk, heaving with breath, limbs covered in cuts and wounds from the onslaught. Her clothes looked like they'd been through a shredder.

Andrika cowered in the bed. "Is he gone?"

Lily nodded with exhaustion.

The woman climbed down from the bed and grabbed the puppet by the foot, holding as little as possible. She dangled it over the sharps bin and shoved it inside. The puppet was too large, so half its body stuck out, but then she ran back to the bed and held her covers up like a shield.

"Maybe I try acting."

Lily tested her shoulder, which had taken a beating when she'd been thrown into the drawers.

"Probably a good idea."

"You're bleeding," said Andrika.

Lily checked to find her scrubs were covered in blood and cuts. She climbed to her feet, wiped the hair stuck to her forehead away, and after chugging a blood coagulator, stumbled out of the room.

Nurse Tishanti and the rest of the nurses at the station watched her approach with wide eyes. No one made a move to help, but she didn't blame them. They were as stunned as she was.

"The puppet's no longer a danger, but you should probably take it down to the incinerator. Just in case."

"Are you okay?" asked Nurse Tishanti.

Lily gestured randomly ahead.

"I'm going to get a shower and a change of clothes."

She left the nurses station and passed other doctors and patients who gave her a wide berth as she stumbled towards the Aura Healers section of the hospital. As she rounded the corner, she found a stern Biddy walking the other way.

Her eldest sister crossed her arms and prepared to deliver another lecture, but Lily held up her hand.

"I'm not in the mood, Biddy."

Biddy's mouth hung open in confusion as Lily shuffled past, making her way inexorably towards the showers.

FOURTEEN

The warm tones of laughter made Remi smile despite her exhaustion as she stepped onto the Children's Supernatural and Virology Ward. The walls were decorated for Halloween, which was only a week away, and the nurses were wearing costumes. Remi spotted a werewolf, two different versions of Patron Celesse D'Agastine, and a city Fae with chalky gray skin.

A nurse at the station sent Remi to a room. She found Dr. Lara Vista seated on the bed next to an emaciated girl no older than twelve with lilac-colored skin that glowed faintly in random spots. The head of the department wore fairy wings that fluttered lightly, spilling sparkling dust behind her that disappeared before it hit the floor.

"You must be Remington," said Dr. Lara Vista with an earnest smile.

She had lush blonde hair and the kind of doey-eyed softness that reminded Remi of a kindergarten teacher, but she knew that couldn't be the case as the head of a department. Remi figured she was made of steel beneath that gentle exterior.

"Just Remi is fine, Dr. Vista."

"Call me Lara, or Dr. Lara if you must. Please come in." She gestured towards the young girl in the bed. "This is Prim. She's staying with us while we figure out how to fix this nasty curse. Isn't that right, Prim?"

The girl in the bed giggled when Dr. Lara shook her arm gently.

"Yes, Dr. Lara."

Remi realized she was standing too far away, giving the impression she was concerned about the girl's affliction, so she stepped to the chart at the end of the bed.

"You don't need that," said Dr. Lara. "Prim, tell Healer Remi what happened."

The girl sat up straight in bed as if she were about to give a formal speech. Her brown eyes stared at the ceiling as she repeated a story she'd clearly told dozens of times.

"I was playing in the park in the eleventh ward when I saw a creature that looked like a cross between a dog and an elk. I followed it into an old building where I found a circle of mushrooms with an amulet inside. I put it on and then I woke up in Golden Willow like this."

Remi searched Prim's face, trying to understand if this was the truth. She didn't sense a lie, but it didn't feel like fact either.

"What's the prognosis?"

Dr. Lara wrinkled her nose playfully at the young girl. "That's what we're trying to find out. Right, Prim?"

"Aye, aye, Dr. Lara," said Prim, adding a salute.

"Alright, Prim. I need to give Remi a tour of the ward. She's deciding if she wants to work here for her final two years of Aura Healers."

Prim gave an enthusiastic wave. "I hope you pick us! We're lots of fun."

Away from the room, Dr. Lara's expression faltered.

"Not good?"

"Not bad, but we haven't determined what's wrong with Prim."

"What about her story? Something seemed off," said Remi.

Dr. Lara sighed.

"Your instincts are sharp. Her parents told us there was nothing of the sort near the park. She'd disappeared for five minutes and then came wandering back looking like she is. We don't know if it's a curse or a virus, or what."

"That's terrible."

Dr. Lara smiled wistfully. "Let's not dwell on difficult problems. I'd like to show you around the department, give you a feel for what it might be like if you choose to join us for your final two years."

For the next hour, Remi met the staff and patients. There were a lot of stories like Prim's, which seem to hit harder than they would in the adult wards.

"Are they all like this?" asked Remi after they heard a particularly sad story about a boy who'd been attacked by a banshee and could no longer see.

"Like what?"

Remi struggled to articulate her feelings. "Depressing?"

"We have a higher rate of positive outcomes than the adult wards. Kids are more resilient than older patients, and they follow directions better. You'd be surprised how many adults sabotage their own care because they think they know better."

"I'm not surprised at all."

Dr. Lara pursed her lips. When they were with the kids, she maintained a cheery exterior, but Remi saw the serious professional standing before her.

"I read your background."

"I know," said Remi, nodding. "I come with a lot of baggage, but I assure you that those days are long behind me."

"My one and only concern is the well-being of the kids. I would do anything, and I mean anything, to heal them. This is my life's work. When I had the opportunity to take over from Dr. Fairlight when she became Chief of Staff, I jumped at the chance and moved back to Invictus. My husband didn't want to live in the city of sorcery because he was afraid that the Event might happen again, so we had to get divorced. Do you understand what I'm saying?"

"That if I came to your ward, I would have to put the kids first."

Dr. Lara's eyes rounded. "If you say your past is behind you, I would take you at your word. But I cannot always say the same for the parents. You have to understand that the best part of this ward is the kids, and the worst part is their parents. They can be very protective, sometimes to the point of interfering with care. They will find out who you are, and that will be a deal breaker for some of them. Others will be downright abusive, thinking it will earn them better care for their child, and once those parents find out what you did in Utica, they might ask that you be removed from the care team."

A knot of anger twisted in Remi's chest. She never seemed to be able to escape her past, even as she was trying to remake herself.

"How do you know what I did in Utica? That's supposed to be sealed because I wasn't an adult."

Dr. Lara squeezed her lips with sympathy. "I'm sorry, Remi. It's not that hard to find out with a little digging. I was able to learn what happened, so you can be damn sure that some parents will as well. You put a girl in the hospital, and as far as I understand, she was permanently changed because of it."

"It was in self-defense. They hurt one of my friends and I baited her into attacking me instead, but when I pushed her, she tripped over a curb and cracked her skull wide open. I didn't mean for her to get hurt."

"Now tell me, Remi. If you were a parent, what would you think about that story? Would you believe it?"

Remi looked away as heat burned her cheeks. The only thing she could think of was how her parents had used her and then when she'd gotten caught, abandoned her to the correctional system.

"I don't know how parents think."

"I do, Remi. I know all too well," said Dr. Lara. "The tough ones operate on fear. Fear that their child is hurt and they can do nothing about it, but they try anyway. For better or worse, they will see anything as a threat to their child's safety and take appropriate action."

"Do you not want me in your ward?" asked Remi, trying her best not to cross her arms defensively.

"If you choose this ward, I will make it happen. But you're going to have to eat a lot of shit from some parents and every mistake you make will only reinforce their prejudices. I'm sorry, Remi. You have a lot of baggage. I believe in second chances, but not everyone does."

The truth in her heart was that she was hesitant about the Children's Ward. Growing up, she'd never hung around her peers, so she didn't know how to act around kids. Remi knew more about navigating broken people or criminals like Warnock or the Scythe Sisters than regular children.

But hearing Dr. Lara's blunt analysis made Remi long for a life she'd never been given the opportunity to have. Her parents had taken that from her when they'd signed her up for a life of petty criminal activity.

"I understand," said Remi.

"Whatever you decide, I will support you," said Dr. Lara. "And if you want to come back during the year to spend more time on the floor with the kids, let me know and we can set that up. But I want you to make the decision understanding the full scope of what it's going to be like."

"Thank you, Dr. Lara. I appreciate it."

To Remi's surprise, Dr. Lara pulled her in for a warm hug. She didn't know what to do with her hands and the embrace was over before she figured it out.

"I have to head to a staff meeting, but feel free to hang around longer if you want. Good luck, Remi."

Dr. Lara left her in the middle of the hallway. The twin sounds of a child laughing and another one crying came from different directions. The noises were a language she didn't understand. Remi listened for another minute before heading back to the Curse Ward.

FIFTEEN

Lily spotted Neko sitting on the nurses' desk cleaning his pointed face. No one was nearby for the moment, as the nurses were in back drinking punch and eating snacks in their costumes.

"You can't be here," said Lily, glancing around nervously. "Not only is Dr. Decker going to kill me, but if my sisters see you..."

Neko stood on his haunches and made grasping motions with his tiny rat hands. She knew what he was intending. He missed her. Normally, he spent half his time hiding in her hair, which was a comfortable kind of existence.

"I know, little one. But if they catch you, they'll send you back and I'll never get to see you again. Until my sisters leave, you have to hide."

Approaching laughter had Lily grabbing Neko and hiding the white rat behind her back as one of the nurses dressed like a mummy came back to the front to grab a drink that she'd left on the desk.

"Can I help you, Healer Lily?"

Lily kept her face neutral. "Just takin' a breather."

"Ain't no more puppets on the loose, are they? You look more puckered up than an asshole at a proctology exam."

"I'm green as gold."

The nurse made a noise under her breath that suggested she didn't believe her. As soon as they were alone again, Neko leapt out of her hands and scurried down the hall, right past a pair of orderlies pushing mop buckets. Neither saw Neko, but only because he maintained a Fae aura that kept him from being seen by normal people easily.

"Got your hand in the bin again?"

Lily spun around to find Biddy across from her with Alice at her side. The younger de Meath was in a green cotton dress rather than the more modern clothes she'd been wearing since she arrived in Invictus.

"You can't go creepin' around the hospital like an apparition, Biddy," said Lily.

Biddy looked past her shoulder as she sniffed the air. "I smell your changeling."

"Bugger off, sister, I have work to do."

Her eldest sister flattened her lips. Her judgmental gaze had been honed to a fine point.

"You'd make a good principal," added Lily.

"I would."

Lily wished she had a clipboard, or something to do with her hands. She started to grab a stack of papers on the nurses station, but realized it was a fashion magazine.

"When I find your rat, I'm going to send him back home where he belongs."

"Why are you really here, Biddy? You've been here two months and you've done nothing but bother me."

"I've been busy in the city unlike you, wasting your time in a hospital. I spoke to Lady Nimueh and some other professionals."

"And you're no further than I am," spat Lily. "And I'm not wasting my time."

Biddy screwed up her face. "You're an ungrateful brat with an over-inflated sense of entitlement because everyone always praised the little witch who was ahead of her time. But everything you've always done was for selfish reasons, while I've maintained our traditions in the face of our slow-motion family tragedy."

"Sisters," said Alice softly, keeping her head down. "You shouldn't fight like that."

For the first time, Lily noticed the early gray in Biddy's hair and the bags around her eyes. The eldest de Meath sister had always been an old soul, but this seemed different.

"What do you want?" asked Lily. "You clearly came looking for me. *Sister*."

Biddy's gaze bored right into her. The intensity was unsettling, but Lily refused to look away.

"I need you to come with us."

"I'm on shift."

"You're always on shift," said Biddy. "I heard one of the nurses say this is the calmest Halloween they can remember."

"How much time is this going to take?"

Biddy turned on her heels and marched the opposite direction, wooden heels ringing on the tile. Alice shrugged and followed, checking back to see if Lily was coming.

She sighed and strode after, keeping her distance as they navigated the maze of hospital hallways. Eventually Biddy led them down flights of stairs until they were in the maintenance basement.

The hum of equipment made her teeth ache. They passed a doorway covered in runes that led to one of the hospital wardings that helped protect them from an abundance of ghosts. Around the corner, in a side room that had been cleared out, sat a single potted tree. For a moment, Lily thought it was the same one from the chapel that she'd used years ago, but realized it was too large.

"You can't go around stealing trees."

Biddy crossed her arms. "You forgive your roommate a little theft but not your sisters? We're not eejits. We'll put it back after the ritual."

"The ritual?" asked Lily, tilting her head.

"You need to see, Lil, or you won't understand."

Lily squeezed her hands into fists. "Don't call me Lil."

Alice stepped forward. "Lily, please. Biddy's right. You need to see."

If it'd only been Biddy, she would have refused her on principle, but it was hard to say no to her younger sister.

"Fine. Let's be quick about it."

The tree already had the runes carved in the trunk. The three of them made a circle around the plant, holding hands and speaking in concert.

The ritual was simple, born of their family history and connection to Medb. Repeating the words with her sisters, however strained her relationship with Biddy, still brought a sense of longing for the Old Country.

The tug was brief.

To Lily, it felt like a hook had been gently set in her breastbone and then she was yanked forward.

She passed through a bright mist. Lily could only see a few feet in front of her, but enough that she felt her sisters to either side.

Leaves crunched beneath her feet, which were barefoot now, because this wasn't physical. They'd traveled to see Medb through a spirit channel. It was only her mind in the Old Country.

The longhouse appeared out of the gloom, surrounded by ancient trees covered in moss that hung down like green vines. The moss slapped against her shoulder as she passed, feeling both damp and warm.

A shield adorned the spot above the fur-covered door. The sigil on the shield was a bull and a flagon. Lily pushed through the furs.

The forest outside had smelled soggy with a hint of rotting vegetation, but inside the longhouse the scent of burning wood and iron remained.

Lily passed the central fire. Burning coals crackled with reddish-orange heat. The smoke parted to reveal a fair-haired woman lounging on a wooden throne. A spear and shield lay near her feet.

Lily fell to her knees, inclining her head. Her sisters did the same.

"Lilith. My lost child. Are you well?"

The words were in the Old Tongue, but her mind translated them quickly.

"I'm sorry, my queen. I have not found an answer, but I believe I'm searching in the right place. There is a mystery at the heart of the city of sorcery."

"Look at me," said Medb.

Lily lifted her chin. It wasn't the first time she'd been in Medb's presence, physically or spiritually, but she felt the difference right away. The beauty and vitality that normally assaulted the senses was muted. It was like looking at a fabrication of the real thing. Medb's golden hair appeared thin and her cheeks gaunt. The shield on the ground was tinged with rust and the wooden shaft of the spear was cracked.

"I'm lookin' for a cure."

Medb shifted forward, leaning her forearms on her knees. The intensity of the goddess' gaze made it hard not to look away.

"You're not trying hard enough. The corruption is deep. I won't be able to protect your family, your sisters, much longer."

"If I knew why the corruption is happening, I might be able to figure it out."

The crackling of bones made her look away.

Lily squeezed her eyes shut and spoke again. "We stopped a White Worm. A Green Man that had been corrupted."

"I know this already, Lilith. The Green Man was a symptom of the problem, not the root cause."

"Then what does the Oak Father say? It's his realm that is corrupted. Why is *he* not fixing it?"

The anger and frustration slipped out before she could rein it in. The longhouse trembled with Medb's rage.

"You dare question the Oak Father? Even in absence, I'm certain he toils after a solution. He wouldn't abandon us like you have to this abomination of the Halls."

Before she knew it, Lily was lifted up by her neck. Medb had her by the throat. She couldn't breathe, and if she died in the spirit world, her body would cease living back in Golden Willow. Her instinct was to fight, but she knew that would only further enrage her former patron.

Lily hung from Medb's arm while her life was slowly being choked from her. From up close, she saw the dark lines haunting Medb's normally perfect face. The tendrils of corruption had captured the old queen.

Right before Lily thought she would black out, Medb dropped her to the dirt and returned to the throne. The look of fear in Alice's eyes told her how close it'd been.

Lily swallowed painfully and placed her forehead against the wooden floor. "I meant no disrespect."

"Yet your lips gave it."

Silence followed. Eventually Lily dared to peek, finding Medb staring into the distance.

"I cannot reach him," said Medb eventually. "He is hidden from my sight. For reasons I do not understand. And all the while, his lands rot without his attentions."

"I know it doesn't seem it," began Lily, "but I think the city of sorcery holds the answers we seek. There have been too many coincidences. The Green Man. The heir of King Nuada in the same hospital, and lately, I've sensed something older. Brimstone and hate. Fleeting, but I catch it sometimes."

"The Fomorians, despite being his ancient enemy, could never have affected the Oak Father as such. Nor can they be the cause of the Great Corruption. The only thing they ever succeeded in doing was to destroy their own lands."

"Yet they persist in our world."

"No more or less than the other ancient beings roaming the lands in search of power and profit."

Medb leaned even further, making it feel like she was right in Lily's face.

"Whoever has perpetrated this crime is more cunning, more powerful than the Fomorians."

"Who?"

Medb sat back in her throne. "I do not know."

"What do you want of me?" asked Lily.

The golden-haired figure upon the throne pursed her lips. "I want you to find the source before we meet our untimely ends."

For the first time, Lily sensed doubt from the ancient queen. After many centuries of life, she sensed a looming end and it frightened her.

"Déanfaidh mé iarracht níos deacra," said Lily, inclining her head.

When she looked back up, the smoke swirled before her eyes, burning until the longhouse faded from view and Lily found herself back in the hospital basement, holding hands with her sisters.

Biddy was the first to let go. "You see now? Time is at the quick while you play games in this hospital."

The eldest de Meath sister stormed out of the room, leaving Lily with Alice, who looked on with rounded eyes.

"She's a bitch, but she's right," said Alice.

"I'm trying, Alice. I truly am."

Alice reached beneath her dress, pulling out a pendant. She breathed on it and the glamour faded, revealing a different version of her youngest sister. Her eyes were gaunt and her hair thin. The vitality that made Alice a joy to be around had been sapped away. She looked like she'd barely survived being stranded on a desert island.

"Alice..."

Lily reached out her hand.

"We don't have much time, sister. I know you're trying, but please, for the sake of all of us. Try harder."

Alice brushed past, leaving Lily alone in the basement staring at the rune-covered potted tree.

SIXTEEN

The dead mouse leaning against the threshold of his door was suspicious. Damon lifted it by the tail, examining the creature, which had been killed by a sharp knife or talon. He smelled the feline and something sweet.

Damon tossed the dead mouse out the window. It'd been a long shift and he was looking forward to sleep, but as soon as he lay on the bed, his mind snapped awake.

"Blood and bone."

He wrestled with the idea of slumber until he realized he couldn't achieve it.

Standing in the doorway, he looked both ways and inhaled deeply. At the apex of in-breath, he could smell a sweetness in the air. Perfume.

A glance discovered a paw print along the baseboards. Faint, but his werewolf eyes could detect them when normal eyes would struggle.

"If I'm not gonna sleep..."

Damon threw on a fresh pair of scrubs and followed the prints. He could only see the occasional mark, but it was enough for him to track through the hospital.

When he came upon an orderly mopping the floor, the scents of pine and cleaning solutions thick in his nose, Damon searched two different hallways, finding nothing.

"Have you seen a black cat?" he asked a group of nurses on their way to the cafeteria.

He received a bunch of chuckles and smirks for his question, leaving him without an idea of which way to go.

"I should just go back to bed."

He took two steps before turning back. Damon reached into himself, drawing forth the rage that helped him transform. Claws stretched from his fingertips, but he let himself go no further.

With senses heightened, Damon examined the tile floors again. He went back to a different cross-hallway to find the sweet perfume that reminded him of lavender and blackberry wine. A single feline paw print was the reward for his search.

The trail led him to the stairs, and after descending to the lowest level, he found himself outside Bob Morehouse's testing laboratory. The irascible head of the department glanced up as he sprinkled glowing dust into a petri dish with a pair of plastic devil horns on his head.

"Oh, it's you. We don't do treats or tricks down here."

Bob frowned and went back to his work.

"You haven't seen a black cat by any chance?"

"You been drinking the punch from the Death Ward? They like to spike it with shaman potions. One of the orderlies thought he was an ice cube and kept trying to crawl into the freezer last year."

"No, I haven't been up top."

Damon half-turned when he saw an attractive woman with jet-black hair pulled back into a ponytail in the back of the laboratory. She was mixing a pale greenish liquid in a glass beaker.

As soon as he laid eyes upon her, his heart thumped uncontrollably in his chest.

She glanced in his direction, glossy red pouty lips curling upward at the corner, which sent a shock through his system. He didn't recognize the lab assistant, but then again, he hadn't been in the basement laboratory for months.

Damon marched into the back, standing opposite from the dark-haired woman as she finished mixing. A meticulous eyebrow arched upon his arrival.

"Can I help you?" she asked with a slight smirk.

She smelled like lavender and blackberry wine.

"Are you new here?"

The question tasted like ash as soon as he'd said it. The woman straightened her white lab coat. Her red-hot fingernails clacked against the glass.

"Did you need something?"

"I was looking for a black cat."

"A black cat? Shouldn't you be helping patients, not tracking down errant kitties?" she asked in a melodic voice.

"This one left a dead mouse on my door," he said, crossing his arms.

"I've heard such gifts are a form of endearment. Perhaps this feline has taken an interest in you."

"You're not wearing a name tag."

The woman extended her hand. "I'm Regina Felidae."

"Damon Wolfhard."

Her eyes glittered with interest. "You're the werewolf, aren't you?"

Their palms still touched, which sent a pleasurable shock up his arm. He felt like he should release her hand, but it was warm and he couldn't quite think.

"Guilty as charged."

"I'm sure you're guilty of a lot of things," she said.

"It's not just about the mouse. The cat led me to a missing healing stone and some reagents that helped one of my patients. I wanted to thank this feline for her help."

"Her?" she asked with a raised eyebrow. "Are you certain it's a female?"

"Fairly."

"And what would a cat care about one of your patients?"

He shifted his hand, which only gave the impression he was giving her a soft squeeze. When she smiled, he released her hand and let his rest on the counter.

"That's what I'd like to find out."

She cocked a winsome smile. "I may or may not know something about this supposed feline. Perhaps you could take me out for drinks and I could tell you everything I know."

His cheeks were flushed. He'd never been one to lose himself around women, but Regina seemed to be scrambling his thoughts.

"I would—"

The word *love* dangled at the end of his tongue. He swallowed it away.

"I probably can't. The hospital keeps me busy."

"Probably? And that's not what I heard about you and the big Krak woman," said Regina, studying him intently.

He felt like a bug under a microscope, or a mouse about to be pounced upon by a cat.

"I need to...change, or shower I mean."

"Which is it?"

"Shower."

Her generous red lips shifted to the side. "Enjoy the steam."

Regina returned to her testing beaker, leaving Damon reeling with confusion. He took a step away and paused, expecting her to say something more, but when she didn't, he kept going.

Before he made it out of the lab, she called after, "I'm available for drinks anytime. I don't even bite. Not on the first date at least."

Bob Morehouse rolled his eyes and Damon went straight up to his room, grabbed his kit, and took the longest cold shower in existence.

SEVENTEEN

An early November snow blanketed the parking lot in a covering of soft white. Remi sipped her black coffee at the cafeteria window, watching the snowflakes drift lazily in corkscrew patterns. It was peaceful and made her wish she had time to head into the city. She'd heard some enterprising Oestomancer students were encasing themselves in snow and wandering the streets as abominable snow people, but with a circus twist—shooting off illusionary sparklers or performing acrobatic tricks. It made her smile to think about the playful mischief of some of the smaller Halls.

Growing up, she'd rarely interacted with the white stuff. Her parents stayed away from the northern climes in the winter, claiming that the cold was hell on thievery. So it was pleasant watching the cars in the parking lot get coated by a layer of white.

Remi was about to turn away when she caught sight of Damon running along the sidewalk, laughing as he threw a snowball behind him. She was expecting to see one of their fellow third years, but when Remi saw a dark-haired woman in a puffy white coat throw a snowball back at Damon, the tile floor turned to quicksand.

Even from the third-floor window, Remi could tell the woman was beautiful. Her dark hair was raised into a high ponytail and her lips were coated with a crimson lipstick. She looked like the kind of woman who had a thriving social media presence and a healthy bank account. The impromptu snowball fight ended when Damon headed into the automatic ER doors while the woman turned to the parking lot. Before she slipped into a sleek black sportscar, she took off her puffy coat, revealing a lab tech white coat.

"I shouldn't be jealous, it's not like we're dating," Remi told herself.

She'd intended to head to the hospital library for some more readings about ghosts and apparitions, but her heart wasn't in it now. She dumped the half-drank mug into the bin and grabbed a quick cup of ice cream before heading back to her room. Lily was on shift with Dr. Martinez, so maybe she could catch a bit of shut-eye before her next shift.

Coming around the corner two turns from her room she ran into Alice, the youngest de Meath sister, who was pacing the hallway.

"Hey Alice, you okay?"

She was wearing a Hall hoodie and jeans, rather than the regular peasant dress, and looked almost embarrassed about being seen.

"Hey," said Alice with a weak smile, then swallowing hard. "Ice cream?"

Remi spoke around the mouthful of caramel chunk. "It's better than therapy."

She took a step towards her room when Alice stepped in her way.

"Have you seen Lily, Remi?" asked Alice in an overly loud voice.

Remi frowned. "You're not very good at this, Alice."

"What?"

Remi feinted left then ran around Alice. Biddy was standing at her door with her hand glowing faintly over the handle.

"You're not getting through that door," said Remi, startling the older de Meath sister. "I put a warding lock on it."

Alice's sneakers squeaked to a stop. "I'm sorry, Biddy."

"Do you not understand what being a lookout means?" asked Biddy with a furrowed forehead.

"I spoke really loud so you could hear me."

Remi marched up to Biddy as she shook the golden light from her right hand.

"I know a bully when I see one. You might be Lily's sister, but you're not acting like it."

Biddy glared with the intensity of a thousand suns. "You don't understand what you're talking about."

"Probably not, but I know Lily and I know when she means to help someone she does it, so if she's here in the city of sorcery trying to find a cure for your family's problems, then I trust her to do it. You're just getting in her way."

"You're a baby mage without a clue of how the real world works. We learned to use faez as young children, so don't lecture me about my sister," said Biddy.

"You're right, I'm new to magic, but I know people and I know when someone's acting the bully. That's you."

Remi tapped her finger in the middle of Biddy's chest. The sharp scent of faez followed and an invisible hand pushed Remi across the hallway, despite her never seeing Biddy move a finger.

"See, I told you, you're a bully."

Biddy's cheeks turned crimson. She raised her hands and Remi realized she'd pushed her too far, but then Alice threw herself in the way.

"Bridget! This is a hospital. What would Mother think if she could see you?"

The eldest de Meath let her hands drop, but continued shooting daggers with her eyes. After a long staredown, she grunted under her breath and marched the other way.

Remi blew out a breath. "Thank you."

"She means well, I swear. She's just looking out for our family."

"She has a strange way of showing it," said Remi.

"She's under a lot of pressure as the eldest sister. Our family has the strongest witches of any family line, so we're looked upon to be the ones to put the party back in the rave...or something like that."

"Then it might help if she treats Lily with the respect of an equal rather than like a child," said Remi.

Alice squeezed her eyes shut for a moment. "I know, I know. Bridget's hard to manage."

"Why are you here, Alice? I don't think they would have sent the youngest to manage the eldest, especially as headstrong as she is."

"Biddy wanted to come alone, but I volunteered."

Remi took a long look at the youngest de Meath in her street clothes, looking like a regular student at the Halls. Even her accent seemed to be toned down as if she were trying to fit in.

"It wasn't to keep an eye on your sister," said Remi.

"I wanted to see the city of sorcery," said Alice breathlessly. "And it's been everything I hoped it would be."

She sighed with lovesick energy, and for the first time Remi saw Alice as her own person rather than an addendum to her oldest sister. The Hall hoodie, the improper use of local phrasing, even the smoothing of her accent—her heart's design was awkwardly clear.

"You don't want to stay in Ireland."

Alice glanced nervously down the hallway. "Please don't tell Biddy."

"Why? I would kill to have a group of siblings to share my time with, and I'm sure Lily would love to have you around," said Remi.

"I love each and every one of them with all my heart, but I want to do something different."

"Join the Halls?"

Alice shook her head. "No, not that. I mean, unless..."

"Unless you can't find a cure for the Great Corruption."

"Biddy would bloody kill me for even thinking it," said Alice in a quiet voice. "And it's not just because of our family problems. Even before this happened, I wanted to see the world, figure out what I want to do with my life."

Remi snorted softly.

"Don't make fun," pouted Alice.

A smile rose to Remi's lips. "I'm not making fun. I get what you're saying. I'm supposed to pick a focus for my final two years, but I can't decide between them. How does one do that? Make a decision that will affect the rest of their life? Sometimes I wonder if I'm made out for this sedentary life."

"Sedentary life? Why did you join the Halls then?" asked Alice.

Remi laughed. She'd forgotten that everyone didn't know her sordid past.

"Because I wanted a shortcut to a better life, and I really didn't have anywhere else to go."

"I don't understand."

Remi gave Alice the short version of her past, leaving out the pendant, the Scythe sisters, and any other details that painted her in a less favorable light. By the end, Alice stood silently across the hall with her hands clasped in front with glistening, rounded eyes.

"I understand," said Alice, grabbing her hands and squeezing them tight.

Then she put her arms around Remi and held her close for a long hug, before releasing her.

"Truly. I understand," repeated Alice. "If it's drowning you're after, don't torment yourself with shallow water."

Mystified by the phrase, Remi stayed silent while Alice headed in the same direction as her older sister.

After she was around the corner, Remi shouted after, "If you understand, could you explain it to me?"

When no answer came, Remi disabled the wards and entered her room, tossing the remnants of the melted ice cream in the trash can. Then she sat on the edge of her bed and watched the snow fall, wondering how she'd gotten to this place in her life.

EIGHTEEN

A heavy crash echoed down the hallway, reaching Lily, who was speaking with the duty nurse about adjusting a patient's care. She ran to the room with the nurse on her heels, finding the older man with liver spots crouched in the corner.

The entire room was upended. The monitoring equipment had been knocked over. The patient's lunch was splattered across the window. Even some of the ceiling tiles had holes in them as if a pole had been stuck through them.

"Mr. Drexel, are you okay?" asked the nurse as she collected him from the corner.

"I don't want to be here anymore," said the older man, staring at the ceiling where the holes had been created.

Lily knew that she should have been checking on the patient, but the scene and the smell had her perplexed. The scent of burning metal was in the air like an electrical fire or a crucible of sulfurous iron. It coated her nose like heavy oil.

"What happened?" she asked the patient, receiving a glare from the nurse as she was trying to lead him out of the room.

"I don't know. I was half-asleep, those elixirs make me tired, and then all hell broke loose. It was like the Event all over."

Lily grabbed the patient's arm. "What did you see? Please. We need to know."

"Healer Lily," admonished the nurse.

"I...I don't know," said the patient, eyes searching the room as if he expected a second attack.

"Did you see an apparition or ghost?"

"Please, I just came to the hospital to be fixed, not to be interrogated like a criminal," said the old man, pulling away.

As he started leaving the room with the nurse, Lily said, "Did you see eyes? Red eyes, hovering in the air?"

The falter in his step told her the truth. He turned his head slightly.

"I did, and I never want to see them again."

Lily paced the destroyed room alone, trying to figure out why she was smelling Fomorian blood now when she hadn't in the past. Was the ghost a creature from the realm of Mara? The land of nightmares? Did this have to do with her and her connection to the Fae? It wasn't just a coincidence that these things were happening to her.

The squeak of a shoe alerted her to the presence of another person. She turned to find Dr. Decker staring into the destroyed room from the threshold. His eyes were bloodshot and he looked like he'd just woken up from a three-day bender with his hair mussed and sticking out in random directions.

"What the hell did you do, Lily?"

"This wasn't me, and I don't appreciate that you thought it was," said

Lily, still trying to piece together her thoughts.

"Not the room, the patient. He's asking to talk to Dr. Fairlight. He's unhappy about the way you treated him and he's a donor. We try to give them special treatment, you know."

"I'm sorry, Dr. Decker, but look at this," she said, gesturing randomly. "This ain't the first time and it ain't going to be the last. There's a bloody apparition on the loose and not the run-of-the-mill type. I thought it might be Martin Freely, but now I'm smelling brimstone, the mark of the Fomorians."

"What did you say?"

Dr. Decker glared at her from the doorway.

Lily swallowed, remembering who she was talking to. She'd been so deep into figuring out the identity of the apparition, she'd forgotten the serial killer's connection to their lead instructor.

"I'm sorry, Dr. Decker. 'Twas a mistake. A bloody foolish one. I shouldn't have brought up that name."

Dr. Decker's eyes darted in all directions while his jaw pulsed.

"I forbid you to ever speak that name again. Do you understand? You don't know anything about it, so if one of the staff, or that conniving prick Brennan put you up to it, stop right now. I...I can't—"

He fled from the room, sweeping down the hallway and nearly knocking over an orderly pushing a rolling shelf of food trays.

"What in the bloody hell is going on?" Lily asked herself.

She started putting the room back together, but the smell of brimstone was distracting. It made no sense that a ghost was haunting the hospital. The wards should prevent it. Unless it was a more powerful apparition that had ties to Mara? A Fomorian ghost with a grudge? Or was there something about Martin Freely that tied him to a more unusual past?

Head full of thoughts, Lily headed out. She needed to talk to someone about what had happened. Remi preferably, but any of her classmates would do. She made it halfway down the hall when she heard the heavy wooden clop of Biddy's shoes headed her direction.

Lily ran the other way, finding herself practically back at the patient's room before darting into one of the random conference rooms for telemedicine events. She had the door slammed closed before she realized there were others in the room.

"Is there a problem, Lily?" asked Dr. Martinez.

She turned to find the head of the department leaning against the big wooden table in the center of the room with Brennan only a few feet from her. She sensed they'd been flirting before she'd come in by their nearness and the way Dr. Martinez's shirt was open a few extra buttons than normal. She looked flushed.

"Fooking ghost destroyed my patient's room."

Dr. Martinez stiffened.

"A ghost? Is it rampaging through the hallways?"

Lily shook her head. "Sorry. I'm hiding from my sister."

"What's this about a ghost?" asked Brennan. "I thought the hospital wards protected from that sort of thing."

"They should," said Dr. Martinez, forehead hunched.

"Aye, they should, but this ain't the first time I've seen it. Remi too. Heard other reports from the staff as well."

"How is it appearing? A phantom? Or is it completely incorporeal?" asked Dr. Martinez.

"Menacing red eyes." Lily thought about it for a moment. "And today there was a new element. Sulfur and brimstone. Like an electrical fire."

"Or a Fomorian," said Dr. Martinez.

"Yes, a Fomorian," said Brennan.

"You can still smell it," said Lily, sniffing the air. "Though it's less than it was before."

"Can you tell us more about this ghost?" asked Brennan.

Lily gave them both a complete rundown of what they'd learned so far, including their suspicion about Martin Freely.

"Oh Merlin," said Dr. Martinez, shaking her head. "As if Oren isn't hurting enough."

"Aye, I'm a bloody fool for bringing it up. I'm sorry, Dr. Martinez. I should have been watching my mouth, but I was too busy thinking about what had happened."

Brennan nodded sympathetically. "I wish there was something we could do for Oren, but there is something I can do about the hospital wards. A ghost like that shouldn't be able to affect the hospital, not if the wards are active."

Dr. Martinez turned. "They're old. The maintenance team does the best they can, but it might be time for a complete rebuilding."

"Which means more money to raise," said Brennan with a sigh.

"You signed up for this," said Dr. Martinez.

Brennan grinned, laughing slightly. "I know, I know. I just didn't realize how deep into everyone's pockets I would need to dig." He tilted his head with a smirk. "But I have ideas. Maybe a few things that might pick the locks that some of our wealthy friends have put on their wallets."

"Lily, thank you so much for bringing this to us," said Dr. Martinez. "In fact, if you learn anything more, please bring it to me right away."

The welcoming encouragement from Dr. Martinez as opposed to Dr. Decker was refreshing, especially after a difficult morning. She'd felt like things were getting worse. But while having the support of the ward staff and the hospital's biggest donor might help with a breakthrough in hospital facilities, it wasn't going to solve the immediate problem. They needed to catch the menacing apparition before it caused any more issues.

NINETEEN

The wrinkly, desiccated monkey paw sat on the table surrounded by other accoutrements like silver dust, a jar full of paint markers, two pickled manticore eyes, and demonic bone dust. Damon poked the shriveled hand with his divining rod, expecting a finger to move on its own.

"Are we putting a hex on someone, or tracking down a ghost?" he asked, receiving a glare from Lily. "And where did you even get half this stuff? It certainly didn't come from the hospital stores."

The Irish witch was wearing her dark green peasant dress and she'd tied smaller items into her enormous mess of rainbow-colored hair.

"The city is full of places that provide the more exotic reagents, and we don't know what kind of bloody ghost it is so we need all the help we can get. The silver dust is for banshees, the manticore eyes when crushed help with spectre bites, and the mystdrakon scales any of the vengeful types."

"But a monkey paw? I thought those were for granting wishes, or something."

"Don't be an eejit, Damon," said Lily, punching him in the arm. "Wishes are an urban legend. No magic is strong enough to be able to do anything like that."

Remi was scratching the back of her head. "Our wolfish friend has a point. What is all this? I've spent the past two and a half years learning how to be a healer, but I don't know a thing about banishing a ghost. Banishing? Is that the right verb?"

"Aye, banishing," said Lily with a frown.

Damon poked the monkey paw a second time just to be sure it wasn't going to move on its own. He checked back to Remi, expecting to share a secret smile with her, but she was staring at him in a way that made him feel like he'd done something wrong.

"How's this going to work, Lily?"

"Aye, a good question. We're going to have to improvise. I'm sure I can count on you both for that. There's gonna be two problems. The first is we don't know what kind of ghost it is, and the second is we don't know where it is. The only thing we have going for us is that we know it's in the hospital and that any incorporeal being must maintain a link to the Veil."

"How does that help us?" asked Remi.

Lily spread her hands on the table. "The Veil is the realm between the living and the dead. The beings that count it as their home have a certain signature that we can use to track. With the three of us, we can triangulate its location in the hospital using these three stones I've enchanted."

Damon grabbed one of the smooth stones and held it up. On the side, it read in fancy painted calligraphy: Agnes.

"Is this from the gift shop?"

"It works best if the stones are identical," said Lily.

Remi picked up a stone and held it for the others to read. "Can I be

Beatrice?"

"Of course. I'll be Josephine then. The stone will vibrate and put off a soft glow the closer you get."

Lily held up three small jars. "This is demonic bone dust. It has a high concentration of inactive faez. If you come near the ghost, throw a handful at it. The dust will make it visible and make it harder for it to escape. It will, however, make it very angry, so be prepared."

"I mean, how much damage can a ghost do?" asked Remi with a shrug.

"A vengeful one can kill you, and if this is truly Martin Freely, the Golden Willow serial killer, then you can be certain he's going to try and end you," said Lily sternly.

Damon bit his lower lip. "Shouldn't we get more help? Involve your sisters at least?"

The heat-seeking glare he received from Lily was enough to get him to raise his hands.

"Sorry I asked."

"Any questions?" asked Lily tersely.

"What do we do once we trap it?" asked Remi.

"Hold it until I can get there," said Lily. "Unless it's something more powerful than we think, then I should be able to sever its link to the hospital and end its destructive reign."

The way Lily explained it made him feel like she was holding something back.

"What would be too powerful for you to banish?" asked Damon.

Lily frowned.

"If it were a nightmare from the realm of Mara, or any being that was more powerful in life than the typical person," said Lily.

"A nightmare?" asked Damon. "Like a bad dream?"

"Nay. A nightmare is a kind of apparition from the realm of Mara, the land of the Fomorians. It's not quite a ghost, but our tools should still affect it."

"Great," said Remi with a roll of her eyes.

Lily checked the clock on the wall. "We should get going. Only have a few hours before our next shift. Keep in touch on our phones, let us know where you're at, and anything you might see."

As they headed out of the break area, Damon caught up with Remi.

"Hey."

"Hey?"

"Is there something wrong? I feel like you're avoiding me, but I can't figure out why."

The blank look left his stomach in knots.

"You heard Lily. We only have a few hours. Let's get to work."

Remi headed the opposite direction, leaving Damon with a gut full of indigestion.

He headed towards the far end of the hospital where most of the normal care was given. While Golden Willow specialized in supernatural treatment, not everyone required the unusual spells or elixirs that came with that side of the hospital. Many procedures like childbirth or wound care were administered by regular doctors and nurses.

The faces of the staff were less familiar than his side of the hospital, but he was wearing scrubs and a name tag, so he was given a lot of head nods on the way.

"Anything yet?" asked Lily over the phone.

"Beatrice hasn't seen anything," said Remi. "What about you, Agnes?"

Damon sighed. "Nothing."

He wandered the maternity ward, poking his head into rooms while keeping an eye on the stone. A few times, patients tried to corral him for questions and he had to promise he'd send their doctor in later so he could keep moving.

After an hour of wandering, Damon thought the whole exercise was going to be a bust. He was heading past the newborn feeding room when he felt the stone vibrate against his palm. He almost said something to the others, but wanted to confirm that it wasn't his imagination first. He feared it was like the phantom buzz he felt when his phone was in his pocket, but when he checked it, there was no message or call.

Damon pushed through the swinging door into a room full of women with infants in their laps or nestled against their chests. He scanned the room, especially the ceiling area.

"Hey doctor," cooed a voice from his left.

A tired, but attractive looking woman with her hair in a messy ponytail and bags under her eyes with an infant pressed against her chest glanced up.

"Uh," he said, trying not to stare.

"It's okay, I don't bite." She grimaced slightly, adjusting the baby. "But he does."

Another woman from across the room said, "Don't listen to Jessie. She's just looking for a better baby daddy."

"Hush, Maria. Not everyone has a great husband like yours."

The Agnes stone vibrated again, leading Damon further into the room.

"I promise I'm not this forward," said Jessie from behind. "It's the lack of sleep."

"I'm sorry, ladies, I'm just doing some routine checks."

The stone had a faint orangish glow. He turned to his left and right, feeling the way the stone vibrated as a method of detection.

"I think I have something," he whispered into the phone.

"If it tries to escape, hit it with that dust I gave you," said Lily. "It'll help us keep track of it."

Damon checked around the room. The entire collection of mothers was staring at him suspiciously.

"Hey doc, nothing's wrong, is it? You're kinda giving us all the creeps," said Jessie.

He half-turned at the moment the red eyes appeared above the soda machine. Damon tossed the stone and phone onto a table and reached for the demonic bone dust bag in his pocket.

The new mothers started raising their voices at him and he thought a few might have seen the eyes, but he was too focused on the apparition to pay attention. Right as he had the baggie open and in his hand, the red eyes flashed menacingly and sped past him, raising a cry from the room.

He tossed the baggie at the ghost, coating it in pale dust.

"I got it!"

Then he remembered he'd dropped the phone. He grabbed it and the stone and repeated, "I got it!"

Running after the ghost, he saw it fleeing down the hallway, then disappear around the corner. He checked the stone to see a more confident glow that was quickly receding.

"It fled the area. I think it's headed your way, Remi."

"I'm starting to see a glow," said Remi through the phone. "On it."

#

The glow on the Beatrice stone increased in intensity as Remi crept through the kitchen for the hospital cafeteria. Workers gave her side-eye as she moved past them while they prepared the special dietary plates that would get sent to patients across the hospital.

"What do I do if I find it?" asked Remi.

"Keep it there. I'm headed your direction from the opposite side of the hospital," said Lily.

Remi shook her head and toggled the microphone off. "Keep it there? Like I have the slightest clue how to do that."

A dropped pot startled her. She paused, closed her eyes momentarily, and uttered a curse before moving on.

When she reached a locked door, she reached for her lockpicks but remembered she hadn't grabbed them.

She turned to one of the kitchen staff. "Hey, can you help me get through this? I need to check on the fire suppression equipment. There's an inspector coming by this afternoon."

The worker screwed up his face. "Why are you wearing scrubs?"

Remi sighed and rolled her eyes. "I'm part of Aura Healers. We have to learn all sorts of things about hospital administration."

"Oh, yeah, that makes sense."

He grabbed a key chain off the wall and tossed it to her. Once the door was open, she gave it back.

The interior was larger than expected, with rows of shelves containing boxes of food. A slight hum registered at the high end of her hearing. She thought a motor was out of balance until she saw the pulsating runes on the shelves.

The stone vibrated against her palm, making it itch. She craned her neck in all directions.

"What the hell am I doing?" she asked herself as she crept through the aisles.

An itchy feeling between her shoulder blades had her turning around. She couldn't figure out where the sensation was coming form until she spotted faint movement near the ceiling.

The apparition was vaguely human shaped. The red eyes that she'd seen before were focused on the runes of the shelves.

"I see it," she whispered after toggling the microphone back on.

"I'm almost there. Two minutes," said Lily with heavy breaths, clearly running. "Keep it there."

"How?"

"Use an anchoring hex or...never mind, just try," said Lily.

Remi shoved the phone in her pocket and raised her hands like a boxer about to get into a fight.

"Hurry up, Lily."

About ten seconds after she put the phone away, the apparition slowly turned. Remi sensed that she'd been detected.

"You might be wondering why I brought you here," said Remi.

The menacing eyes flashed a deeper red. She couldn't quite make out the form, but it looked like a man. The newspaper pictures of Martin Freely showed him as a shorter fellow with dark hair and a brooding expression. The ghost was too faint for her to make out the details.

"Are you Martin Freely?"

The floating ghost made no signal of recognition.

"Maybe you don't remember? I guess it'd be all hate keeping you in the Veil."

She checked over her shoulder.

"Come on, Lily."

When she turned her head back, the ghost was streaking towards her. Remi blasted it with a force bolt, which only slightly deflected the oncoming apparition before it hit her in the chest.

Remi found herself flying through the air, slamming into the shelves and having the wind knocked out of her chest. Before she could cast another force bolt, the apparition was upon her like an invisible vise. Ghostly hands wrapped around her neck. She couldn't breathe.

As the spots started to connect in her vision, she heard the sound of pounding shoes. A male voice shouted something and then the vise was no longer around her throat.

"Remi, are you okay?"

She looked up into Damon's worried face and reached for the phone in her pocket.

"Lily, it left the cafeteria."

Damon grabbed her phone. "It went through the floor, which I think is where the earth protective ward is located."

"Headed that way!"

Damon helped her to her feet. She rubbed her neck and tried to swallow, but the constriction had bruised her throat.

"Let me fix that with a spell."

"No time. We need to catch up to that ghost."

§

The sight of a woman in a green peasant dress running through the hallways brought questioning stares, but no concern, which was why she'd chosen not to be in her scrubs. Nothing sent heart rates soaring like a member of the medical staff at a full sprint.

Lily threw herself through the stairwell door, beating feet until she reached the lower level. She paused to catch her breath, hating how out of shape she was from working in the hospital. Back in Ireland, she spent a lot of time wandering the region collecting reagents, or helping folk in other counties. Some days she walked twenty kilometers.

The door blocked her passage. She thought about waiting for Remi, but didn't want to give the ghost a chance to get away. Lily focused her faez until she formed a force-hardened wind-spear. The blast snapped the lock and the door swung open lazily.

The stone in her pocket vibrated against her leg, but she didn't need it. She could feel the presence of the ghost in the room beyond.

The maintenance area was filled with huge boilers and other equipment humming from use. She crept forward carefully.

The lack of brimstone was curious, given her previous interaction with the apparition, but it wasn't unusual for the incorporeal to present differently depending on their linkage to the Veil.

As she crept through the machines, Lily felt pressure on her entire body. The ghost was more powerful than she first thought. As she rounded the corner, she came face-to-face with the apparition floating right outside the room that held the earth ward.

The faint outline suggested familiarity. Her pocket mumbled with the voices of her friends but she was too focused on the apparition to reach for the phone.

"Who are you?"

The menacing red eyes flashed with intensity. The longer she stared at the figure, the more she knew she should recognize it. He was wearing an old tweed coat, but his hands were covered in runic tattoos.

"You thwarted me."

The voice froze Lily's heart. It was crystal clear. No wavering Veil static.

And it knew her.

"You're not Martin Freely."

"And you're Lilith de Meath, meddler in chief. You dragged me back from the edge, and then stole my chance at vengeance and left me stuck here to rot the endless days. Now I have no course but to punish you in his stead."

Recognition hit her like a stone to the face. She remembered his hate like she knew his face. It was the mage that had created Sammie, the patient last year she'd freed from his cursed blood.

When she'd summoned the link to figure out what was wrong, she'd had to fight for her life to banish him, using an old Roman coin. But it hadn't done the job completely.

The mage was back, causing havoc in the hospital.

Lily raised her hands, preparing a binding curse to hold the ghost in place until her friends could arrive.

"I know your tricks, Lilith de Meath. I've been watching you from the shadows. I may not be able to get my revenge against that twit Sammie, but I can surely make you pay for his sins."

As Lily reached the culmination of the spell, the ghost mage gestured with his hands and an invisible fist punched her in the stomach, interrupting the spell and leaving her doubled over. The mage surged forward, before looking up.

She heard her friends running through the room as she tried to yell out her location.

"This isn't over by any means. After I'm done with you, you'll wish you'd stayed in the Old Country."

Lily struggled to her feet as the ghost faded from view. It shouldn't have been able to retreat back to the Veil, but she knew that was exactly what it had done, which told her it was even more powerful than she first expected.

Her friends appeared around the corner out of breath.

"Are you okay?" asked Remi.

"You look like you've seen a ghost," said Damon, wryly.

Lily frowned.

"Worse than that. I know this ghost."

"Martin Freely?"

Lily shook her head. "You remember Sammie from last year? When I tried to figure out what was wrong with him, I followed the link from him to the Veil. What I ended up summoning was his maker, the old mage that had experimented on him and kept him a prisoner."

"That's who the ghost is? Oh shit, we need to tell Dr. Decker," said Damon.

"No, please no."

"Why not?"

Lily squeezed her lips tight. "Because I did that without permission from the hospital. Summoning rituals like that are forbidden for a reason.

They'd be forced to kick me out if they learned what I did."

"What are we going to do?" asked Remi.

"I don't know. I'll need to think, do some research," said Lily.

"And let this evil ghost roam the hospital causing trouble?" asked Damon.

"It doesn't care about anyone else but me. It might cause some minor inconvenience, but it's me the mage wants. I'll have to increase my personal protections until we can figure out how to get rid of it."

Damon frowned. "I'll keep your secret for now, but if it starts harming patients, we need to tell someone."

Lily nodded tightly. "If it gets to that, I'll tell Dr. Decker myself."

TWENTY

A blue truck slid around the corner at the entrance of Golden Willow. The snow-slick streets were a mess. The ER had been receiving howlers all afternoon, but that wasn't Remi's problem as she waited near the sidewalk.

A woman's voice carried to her from the side entrance. Remi reflexively ducked behind a car, seeing the gorgeous woman with dark hair in a lab coat standing outside talking to Damon. Her name was Regina Felidae. Remi had looked it up after the last time she'd seen them talking.

The incoming ambulance made it too hard for her to hear what they were talking about, but then Damon went back inside and Regina stalked to her vehicle in the employee portion of the parking lot. Remi chewed on her lower lip as she tried to convince herself she had nothing to worry about.

"It's not like she's not drop-dead beautiful."

The scuff of a boot brought Remi's head up.

"Hiding from someone?"

Alice had her hands in the pockets of her puffy white coat. The cold air turned her cheeks pinkish.

"It's not important."

Alice shrugged while wearing a wry grin.

"So where are we going?"

"There's a bar in the fourth I heard from one of my patients called the Amber & Smoke."

The trains were packed as most residents sought to avoid the messy streets. The snow came in fits and starts, leaving the city covered in the white stuff. As the train passed Stone Singer Hall, which was an enormous building in the shape of a flower, they watched as students created intricate architectural buildings out of snow using only their voice. A trio of students had recreated Notre Dame while two others had made an elephant battling a manticore.

"I wish I could do that," said Alice brightly.

"Thinking of joining the Halls like your sister?"

"I couldn't."

"Don't want to give up your patron?"

Alice giggled. "I have the voice of a necromancer. My mother always said I could summon the dead with my singing."

The Amber & Smoke had a line waiting outside to enter. The people in back said they'd been there for an hour already.

"We can go somewhere else," said Alice. "I'm just happy to be out in the city with someone other than Biddy."

"Get your fill of beating up orphans and kicking the homeless?"

"She's not that bad, you know. Or used to be. Biddy could be quite funny. She could act the eejit when it was just us sisters together."

"I'm sorry, I shouldn't have said that. I think I'm jealous of you and your siblings. I think I could put up with having a Biddy if I had an Alice and a Lily too."

"That's awfully sweet, Remi."

"Come on," said Remi, grabbing Alice's hand. "We're getting into this place."

The back of the building had a high brick wall with a wrought-iron fence. A breath of faez revealed arcane protections on the locks, but Remi was more studied now than when she first came to the Halls. Using a piece of gold wire and a short spell, she bypassed the alarm and picked the lock in a few seconds.

A back door led them into the bar proper. There was an upstairs, but Remi wanted to get the lay of the land first. At a glance, she saw loads of magical trinkets, expensive watches, and the latest fashions.

"I don't think we're in Kansas anymore," Remi said as she pulled Alice through the crowd to a spot along the bar.

When the bartender didn't give them service right away, she waved a hundred-dollar bill. He rolled his eyes and moved to another customer at the other end.

"What was that about?"

Remi leaned against the bar and examined the clientele of the Amber & Smoke. After a minute, she realized her mistake.

"This is a Coterie bar."

"Coterie of Mages?"

"Yeah. Not all of them, I see an Alchemist and an Assassin student, but this is probably where some of the Societies hang out. That's why the bartender didn't care about my money. Everyone here is rich. It's their influence that matters more."

"You know a lot about them."

Remi lifted a shoulder. "Not directly. Let's just say I spent my life studying people like this."

A rap of knuckles on the bar had them spinning around. "Can I get you ladies something?"

"A couple of smokes. Whatever the latest trend is," said Remi.

When the bartender was finished, he slid two intricate glass mugs in the shape of a howling face filled with billowing smoke. A stainless steel lid contained the swirling gray mist.

"What is it?"

The bartender smirked. "The Beast."

Remi was going to ask, but decided she didn't care. Besides giving Alice a night on the town, she wanted to feel like a regular student of the Halls.

"Were you really a thief?" asked Alice after taking a big inhale of the smokey mug.

"I was."

Remi shoved her nose into the cool smoke and let the mixture drift through her nostrils. When she was feeling content, she sniffed hard, sending a shot of alchemy into her brain. As she pulled away, she was filled with a sense of confidence and belonging. The entire world felt right as if it'd been created just for her.

"A chacc cuirre uidre ittige," muttered Alice with her eyes wide. "I ain't felt this good in years."

The colors and smells in the bar came into sharp focus.

"What kind of people did you steal from?"

The question filtered through her brain. Remi jawed at the empty air before answering.

"The bigger the score the better."

"The lot of 'em here?"

Remi nodded. "Yes. Filthy rich."

"Probably wouldn't even miss it."

"I wish that were true. These assholes are like dragons and their hoard. They know every coin and bill like it was one of their children."

This wasn't entirely true, but Remi was feeling so good after the alchemical smoke that it felt true. And wasn't that all that mattered?

Remi didn't realize Alice was tugging on her arm until the youngest de Meath leaned into her ear.

"Think you could steal from one of them here?"

Under normal circumstances, Remi wouldn't have considered it, but the alchemical smoke had her feeling good and she wanted to make Alice's night on the town a memorable one.

"Easy as pie."

"Would you?" asked Alice with eyes wide.

Remi canvassed the bar. The clumps of students were no good. Too many chances for a friend to notice her sleight of hand. Then she spied a lone student at the end of the bar, waiting for his drink. She hadn't seen him before, suggesting he'd just arrived. He was fairly well dressed in a navy button-down, with an expensive watch on his wrist. With his slicked-back hair, he looked like he was trying to get into finance.

"Watch this," she said, pumping her eyebrows at Alice before sidling next to the finance guy as if she were waiting for the bartender.

She caught him glancing over. The look in his eyes suggested he was about to hit on her, and the last thing she wanted to do was get bogged down in conversation with a mark.

"Slowest fucking bar ever," she muttered, before turning and bumping into finance guy.

With the expensive watch in her pocket, she was halfway back to Alice when a crimson glow rose up around her. A pit formed in her stomach. She shouldn't have been so quick to show off without checking her mark for defensive spells.

"Hey, you, mullet girl!"

Remi turned slowly. Finance guy was pointing at her, not that it was necessary since the crimson glow had identified her clearly in the crowded bar.

A bubble formed around her as finance guy stalked forward, joined by three other similarly dressed guys who stood by his side. She hadn't seen them because they'd been upstairs, she realized.

"She stole my watch. It's protected with a Dye Spell," said finance guy loudly to the now quiet bar.

Remi pulled the watch out of her pocket, twisting the band with her fingers. "This? I found it on the floor. You must have damaged the band and it fell off. I was going to give it to a bouncer."

She held the watch out in her hand, hoping he'd take it back. He took one step forward then glanced around at all the eyes upon him. Remi knew at that moment she was screwed. It wasn't about the value of the watch, but the hit to his reputation.

"Look at these two, Geoff. I don't think they belong here," said one of Geoff's friends.

Remi shook the watch again as the crimson glow faded from her body.

"You're probably right. I don't think this is our kind of scene. It's probably a good time to leave," she said as she sensed the crowd hardening against her. She tossed the watch back to Geoff.

Remi turned towards the front with her heart in her throat. She thought she might make it out, when one of Geoff's friends hit her with a limb-lock spell that momentarily froze her. Then they had her by the arms, dragging her towards the back.

"Let's take her to the patio."

A parade of students followed Geoff and his friends out back. Remi glanced around, but she didn't see Alice. She wouldn't blame her if she'd headed back to Aura Healers. This wasn't exactly what she'd signed up for in coming out tonight.

Remi just hoped the punishment wasn't going to be too severe. It wouldn't be the first time she'd taken a beating, and she worked at the best place possible for recovery.

"You might be wondering why I brought you all here," she said to the crowd when they released her arms.

Geoff turned to the crowd. "Does anyone know mullet girl?"

No one answered.

"Then she snuck in somehow. I don't know who you are, but this is a Society bar. Not only shouldn't you be here, but you tried to steal from me and now it's time to pay the piper."

Remi feigned reaching into her wallet. "Cool, cool. Which one's the piper? Is it that tweed asshole to your right? I don't have a ton of big bills, but I'll do what I can."

Geoff furrowed his brow as if he didn't understand.

"What should we do to her?"

The crowd shouted suggestions as if it were a game show: "Shaky Leg Curse!" or "Turn her skin blue!" or "Luxus Remedial!"

The punishments kept coming until a strong voice echoed over the crowd.

"Verum Loqui!"

Geoff snapped his fingers. "What a great idea. Verum Loqui it is. You're going to tell us all your secrets. Every last one."

Remi's heart sunk. A few punches to the ribs was what she'd been expecting, but she should have figured the Coterie crowd to be more ruthless than that.

She tried to send out a scattered force blast to give herself room to run, but someone punched her in the side, ruining the five elements spell before it completed.

"Grab her arms," said Geoff.

Once again, she was being held fast, but this time Geoff approached with a menacing grin.

"You don't fuck with Coterie, or the Societies. We're going to teach you a very important lesson that I don't think you're ever going to forget."

Remi glanced around, seeing her window of escape had closed.

"Let me get this straight. The big, bad Coterie mage is going to have me held down and put a spell on me? I thought you guys were ruthless. Not chickenshits who gang up on a single girl. Maybe that Coterie reputation is bullshit. I've had more intense run-ins with the plant Hall, or are you afraid to duel a girl?"

She had no idea if dueling was a thing, but her comment got a reaction from the crowd. Geoff glanced around nervously. As scared as she was, he was surprisingly worried. Remi guessed he wasn't the hot mage he thought he was, because mommy and daddy had gotten him an invite to the most prestigious Hall in the university.

"Nice try, you twit," said Geoff, breathing heavily. "You're not getting out of your punishment that easily."

Remi cursed under her breath. She'd rather have her hair singed off than reveal her secrets, especially in front of this crowd.

Geoff approached her and began the incantation. His finger gestures were slow and sloppy—either from nervousness or a lack of skill—which helped her understand why he hadn't taken her challenge. As the spell neared completion, she fought against the guys holding her arms.

"You're going to really regret this," she said.

The second spell didn't reach her ears until she heard the chatter rise to a crescendo behind them. When her captors glanced over her shoulders, Remi used the distraction to kick Geoff in the knee hard enough to break his concentration.

"You fucking bitch."

The identity of the speaker was easy to determine unless there was another Irish woman in the crowd. Remi saw Alice with her arms flowing through smooth motions and her voice rising with intensity, speaking in the language of the Fae.

A shiver went down Remi's spine at hearing the faerie words. The moment of transfixed observation was broken when Geoff called out.

"Someone stop that spell!"

A few members of the crowd went after Alice, but a booming crack startled everyone, freezing them in place. The youngest de Meath jammed her fist downward, and a greenish light slammed into the patterned concrete, pulsing outward in waves.

Everyone stared at the ground as the earth shook. Remi had no idea what was about to happen, but used the distraction to check her surroundings for an escape route should one present itself.

"Fine, I'll do it myself," said Geoff, marching forward.

Then the concrete cracked and dozens of sinuous vines came undulating out like snakes.

The party turned to mayhem as everyone tried to get away from the grasping plants. Everyone was out for themselves, knocking each other over in an attempt to escape the patio.

The vines grew tall, grabbing people and tossing them aside. Remi head-butted the guy holding her right arm, which brought stars to her eyes, but she turned and jammed her freed fist into the second guy's crotch.

"Let's get out of here," she said to Alice, grabbing her hand and leading her towards the tables in back.

Geoff tried to get in their way, his face breaking with anger.

"I'll send your souls—"

Twin force blasts sent Geoff tumbling over a drink cart, spilling alcohol all over his button-down, leaving a clear path to the back.

Remi helped Alice climb onto the bar structure, which gave them a way to climb onto the brick wall. The landing rattled her knees, but they were running down the alleyway to the opposite street in no time.

A circling taxi gave them a quick escape. Remi had the driver drop them off at the train station. She didn't want anyone to be able to track them back to Aura Healers.

Once they flopped onto a seat on the train, Remi burst into laughter along with Alice.

"Bloody hell, Alice. You saved my ass back there. What was that spell?"

"A little gift from Medb. It was harder given it's the city rather than the forest, but I couldn't let anything bad happen to you since you were trying to show me a good time in the city."

Remi pulled Alice close to her. "I'm glad you're on my side."

Alice leaned her head on Remi's shoulder. "Did you see the look on Geoff's face when we both hit him with those spells?"

"I won't forget it." Remi chuckled. "Sorry our night has been cut short. I should have been more careful about stealing his watch. That Beast smoke muddled my brain."

"Not a bloody word," said Alice, grinning. "This is the best night since I arrived in the city. I could stay out all night."

Remi had a shift in the morning, but she couldn't help being pulled along by Alice's good mood.

"I know a bar down the street from Golden Willow. Let's swing by there and enjoy a beer or two. I promise it's a normie bar and I won't steal anything."

"You don't have to on my account."

Remi grinned despite herself. "I put that life behind me. But I'm happy to share a drink."

The train rumbled around the tracks as Remi watched the city slide past with Alice leaning against her shoulder.

TWENTY-ONE

Lily was halfway out the door when a sleepy Remi stirred from her bed. Strands of her dark hair were stuck to her forehead as she rubbed the corner of her eye with a knuckle.

"Where are you going in those clothes?"

Lily had chosen her scavenging dress. The one she wore when she was meandering the forest looking for plants and mushrooms for their elixirs. The green and brown absorbed the dirt and smudges from the greenery easily.

"I have a meeting in the city."

"With who?" asked Remi, sitting up. "You look like you're going to a sacrifice with those bones around your neck."

Lily put her hand to the bone necklace. "Is it too much?"

"Who do you have a meeting with? The Honorable Order of Witch Doctors?"

"There's such a thing?"

Remi screwed up her face. "I was making a joke."

"Oh." She sighed. "I don't actually have a meeting, but I was hoping that if I looked more like my old self I might get a chance to speak to Sebastian Hollow. He's the Patron of Umbra Velum."

"Umbra Velum? Does that have something to do with paper?"

"They're a small Hall that deals with the Veil."

"You want to talk to him about the evil mage ghost. Do you want me to come?"

"That would be great."

After Remi got dressed, they got on the train, headed to the eleventh ward.

"I take it you don't have an appointment," said Remi as they neared their destination.

Lily pulled a small folded paper from her enormous linen carryall. Inside the folds was an obsidian talon the size of a pendant.

"Whoa, that's wicked," said Remi, stroking the smooth material. "What's it from?"

"A mortanis hound. They hunt the Veil for anything living, or otherwise foreign to their realm. When I was eight or nine, the Veil was acting weird as if no one was in charge of it anymore. Nyx and I found an old nekyia tree that was sickly and we managed to sneak through it into the Veil. We found the talon and escaped back before we were discovered."

The Enochian district had an identity crisis, with every other block looking like it belonged in the inner ring while the opposite ones were in need of repair. The Umbra Velum Hall was an old house with an old factory in the back that looked like it'd been built in the early 1900s.

A knock brought heavy footsteps down a wooden staircase. The door swung wide, revealing a pimple-faced guy with messy brown hair looking like he'd just woken up.

"We don't keep ghosts here, so just—"

He screwed up his face.

"Oh, you're not those damn kids. I can't sleep when they keep banging on the door. Can I help you?"

"I'm looking for your patron."

"Sebastian's busy in back with the Brine Man. He said no one should bother him."

"I didn't come without a gift." Lily unfolded the paper wrapping, revealing the mortanis hound talon.

"Is that…?"

"Aye."

The guy shifted his mouth to the side. "I don't know how you have that, but I know Sebastian would kill me if I turned you away. Follow me."

The brownstone was quaint. A far cry from the enormous building that she lived in at Aura Healers. In another life, a Hall like Umbra Velum would be appealing.

"How many students are in your Hall?" asked Remi on the way through.

"Twelve, but not everyone lives in the house. The others live across the street, but Sebastian likes this location because of the thinness between the city and the Veil."

The old factory building was nearly as large as the house, but not as tall. Thick timbers held up the building while straw and dirt covered the floor. A middle-aged man with the edges of his hair faint with gray sat opposite a ghostly figure who looked like he'd been born at the same time the factory had been constructed.

"What's with the fooking bogtrotter?" asked the apparition as he hooked his thumbs in his suspenders.

The middle-aged man frowned as they approached.

"Teran?"

Their guide held up his hands. "I know, you said not to bother you, but she has a mortanis hound talon."

Sebastian let out a soft whistle.

"Don't let that Irish witch near you," said the Brine Man. "She's full of the forest spirits. Put a curse on ya as simple as shedding a tear."

"I'm only here to ask you some questions in exchange for this talon," said Lily, holding out the paper.

"That's a mighty big gift. I assume these aren't the usual questions like can I talk to my dead grandpa or anything like that."

She glanced at Teran, who nodded and headed back into the house. Sebastian accepted the talon, holding it up to the light before setting it on the table.

"Can you feel your innards boiling?" asked the Brine Man. "Never trust an Irishwoman, especially a witch. She's probably already put a hex on you."

"My apologies," said Sebastian with a sigh as he jutted his head towards the ghost. "He sort of comes with the house and since it's a great location for investigating the Veil, we have to put up with his inappropriate comments."

"Ain't nothing haven't heard before."

"You two are Hall students?"

"Aura Healers. I'm Lily and this is Remi."

Sebastian raised an eyebrow. "Aura Healers? Wasn't expecting that. What's so important that you're bringing me a talon from the Veil?"

As Lily cleared her throat, unsure of how to begin, the Brine Man floated around the table, but Remi shooed him away, a gesture which inexplicably worked. Lily caught the furrowed brow from Sebastian, who clearly thought that Remi shouldn't have been able to affect the incorporeal being.

Remi spoke up. "It's a delicate matter that requires a certain level of secrecy."

"I can't promise that if you're doing something illegal, or someone's going to get hurt."

"I did break the rules, but I think you'll understand why, Patron Hollow."

Lily went on to explain the story of Sammie, his exotic blood, the mage that had made him that way, and how she'd fixed him. Then she told him all about the ghost that had been tormenting the hospital and their discovery of the mage's identity.

Sebastian Hollow sat quietly for a long time after Lily finished speaking, which made her worry that he wouldn't be interested.

"That shouldn't be possible," he said, shaking his head. "Either the wards are damaged or this ghost was a very powerful mage in real life, which probably meant he was old. Ancient even. That's a tricky situation. Are you sure you can't bring this to the administration?"

"They're already raising funds to improve the wards and the hospital in general, and I'd rather not reveal the illegality of what I did for Sammie last year," said Lily.

Sebastian tapped on the talon. "It was very clever what you did to track the ghost down. But the fact that it was able to nearly kill you, Remi, tells me that the normal solutions aren't going to work."

"Why is that?" asked Remi.

"When a ghost remains with more of its earthly powers intact, it means that it planned for this contingency. This mage knew that it might die at some point and wanted to continue even if it meant he was only a ghost."

"Of course that bloody gobshite would do that," said Lily.

"What can we do?" asked Remi.

"You had the right idea with those gift shop enchanted stones, but you'll need more powerful ones to trap him so you can banish him once and for all. I can teach you the rituals, but you'll need to be able to keep him in one place. For that you need a robust arcane scaffolding, or an extremely powerful entity that can do the same."

"Whatever it takes," said Lily. "This mage is causing havoc with the patients. No one has died yet, but I can't imagine our luck will last."

"Luck of the fooking Irish, my ass," said the Brine Man.

"If you give me a minute," said Sebastian, "I can get you some anchor stones. They're not strong enough on their own, but I can teach you how to use the hospital wards to bolster their effectiveness. If you can trap the ghost with the anchor stones, then you can complete the ritual and banish the ghost, once and for all."

"You're a fine stepper, Patron Hollow," said Lily.

"I'll be right back," said Sebastian. "Don't mind the ghost. He's all bark, no bite."

After he left, the Brine Man stared at Lily as he if was going to stab her.

"He's a real treat," said Remi, jabbing her thumb in the ghost's direction.

"Women shouldn't be going to school and messin' up things," said the Brine Man with a snarl.

"What did you do to get stuck here?" asked Remi as she approached the ghost.

"Ain't none of your business, ya fruity broad."

Remi half-turned with a grin hitched to her lips. "Imagine living back when assholes like this were the norm."

Patron Hollow returned with five pale, misshapen lumps. They wobbled on the table when he set them down.

"Those are the anchor stones? They look like old gum," said Remi, poking one with her fingernail.

Lily could sense their power as she hovered her palm over the nearest, feeling a prickle against her flesh.

"These are old bones, I'd rather not say from who or what, infused with threads from a nekyia tree. You only need three, but given your hospital wards, I thought it best I give you all five, one for each element. If you use the wards as a linkage, you should be able to trap anything short of a harrowing."

"Thank you, Patron Hollow," said Lily as she slipped the stones into her carryall.

"They're only on loan. Return them when you're finished, and if you don't mind, I'd love to hear all the details."

"May your ghosts always be kind," said Lily, glancing surreptitiously at the Brine Man.

"Fook you, bog witch," said the ghost. "A deep smoke is comin' for you, born from ashes and fire. Ain't no way you're getting out before the nightmares get ya as you rightly deserve."

Patron Hollow let out a curt laugh, but his flat gaze betrayed a deeper worry.

"Let me walk you out."

He paused at the front door, glancing back to the old factory where the Brine Man was waiting.

"Be careful. You have dark days ahead."

Lily frowned. "The Brine Man is an oracle?"

"I… I don't know, but sometimes the things he says come true. He may see things through the Veil that we can't. That's the only thing I can surmise. Either that, or he's a hateful bastard and life can suck sometimes," said Patron Hollow with a wry grin.

"Thank you, Patron Hollow. I'll bring the stones back as soon as possible."

As they headed back to the train station, Remi checked behind them.

"You believe any of that ghost oracle nonsense?"

Lily put her hands around the bones of her necklace.

"His words reek of Mara, the land of nightmares and the Fomorians."

"But you said after we battled the ghost that it couldn't be from Mara."

"Aye, I said that, but I've also smelled the fires of Mara in the hospital. Sulfur and brimstone. It might be unrelated. In a hospital full of supernaturals, it wouldn't be unusual for someone with a Fomorian heritage to be seeking treatment."

"I see that look, Lily. That's not what you think it is."

Lily paused as her gut tightened with unspecified fear. She stayed silent until they reached the train station. Her pace faltered, prompting Remi to turn slightly with an eyebrow raised.

"Hope, not think," said Lily. "Something strange is going on in Golden Willow. I feel like we're missing an important sign that may doom us in the end."

TWENTY-TWO

Damon was reading his notes about the next three patients when he spotted the glitter smear on the wall. It looked like someone covered in craft supply sparkles had stumbled, leaving a rainbow mark that trailed off at the end.

He thought nothing of it until he saw a second smudge and then a third, which was around the door of a lactation room. His gut told him to check. Damon let his hand hover over the handle, nearly convincing himself to move on, when he heard the soft whistle of birds followed by the crash of glass.

Damon rushed in to find Dr. Decker wearing silvery microshorts and covered in glitter while illusionary birds circled around him. The head instructor had put his fist through a candy machine and was currently chewing through the wrapper of a Bahama Blast.

"Hey-O, Wolfboy," said Dr. Decker with a hazy-eyed wave as blood ran down his wrist.

Hearing a group of nurses coming down the hall, Damon quickly shut the door, locked it, and rushed over to the doctor.

"Dr. Decker, you've sliced your arm pretty badly. And you smell like a strip club and baby lotion."

"Call me Oren." He grinned. "The baby lotion was from the slide."

Damon tried to grab his arm, but he kept moving it as he was eating his candy.

"Blood and bone, Dr. Decker. What are you on? Your eyes are huge."

He swiped at the illusionary birds still swirling around Decker's head.

"Can you make those go away?"

"They're my little friends," said Dr. Decker, slurring heavily.

Damon grabbed the doctor and pushed him into a chair. He used his foot to hold Decker back while he applied a hasty wound closure spell to stop the worst of the bleeding, but it didn't quite hold the flesh together.

"Do you think we get what we deserve?" asked Dr. Decker, wavering on his chair.

Damon checked the dilation of his pupils. "What did you take? It seems to be interfering with my spell."

"It's a party. A big party. There were bubbles, and girls with horns, and a big slide," mumbled the doctor as he leaned his head against the wall.

Damon snapped his fingers before Decker's eyes. Clearly he was seeing things from the drugs he'd taken at the rave.

"Dammit," he said with a sigh.

He didn't think Dr. Decker was in any danger, but he couldn't be left alone. Nor did he want to carry the doctor to his room, letting everyone see what kind of state he was in. After some thought, Damon dialed Dr. Martinez.

"The meeting isn't for another half-hour, Damon. You don't need to let me know that you might be a minute late."

"Not that, Dr. Martinez, but I'm pretty sure I'm going to be late."

"Is something wrong?"

Damon was going to try and explain, but instead he snapped a picture and sent it to Dr. Martinez.

"I'll be right there."

When she arrived, the illusionary birds were no longer circling, but sitting on his shoulders looking sleepy. Dr. Decker was staring into space. No amount of waving or prodding was producing anything other than unintelligible mumbling.

"Fucking hell, Oren," she said with her hands on her hips, shaking her head.

After dialing one of the other doctors to take over the rest of her rounds, she instructed Damon to fetch a gurney. When the hallway was empty, Damon carried Decker onto the wheeled vehicle and covered him with a sheet.

"I feel like you've done this before," he said.

"Not in a long time, but yes," said Dr. Martinez, gaze haunted with the past.

Dr. Decker's apartment in the Aura Healers' side of the hospital was a disaster. Empty bottles everywhere. Messy notes written on the wall in permanent marker and a stuffed tarantula resting on the ceiling somehow. A hookah pipe sat next to the couch overflowing in ash.

Damon set him on the couch after clearing away the bottles and fast food trash. The doctor lay on the sofa like a corpse, but with his eyes wide open, staring at the ceiling as if it held the world's answers.

"You can get back to your rounds, if you want," said Dr. Martinez pensively.

Seeing the pain in her eyes, Damon said, "Let me stay a while. At least until he's coherent."

"That could be hours." She stared back flat-lipped, then exhaled heavily. "Thank you, Damon. Let me make some calls and get your shift covered."

When their hospital duties were settled, Damon asked, "Is this what he was like before? Or I guess, after the Martin Freely thing?"

Dr. Martinez looked away, mouth twisted with anguish. The corners of her eyes glistened. "Worse. I really thought that it wouldn't affect him if I came back. I really did. Maybe I should have given him more time."

"What happened? I mean, I know all about Freely, but what about after? You know, before he went on his walkabout."

Dr. Martinez inhaled deeply through her nostrils. "It broke him, and I couldn't stand watching him suffer. He wouldn't seek help, so he self-medicated, like he's doing again. I tried to tell him it wasn't his fault. But he couldn't hear me. He'd been so sure of himself as a doctor. We all get a bit of a god complex in this position, bringing people back from the brink of death, but for Oren it was more pronounced. He *was* that good. The best I've ever seen."

She hung her head.

"Until he wasn't. I had to break up with him. I thought it might break him out of his spell, but it only made him worse."

Dr. Martinez put a fist to her mouth as she squeezed her lips together.

"I found him above the ER. I was looking for him when he didn't show up for rounds and he wasn't in his room." She grimaced. "He was floating like a ghost. I thought he was dead somehow and had made his body levitate. But it ends up he'd tapped into the hospital wards. I think he'd tried to jump, but maybe part of him knew he didn't really want to die, so he'd used the wards to break his fall."

Damon whistled. The kind of magic required to levitate, even using the hospital wards, was strong. And for Decker to do it in the throes of his self-imposed madness was impressive.

"After we got him down, and he had a few days to recover, he decided he was leaving. He left the next day with only a backpack. That was the last time I saw him until I came back here."

"Do you still have feelings for him?" he asked.

Dr. Martinez looked away. "I never lost them. But I can't risk it again. My patients deserve better."

"Flirting with Brennan is hurting him," said Damon, catching the flinch of her forehead.

"I know, I know, but we need Brennan for the fundraising. I love Oren with all my heart, but the hospital is more important and I don't think I can do anything to fix him. If I could, I would have done it long ago."

"You can stop the flirting."

Dr. Martinez stared back with her jaw pulsing. "I don't think you realize that Brennan wasn't the one with the idea to upgrade Golden Willow. I was the one that went to him, not the other way around as he likes to say. He didn't recruit me, I recruited him when I found out the state of things."

Damon wasn't sure he completely believed that, but she did, so he wasn't going to argue.

"It's killing Dr. Decker."

Dr. Martinez closed her eyes. "I know, but I don't know any other way." She leaned forward on her elbows. "But Brennan likes you. If you took a more active role with him, maybe it would let me pull back."

Damon hated the glad-handing required for fundraising, but he looked to Decker mumbling incoherently while staring at the ceiling.

"I could do that."

"Good," said Dr. Martinez. "There's an event coming up in a few weeks after the new year. You could come along and help me work on him. He likes to talk big, but we're a long way from reaching the goals we need to fix the hospital."

He nodded. "I can do that. I'll bring Remi."

Dr. Martinez's face tightened. "Not her. Brennan mentioned something after the charity event. I guess they do background checks and her past at Utica came up and how she got there. Those are the very people that we're trying to convince to give money. Having a former thief at the party isn't going to help our cause."

"But Remi wouldn't do anything now."

"They don't know that, even if it is true."

"He hasn't said anything?" asked Damon. "She has a hard enough time in the hospital."

"No, I made Brennan promise to keep that to himself."

Damon exhaled with relief.

"Good."

"What about Lily then?"

The frown on Dr. Martinez's lips told him the answer. "I don't know why, but Brennan has made some disparaging remarks about Lily on more than one occasion. I don't think he trusts her background, or assumes she has divided loyalties. I'm sorry, Damon. I don't think that at all, but he's the one with the deep pockets."

Her phone buzzed, so she got up to take the call in another room while Damon stared at Dr. Decker. He was mumbling and staring wide-eyed at the ceiling. Damon thought he could understand what he was saying, so he moved in close, putting his ear up to the doctor's moving mouth.

"...to have and to hold..."

Damon wrinkled his nose, trying to understand what he was saying.

"...and in health..."

Dr. Decker raised his hand as if he were putting something small on an extension.

"...until the end of days with you, Christina..."

Damon sat back with the realization of what Decker was saying. He checked to make sure Dr. Martinez was in the other room still so she didn't hear it, but then she came through the entryway, shoving the phone in her pocket.

"Did I miss something?" she asked with head tilted.

Damon checked back to Decker to see he was snoring with his eyes open.

"Nope. I think he's asleep."

She stared at the motionless Dr. Decker with apprehension.

"If you have to go, Dr. Martinez, I'll stay and watch him until he's coherent."

"Are you sure?"

"Positive."

Dr. Martinez let out a little sigh. "Thank you, Damon. I have to meet with Dr. Fairlight about a maintenance issue in the ward."

After she left, Dr. Decker snorted again and a last exclamation slipped out his lips.

"It's only you, Christina, until the end of days."

TWENTY-THREE

The City Library was a mammoth structure with multiple wings full of mundane and arcane knowledge. The magical sections were only second to Arcanium Hall in the world. Lily had spent every spare moment of her free time trying to figure out the identity of the ghost mage, but if those books held his secrets, they weren't revealing them.

Lily was sure that a mage that had collected that much power and lived that long would have left signs of his existence in the history books, but if he had, there was nothing she could find that tied him to a specific name.

"He's a ghost of a ghost. A fooking mirage. If I hadn't seen him myself I wouldn't have believed he existed," said Lily, slamming the book closed.

She leaned back in the chair. The private research room had books scattered about the table and her notepad was covered in pages of scrawl.

As she gathered the tomes, Lily couldn't help but worry that the reason the identity of the mages was hidden was because he had some tie to the realm of the Fomorians. She didn't think that was quite it, but she didn't have a better working theory.

When the door opened, Lily said without looking up, "I've got another ten minutes. I'll be cleaned up and out of the way by then."

The heavy clop of wooden shoes and the chill in the air clued Lily to the identity of the person, though not how she'd found her.

"This doesn't look like research for Medb or the corruption," said Biddy, flipping through books randomly, a scowl perched on her thin lips.

Her eldest sister looked like she was ready to put the cane to a group of unruly students in a one-room school.

"That's not the only problem that needs my attention," said Lily.

"What could matter more than the fate of our entire family? Imagine how many people will die without our help. Are you prepared to watch your sisters wither and fade to the corruption? Or turn into hags with madness-addled brains, dispensing our wisdom in hateful ways? Do you want to see Alice waste away or become a fiend? Is that what you want?"

"Of course not."

Lily snatched a book from Biddy's hands and placed it on the pile.

"But I can't turn away from this problem."

Biddy made a noise of derision. "There are others in the hospital who can accept your problem, whatever it is. Let the thief or the werewolf do it. They seem moderately competent. I'm sure they can fumble their way through it."

"Get off my fooking back," said Lily, growling as she slammed another book onto the pile. "You're not my fooking mother, and if you were, I'd cut my own throat in shame."

Biddy's expression cracked with glee. "Are you defying me? You saw our queen with your own eyes! You saw how the corruption has affected her. You heard her demands and still you choose your own path? You were allowed to come to the city of sorcery because we thought you would toil on her behalf, not delve into your own interests."

Lily tried to move past Biddy, but her older sister stepped in the way. The standoff was truncated when Lily raised her hands, determined to nudge her sister out of the way with a force push, but Biddy was faster. Lily spun into the table, knocking over the tallest pile of books.

She faced her sister.

"I don't have time for this, you eejit."

The next spells came at furious speeds. Lily was fast, but her sister beat her to completion. A viny appendage whipped from the ether, slapping Lily across the cheeks and interrupting her spell. Before she could start a second, Biddy extended her arms and a wind gust slammed her into the wall.

Leaning over and trying to catch her breath, Lily worked to make herself erect as Biddy stalked forward.

"Of all my sisters, you're the most arrogant, most spoiled, self-centered brat. You've taken Medb's gifts and wasted them on this place. They've hundreds of doctors and healers, but we only have one Medb. Can you bloody understand that?"

"I do," wheezed Lily, holding her gut.

When Biddy got in her face, both their hands went up. But instead of casting a spell, Lily clocked her sister in the jaw.

The next thing she knew vines had grown out of the wall and slammed her against the surface. Lily was being held two feet above the ground. A single vine was wrapped around her neck, but had yet to squeeze, but she could sense that Biddy might unleash it at any moment.

Before her sister could act, the door flew open, revealing a concerned librarian with two security guards behind her.

"What is happening? This is the City Library, not a dueling ground."

Biddy glared at the librarian, who took a step back while the security personnel reached for their batons.

"I was having a conversation with my sister." She snapped her fingers and the vines dissipated into mist, letting Lily crash to the ground. "But we're finished. I'll make sure she cleans up her mess. I always do."

"Oh, okay," said the librarian nervously. "Just no more shouting. You're disturbing the other customers."

The librarian and her two security guards backed away, leaving them alone.

Biddy extended her finger, pointing it right at Lily's chest.

"You might be quick, but I still have Medb's backing. I can take you anytime I want. So if you don't change your priorities, then I'm taking you back home. Neko too. And putting him back where he belongs."

Her sister stormed off, leaving Lily alone in the room with a table full of scattered books. The ache in her chest went deep. More than the physical pain of getting thrown around by her sister's magic.

For the first time since she'd made the decision to come to the Hundred Halls, she felt like an outsider to her own family.

"I only want to fix things," she said to nobody in particular.

TWENTY-FOUR

A buzz in her pocket distracted Remi as she was strategizing with Nurse Tishanti about the care of a patient who'd come in contact with a strange slime on the streets in the seventh ward. Their skin was turning scaly and they were coughing uncontrollably.

"…needs a wash spell and a dehexifier... Are you even listening, Remi?"

"Huh? Oh, sorry."

The lights flickered in the hallway and a cold spot traveled past them. Even Tishanti shivered and scowled randomly.

Remi pulled the gift shop stone out of her pocket. The glow was fading, but she spotted lights flickering further down the hall.

"Hey! Where are you going?" asked Tishanti.

Remi half-turned as she continued running.

"I have to check on something. It's important!"

"Merlin's balls, you student mages are a pain in my rear," said Tishanti, shaking her head and storming the other direction.

Remi hurried after the apparition. She made it to the elevators before the stone no longer glowed.

"Dammit."

A family with a small child made weird faces in her direction.

Remi rolled her eyes and contemplated the ghost mage's next move. They hadn't seen signs of it in a few weeks. As far as they could tell, it was avoiding them. And since she hadn't actually seen the ghost, she figured it was either a floor above or below her. Probably above since the ceiling lights flickered with its passage.

"Where am I?"

The family gave her a strange look.

"Excuse me," said the father. "Do you even work here?"

"No, I like to come here and bother the nurses. Sometimes they even let me experiment on the patients who ask stupid questions."

The mother recoiled, pulling her child closer, while the father was looking around for someone to report her to.

"The wards!" Remi exclaimed, remembering exactly where she was in the hospital.

She sprinted to the stairwell, heading up a floor and jogging to a runed doorway near the children's ward. The sign on the front said: Earth Ward – Stay Out – Hospital Maintenance Only.

"I guess that's me."

Remi picked the locks, sliding through the opening before an approaching gurney spotted her.

She let off a soft whistle as she examined the unusual interior. At the center of the round room was a glass box on a pedestal, while inside a chunk of obsidian covered in etched runes pulsed with eldritch light. The hum in the air made the hairs on her arm quiver.

Remi saw no signs of the ghost, but a high-pitched whine at the edge of her hearing suggested something was wrong. She neared the glass box, catching sparks bursting from the corners. Some of the runes on the obsidian stone had lost their luster as if the magic behind them was going out.

The deeper chill near the box had her looking around, but she saw nothing.

"Exspiravit revelare te!"

The ghostly form of the mage revealed itself near the box. The apparition hissed with discovery and fled before she could consider a second spell.

Remi chased the ghost out of the room. It fled down the hallway, past a gurney headed to surgery. She bounced around the nurses, then threw herself up the stairwell when the ghost went through the ceiling.

She passed two more hallways and another stairwell before she was certain the ghost had eluded her.

"Bloody hell," she exclaimed.

A nurse behind the station shushed her and gestured towards the sign near the swinging double doors she'd burst through. It read: "Hospice Ward."

Remi raised her hand in apology as she checked the various directions. The nurse had been doing a crossword when she came in, so Remi didn't think she'd seen the apparition.

She headed past the station, peeking through the open doors at emaciated patients in various states of decline. An old woman lay on her back staring at the ceiling while pink bubbles formed on her lips and lifted into the air, only to be sucked up by a makeshift vacuum line suspended over her head.

In another room, three figures in dark linen robes chanted softly over an unconscious man clearly at the end of the line. Their words weren't magical, but they gave her the creeps regardless.

At no point in her examination did the gift shop stone reveal a glow, which meant that the ghost had escaped to another location. She shoved it back in her pocket and decided to head back to Nurse Tishanti when she saw the placard near the swinging doors.

"Mortui mortui manebunt."

She spoke the words and though she didn't understand, she felt their power in her gut.

A gravelly, meandering voice startled Remi from behind.

"The dead shall remain dead."

She spun around to come face-to-face with a skeletal old man in a white doctor's coat. He had cavernous eyes and gaunt cheeks. The smell of menthol lingered.

"Remington Wilde, I did not think we had an appointment."

"Ahh, how did you sneak up on me like that?"

"You seemed deep in thought," he said at a deliberate pace.

She glanced to his name tag. Dr. Stéphane Morsdux. A memory trickled up from the depths.

"Oh, you're the head of the death ward."

Remi grimaced at her slip of the tongue. Dr. Morsdux smiled like a corpse.

"We prefer the term Hospice Ward. Once our patients die, then we have little more to offer them. What we do offer is a peaceful and dignified end to a bountiful life," said Dr. Morsdux with a faint French accent that had smoothed away with time.

"I'm sorry, I have a loose tongue," said Remi, backing away.

"I've heard that about you, Remington. I've heard quite a lot about you, actually."

"You have? And it's Remi. Only my parents called me Remington."

"How did you come by such an interesting name, if I might ask?"

Remi swallowed. "It's rather personal."

"I understand," said Dr. Morsdux. "I have time if you'd like a tour of the ward."

"I guess," said Remi, trying not to check the stone.

"Come with me. I promise I won't keep you long. I know I'm not a favorite stop of Aura Healers, but I assure you our mission is just as important."

She joined him as he walked slowly down the hall as if it were a funeral procession.

"But you don't fix anything here. I'm sorry, I know that sounds terrible. I'm just not sure what I'd offer."

He gave her a peculiar grin. "You're clearly a student of Dr. Decker. There's never been a patient he hasn't tried to heal."

"Yeah," said Remi. "He does have a bit of a god complex."

Dr. Morsdux stopped at an open door. A woman with glassy eyes was sitting up in bed running her fingers across a book.

"Stéphane? That must be you. I smell the menthol."

"I've brought a friend, Miss Donal," said Dr. Morsdux. "Remi Wilde. A third-year healer who is considering our little department."

Remi moved close to the bed to see that the book was covered in braille dots.

"Hello, Miss Donal. What are you reading? Is that the right term?"

"It's fine, sweetie. I'm reading one of my favorite romance authors. Alice Faris."

Remi nodded. She never had time for reading outside of Aura Healer textbooks. It seemed like a luxury.

"You look much better than the other patients..."

The old woman grinned.

"I assure you that I'm still dying. An uncurable curse that I picked up during the Event. I was lucky to survive an encounter with one of those fiends, but it changed my insides permanently. Including my eyesight."

"That's terrible."

"No one escapes the hand of death, not even you mages with your sorcery-aided long lives."

"Most of them kill themselves from hubris long before then," said Remi. "Or so I've heard."

A pocket buzz had Remi checking her phone. It was a message from Nurse Tishanti wondering where she was.

"I'm sorry, Dr. Morsdux. I have to get back downstairs. I was in the middle of something when I had to come up here. It was nice meeting you. You too, Miss Donal."

Dr. Morsdux walked her to the edge of the department. "I know you can't see yourself in a place like this, but Dr. Decker told me how you comforted Odette before her end."

"I still don't understand what you do in this ward," said Remi.

"We make them comfortable, fix minor things that ail them, provide a sense of peace, and help prepare them for the journey ahead. You could say that we're the first line of defense against the beings of the Veil."

Remi wrinkled her nose. "That's true I guess."

"There are other services we provide. Sometimes patients have accidentally crossed into the Veil, or encounter beings from it. We can help untangle them so they can go on with their lives. I, myself, have been to the Veil on more than one occasion."

"I can see that," blurted out Remi before she realized it might be taken negatively.

Dr. Morsdux put a boney hand on her shoulder. "I understand if you don't choose this ward, but please consider it fully. I think you have more to offer our patients than you realize. You have an air of the Veil around you."

"Thanks?" said Remi, backing through the swinging doors.

She felt relief when she was away from the ward. Then she remembered how she'd ended up there in the first place. The damn ghost.

As she contemplated what it'd been doing at the earth node, and the state of the runes, she realized it was damaging them. But what she couldn't understand was how. The wards should protect against apparitions, not be vulnerable to them. Something strange was going on that made her agree with Lily that their problem was more than just this one ghost. How it all fit together wasn't quite clear yet, but if they couldn't figure it out soon, things might get really bad in the hospital.

TWENTY-FIVE

Lily paced the break room in meandering circles until her friends arrived. Remi was first as her shift didn't start for another hour, while Damon came stumbling in a few minutes later with splatters on his scrubs and hair mussed in all directions.

"We have to deal with this bloody ghost soon, before Biddy gets impatient and takes me back home," said Lily, trying not to let her friends see how frustrated she was.

Remi tilted her head suspiciously.

"Can she do that?"

Lily grimaced. "Were I still connected to Medb, she wouldn't be strong enough, but I lack the power that I had before. I'm afraid if she wanted to, I'd have a difficult time resisting her."

"Can we just knock her on the head and ship her back to Ireland?" asked Remi.

"The thought has crossed my mind, but..."

"Yeah, I know, she's still family. I wouldn't do that either if I had a sister, even if she were an annoying twit." Remi tilted her head at Damon. "Speaking of sisters, how are the twins doing?"

"I got to see them a few days ago. They're doing smashingly, of course. Talia got the lead in a Dramatics play, and Nat won some competition the Protectors have for first years. But as much as I'd like to chat, I really need to catch some shut-eye. I'm doing an early rotation with Dr. Vista in the Children's Ward. She's recruiting me hard."

"I'll get deep in the pond then," said Lily, wringing her hands. "We learned from Remi's little adventure the other day that the ghost is trying to damage the wards, but it shouldn't be possible. The incorporeal, even a mage who prepared his life after death, shouldn't able to affect strong magics like that."

"Which means there's something weird about this mage we don't understand and the normal methods of banishing won't work," said Remi.

"Aye. My research hasn't found anything about him. He might as well be wrapped in clover, for all I know," said Lily.

Damon frowned with his arms crossed.

"I've been meaning to show you both something."

He led them to the roof of the hospital, leading them away from their regular hangout spot with the picnic table. They stood over the ER entrance as an ambulance with the lights on, but sirens off, slid beneath the carport.

"Remember the story I told you about Dr. Decker's past? Right before he went upon his walkabout?"

"Yeah," said Remi, shaking her head. "He's still hung up on Dr. Martinez. What's that got to do with the ghost?"

"Nothing, except for the state that she found him in," said Damon.

He went behind an HVAC unit and dragged a folding chair that someone had been using for a smoking break to the edge. Damon spent the next minute uttering an incantation over the metal chair until points of silvery light glistened at the corners.

"What are you doing?" asked Remi when he finished the spell.

Damon took the chair and lobbed it over the edge. Under normal circumstances, it should have fallen fifty feet and landed on the ER carport, but it only dropped a dozen and then hovered in midair.

"Oh shit, is that the levitation spell?" asked Remi, leaning over the edge.

Lily was frowning. She sensed the change even before the chair shifted downward a few inches at a time.

"It's not working like it should," said Damon. "That chair is only a fifth of Decker's weight and the wards are barely holding it."

Tension formed at the center point of Lily's forehead. She sensed events careening out of control. Right now, the signs weren't visible, but like a tsunami wave, when they hit the shore, they'd overwhelm the hospital.

"We're too bloody late. The wards are already damaged."

"They've probably been trending this way for years, but whatever this ghost is doing is speeding it up," said Damon.

"We need to tell Dr. Martinez," said Remi. "Yeah, I know, me running to the authorities. Who would have guessed. But she has to know what's going on."

"I don't think it's going to change anything," said Lily.

"She's right, Remi," said Damon. "The hospital already knows the wards need upgrading. That's why she came back to Golden Willow in the first place."

"Can't they do something about the ghost mage?" asked Remi.

Lily squeezed her lips flat. "If Biddy finds out what I did, she'll use that leverage to get me kicked out of Aura Healers and sent back to Ireland."

"Not that I want this to happen, but wouldn't that help you focus on Medb?"

Lily shook her head. "I know it doesn't seem like it, but I think the solution is here in the city of sorcery. Too many coincidences for it not to be. But if I can't fix the mage problem, then it won't matter."

"Right. Got it," said Remi. "I guess that means we need to get Brennan to pony up the money for the hospital. Either that or I need to do a lot of thieving."

"Speaking of that," said Damon with a grimace. "There's an event coming up this weekend. I promised Dr. Martinez I'd come along and help sell the need to the rich donors."

Remi scratched the back of her neck. "I guess I can get Dr. Martinez to move my shifts around."

"No can do," said Damon. "Brennan doesn't want an ex-thief at the party. You too, Lily. Something about divided loyalties."

"Is bastard ceart é," muttered Lily.

Remi crossed her arms with a scowl. "Who are you bringing then?"

He chewed on his lower lip. "At first I thought I could bring Alice, but if Lily's out, then so is her younger sister. I tried asking a few nurses, but none of them wanted anything to do with a charity event. Called them bloodsuckers."

"Then who's your date?" asked Remi tersely.

Damon held up his hands defensively. "It's just for the event. There's a girl that works in Morehead's department."

The air between them chilled as if a storm front moved in.

"A girl? She's not a girl. I've seen her."

"Remi...this is for the charity event. I would prefer to bring you. Regina's a nice girl, or woman, but we're just friends."

Remi closed her eyes. "I understand. No really, I do. The hospital is more important."

"Great."

"In the meantime, I'll try to figure out what the best way to banish the ghost is if it's truly as powerful as we think it is. But if I can't find something soon, I think we need to make the attempt," said Lily.

"You know we're there when you need us," said Damon.

Remi was still staring at Damon, but eventually she startled and looked at Lily.

"Count me in too."

A clatter startled them to check back to the metal chair, which had finally loosened from the hospital ward and fallen to the roof of the ER carport. The implications of the weakened wards so visibly revealed was not lost on the three of them.

TWENTY-SIX

The entire ride in the taxi from the hospital to the meeting location was in silence. Damon felt uncomfortable as Regina sat with her thigh pressed to his despite there being plenty of room in the back.

When they arrived at a warehouse with a dozen limousines and black SUVs in the parking lot, Damon was confused because he thought they were going to a dinner in a remote place, rather than the middle of the city.

"I guess this is it?"

He paid the driver and led Regina towards the open entrance. The clop of her high heels ringing against the concrete reminded him that she'd worn them and a slinky black dress despite him telling her they were supposed to wear hiking gear. He had chosen a pair of jeans, a flannel shirt, and a running backpack he'd used in high school.

About two dozen men and women in fancy hunting gear—the kind he would have expected to see on people wandering the moors of Scotland—were clustered around chatting and laughing like old friends. Damon spotted the tall form of Aleksander Grimm, Patron of Arcane Phytology, presiding over the conversation like a maestro.

Damon's gut tightened at the idea of approaching the group until he saw Dr. Martinez' black hair sticking out from the side. Brennan was next to her, heavily engaged in a discussion with a woman with sorcery-smoothed skin and silver hair.

"Damon! You made it," said Dr. Martinez, reaching out to shake his hand. "You're Regina, right? From Bob's group, if I remember correctly."

Regina gave a faux curtsy. "Dr. Martinez. It's nice to meet you formally."

Dr. Martinez frowned at the ground. "Your clothes and shoes, honey. They aren't going to work for today's adventure. Come with me, they have a locker of gear for occasions like this."

Damon was left to lurk at the edge of the circle listening to Aleksander Grimm tell a story about hunting wyverns in Krakatow using spears when Brennan noticed him.

"Damon! I'm glad you could make it. Come. This is Victoria Dreadmarsh. She's an alumnus of Coterie."

The last name had him flinching, which he knew that Victoria had seen. He accepted her handshake.

"You're Aura Healers like Christina."

Damon nodded as he tried to formulate words. Not only was she from one of the most famous mage families in the world, she had an electric presence that reminded him of Lady Nimueh.

"They like to pick one of the current students to abuse on the charity circuit. My name was plucked out of the hat for this year," said Damon.

"I seriously doubt it was random," said Victoria with a laugh. The corner of her eyes creased with mirth. "But you're in for a real treat with today's hunt. Have you ever been to Abhainn?"

"Hunt? I thought this was a dinner."

"Oh," said Victoria, laughing. "There's a dinner at the end, but first we'll be riding dubbers while we hunt hellbenders. Don't worry, these aren't the turn-you-to-stone type. They're more like a dumb land dragon with horrid breath."

"Dubbers? Hellbenders? Abhainn? I'm afraid I still don't understand."

Victoria elbowed Brennan.

"You really didn't prepare him at all. We're traveling by portal to another realm. Don't worry, if it's your first time, you most likely won't get sick. Abhainn is a place of rivers and the dubbers are our mounts. They can easily fjord the rivers, which makes them ideal for our purposes. It's a beautiful realm with lots of fragrant colorful flowers that grow on the banks or trees overhanging the rivers."

Dr. Martinez returned with Regina, who was now wearing gear similar to the others, which prompted a new round of introductions while Damon felt a little sick to his stomach. He hadn't hunted since he was a preteen and the experience of taking another life—even a young deer—had not been pleasant. He hoped he could avoid it on the day's adventure.

"Okay, everyone's here!" called out Aleksander Grimm. "We're heading through the portal. On the other side, there will be attendants to get you set up with your hunting gear and your mount. We'll ride for the day, hunting hellbenders as we find them, and at the end, we'll have a nice dinner on the plateau before we return. Any questions? Good. We're off!"

Damon waited until the end, shuffling his feet as they approached the obsidian pillar at the center of the warehouse.

"First time?" asked Regina.

"Yeah," he said, swallowing. "You?"

Regina paused, looking unsure how to answer before replying, "Not my first."

He didn't get a chance to ask her about it because they were up next to go through.

"It'll activate with faez," said an older man in formal hunting gear. "We've turned off the protections, so you don't have to worry about pass-codes."

Damon turned back to Regina and held out his hand. "Do you?"

"I can manage."

The obsidian pillar was cool to the touch. His face reflected in its surface like a fun house mirror, a mask of concern and duty. He reminded himself that he was supposed to be encouraging these rich folks to give money to the hospital, so he needed to at least act like he was having a good time.

When he sent a little faez into the pillar through his hand, he was expecting an indication that travel was about to happen. Instead, it felt like he'd been placed in a catapult and launched across the universe.

He landed in the grass, stumbling to his knees as he felt his stomach roil. The others glanced back at him with pinched concern. When he made it back to his feet, Regina came through the portal, landing without a wobble and with no signs of vertigo, looking sharp and like she belonged with the others.

"Are you okay?" she asked, touching his arm tenderly.

"Better by the second," he said with a forced grin despite his stomach's unease.

The wind whipped past, reminding Damon he was in another realm entirely. He craned his neck at puffy clouds against a pinkish sky that overlooked rolling green hills dotted with greenery. The air tasted strange in comparison to the city.

Near the portal was a line of elephant-sized beasts with long legs that made them look like they were perched precariously on stilts. Flaccid pouches hung around the circumference of the enormous creatures.

The next few minutes were a whirlwind as attendants in red vests corralled them to the mounts, giving them a musket-like weapon with faintly glowing runes along the muzzle and an enchanted machete for cutting foliage, then led them up a set of stairs to climb onto the back.

Damon saw the problem after they ascended the stairs. The saddle had two sways where they would sit nearly on top of each other.

"I get front!"

Regina hopped into the first saddle position and grabbed the reins.

"This is yours then, sir," said the attendant, handing him the musket once he reached the top.

The weapon felt uncomfortable in his grip. He would have preferred the machete, but Regina had grabbed it right away.

He'd never fired a gun before. If he were going to hunt, he would use his claws and teeth, but he couldn't turn down the weapon without causing a scene. Nor did he want to be defenseless in an unknown realm.

The position of his legs in the stirrups meant they were pressed against Regina's. She held the reins in one hand and ran her fingernails across his thigh with the other.

A streamer of fire shot into the air from the head of the hunting party.

"Let's ride!" called Aleksander Grimm.

The rest of the participants cheered and shot their own magics into the air.

"Come on," said Regina, elbowing him. "Add something!"

He was going to complain but remembered why he'd come, so he raised his hand and sent a burst of earthen magics into the air, which he immediately regretted as small pebbles and dust rained down upon them.

When the hunting party moved forward, it was at a meandering stride. He learned soon after why the mounts were necessary when they descended into the river valley crisscrossed with streams and tributaries. Colorful plants and vegetation surrounded the water, or floated on it in clusters which also held small pink-faced animals with razor-sharp teeth that disappeared into the foliage whenever they got near.

The dubbers' long legs were swallowed by the water, as their flaccid pouches filled, creating a buoyant bulb that helped keep the beast afloat. The depth of their submerging left their boots only a few feet from the river.

The fragrant flowers made the journey pleasant and relaxing, and before long, Damon unclenched his jaw and let out a heavy sigh.

"You two look like naturals," said Dr. Martinez as she pulled up alongside with Brennan at her back. She wore a wide-brimmed hat that protected her face. The two long-legged beasts pushed through the water like barges.

"I think the dubber's doing most of the work," said Damon.

"Speaking of, we have a little while before we reach the hunting grounds. You should mingle with the others. We're not here for fun, after all," said Dr. Martinez, yanking on the reins as the dubber surged forward through the river.

"Bring us up by Victoria," said Damon.

Besides them, she was the youngest member of the hunting party. Regina snapped the reins, but instead of driving them towards the silver-haired Victoria, she sent them bumbling towards the main group. The dubber's rapid forward movement sent a minor wave splashing onto the back of Aleksander's mount, which got a little water on his gorgeous date's pant leg.

"Hey!" said the tall patron with a warm laugh. "We're gonna get plenty wet later, no need to be damp all day."

"Sorry, Patron Grimm," said Damon as Regina brought the mount next to Aleksander's dubber.

Regina leaned back and whispered in his ear.

"His date is the winner of Sorcerous Sweethearts, season nine," she said breathlessly.

The woman with Patron Grimm had the sharp features of someone heavily modified by magic. Her look evoked a falcon, or some other predator bird while still retaining the style of an attractive model. Damon recalled the show involved the contestants modifying themselves using a mix of magic and alchemy.

"Damon Wolfhard," said Aleksander. "How's the hospital?"

"Busy, but not as bad as a few years ago," said Damon, heat rising to his cheeks.

"And the charity giving?"

"Not as much as we need. There are a lot of problems with the old equipment and the Veil wards. We're going to need more money than we first thought."

"Going for the hard sell already," said Aleksander with a laugh. "There'll be time enough for that later. Don't forget to have a good time first."

"Sorry, Patron Grimm."

The tall man looked faintly annoyed and Damon started to nudge Regina away until he remembered his conversation with Patron Grimm at the charity event earlier this school year.

"What are those flowers floating on the river?" he asked.

Aleksander turned with a smirk. "Which ones?"

Damon realized his mistake as he glanced forward to see them coming around the bend. Streamers of colorful flowers clung to vines hanging in the water.

"All of them. I assume you were aware of this realm due to your Hall?"

"I was."

Aleksander gestured towards a cluster of red-orange flowered bushes on the water's edge.

"Those are devil's eyes. Mildly poisonous to humans, but the dubbers use them to aid their digestive system. We also believe that combined with locanath saliva they can make an excellent elixir for improving wound outpatient recovery, but human testing isn't finished yet."

"Wow, that would be great."

Aleksander extended his long arm towards the floating flowers.

"Those are cat's cradles. Home to a lot of insects in Abhainn, but we haven't found a good alchemical use for them yet, though they are beautiful. I have a display of them at my Hall. And then over there, hanging from the vines, are copulets, which are mildly hallucinogenic and an aphrodisiac."

Aleksander continued for another half-hour while Damon asked occasional clarifying questions. The party continued down the river, gently pushing into other streams, but generally heading in the same direction.

After the Hall patron explained the difference between two different strains of medicinal vines, he let out a sharp laugh.

"I know what you're doing, Damon."

He stiffened. "You do?"

"I just remembered my advice to you last year. Well done." Aleksander winked. "Consider my donation to have increased. But you shouldn't focus just on me. We have another short section to cross before we get into hellbender territory."

Regina maneuvered them to the other hunters, but Damon had less success. He spent most of the time listening to them talk about their financial investments, or their complaints about the state of the Hundred Halls.

The hunting party took a short break on a grassy section between two rivers that had ample greenery and flowers for the dubbers to graze. A trio of red-vested attendants that had been waiting for them handed out bento boxes with fresh sushi, steaming rice, pickled vegetables, and bite-sized mochi balls.

"Eat up and make sure you visit the head. We're going to hit the hellbender plains right afterwards and there won't be time for stopping," said Aleksander.

Damon found himself eating alone as Regina went wandering near the water's edge where the dubbers were grazing, which was fine by him. Her constant physical attention was wearing on him. He wished he would have explained he had no interest in her, but he didn't want to create a scene when he needed to be focused on donations.

After leaving the lunch spot, the pace quickened as if the participants were anticipating the afternoon's adventure. Brennan and Dr. Martinez pulled up as they were cresting a short rise.

"Ready to have your blood quicken?" he asked.

"How dangerous are the hellbenders?"

Brennan tilted his head.

"With a party of this size, it's unlikely that anything other than a few quick kills will occur and then we'll make the final leg to our dinner. But. The hellbenders are decently fast and strong. They can sometimes cause a problem if we come upon them unaware. If you find yourself with a hellbender bearing down on you, aim your musket for a spot right behind the neck rather than the face. They're too well armored to shoot directly."

Damon wasn't going to bother asking how you hit a spot behind the head if a hellbender was charging him. He saluted Brennan as they surged ahead to join the others.

"This is exciting," cooed Regina as she leaned against his chest. She smelled sweet, and he was too focused on what was ahead to push her away. Besides, she wasn't all that bad. He did enjoy talking shop with her in the hospital.

The terrain changed as they climbed away from the rivers. Scorched plains that had seen a wildfire in the recent past smelled like smoke. Dust swirled around the feet of the dubbers and occasional updrafts made them squint away the ash.

The ground was cracked in sections, but the long legs of the dubbers crossed the gaps easily. When they came up over a ridge, the hunting party stopped as they spotted a trio of hellbenders about a quarter mile away.

Damon wasn't sure what he was expecting, but the beasts ahead looked like they'd been carved from hot lava and armored with cooled granite. They were the size of rhinos with stocky legs and long thick tails.

The reason for the wildfires became clear when one of the hellbenders exhaled spark-filled smoke, catching the sparse grass aflame.

Aleksander gathered everyone around him, assigning roles for the first hunt. Half the group would make an assault on the hellbenders, while the others watched for next time should they find more.

"Are you sure you don't want to join them?" asked Brennan in the back. "I could get Aleksander to put you in the first group. Would help create some comradery with the others. Help you earn their donations."

The urge to say yes was strong. If it'd been his sisters, they'd have already agreed, but he didn't want to make a fool of himself with his inexperience.

"I'll watch this time."

Brennan nodded, but Damon sensed his disappointment.

"I'm sure you'd do great," said Regina, leaning into his chest and squeezing his thigh.

They stayed near the back of the second group while the others moved ahead to surround the hellbenders. As Damon watched, his pulse quickened, drawn by the violence. His claws wanted to extend, but he buried his fingers into his palms to keep them back.

As muskets were fired, hitting a hellbender that tried to flee from the group unsuccessfully, Damon felt a warm wind on his back. He was so engrossed by the hunt, he almost didn't turn his head until he heard the crunch of dried grass.

The hellbender was only fifty feet away. It must have come up from around the ridge. And it was big. Much larger than the ones being hunted ahead.

"Regina..."

"What, babe?"

Damon bristled at the nickname, but there was no time for correcting.

"Get ready to ride."

"What?"

As she turned to see what he was looking at, the hellbender charged.

"Ride!"

As the beast trampled towards them, Regina grabbed for the reins, which had been resting on the pommel, but knocked them off instead.

Damon put the musket against his shoulder and fired. The blast had a painful kick and the explosive shot hit the hardened ridge near the neck, but failed to slow the hellbender. Before he could fire a second, the creature slammed its head into the dubber's side, sending them over.

Damon rolled down the slope, losing the musket when he hit. He came to his feet halfway down as the injured dubber screamed in pain, while Regina was below and miraculously on her feet looking like she hadn't even fallen off a huge beast.

"Behind you!"

He turned to see the hellbender facing him like a charging bull. Changing form wasn't going to help him, even if he could do it fast enough, but he used his focused rage to reload the magical musket and ready for a second blast.

When the hellbender was charging, he leveled the muzzle at its head but quickly realized it wouldn't do anything, so he adjusted his aim towards a forward leg.

The blast kicked his shoulder back.

The hellbender tumbled forward with momentum. Damon dove to the side as the beast rolled down the slope past him.

Damon bounced back to his feet and hurried after the creature, immediately looking for Regina, but once again, she was safely out of range without a smudge of ash on her clothes.

The hellbender thrashed as it tried to regain its feet on the cracked slope with half its body caught in a small ravine.

Damon tried to reload as he ran forward, but realized the weapon was damaged.

A second blast startled him.

Brennan had come around the ridge. The discharge knocked the hellbender back on its rear, but as Damon stopped to reload, the creature turned and breathed a fiery smoke laden with sparks over Brennan.

"No!"

Damon started to run forward, but remembered he had no weapon. He couldn't see Brennan in all the smoke, but the hellbender looked like it was about to charge.

"Damon!"

Regina threw him the machete in its sheath. He pulled out the blade and ran forward, leaping onto the back of the hellbender. The heat from the beast was unbearable, but he squinted through the smoke and climbed to its neck as it tried to knock him off.

Before the hellbender could rise up, he thrust the blade into a crack in its armor around the neck with both hands. A high-pitched scream was followed by the collapse of the beast's legs onto its belly.

Damon leapt off the fallen hellbender and ran towards Brennan. He reached him at the same time as Dr. Martinez.

At first, Damon thought he'd been burned severely based on the damage to his clothes and was busy thinking of spells to deal with third-degree burns. But then as the smoke swirled away, he saw that Brennan was unharmed.

"I'm fine, I'm fine," he said, climbing to his feet while bits of charred clothing sloughed off his body.

"Brennan?" asked Dr. Martinez with jaw low.

He frowned. "You don't think I'd come to these without the proper enchantments?"

Brennan held up his wrist with a runed bracelet. "Best fire protection money can buy."

Before long, the rest of the hunting party had gathered around the slain hellbender.

"Nice kill, Brennan," said Aleksander, jogging up on foot.

"Wasn't me, Alek. The kid got the beast. With a machete no less."

With adrenaline still coursing through his veins, Damon found it hard to pay attention to everything going on around him, but in that moment he sensed their admiration for his kill.

"That was amazing, babe," said Regina, sidling up against him and rubbing her hand across his chest.

"Now that's how we hunt," said Aleksander, clapping him on the shoulder.

A round of applause broke out.

Dr. Martinez came over afterwards as the red-vested attendants started preparing the two slain hellbenders. Their original mount had two broken legs and was moaning in pain. Damon feared it would be shot, but the beast was given flowers from the river which helped stabilize it.

"You okay?" asked Dr. Martinez, giving him a once-over.

"My eyes are burning form the smoke, but otherwise, I think I'm fine."

She shook her head.

"I really thought I was going to lose both you and Brennan."

"I did too."

Regina squeezed herself to Damon, which brought an eyebrow raise from Dr. Martinez.

"You were amazing."

After a replacement dubber was brought in, the hunting party left the charred plains. The two hellbenders would be brought to camp later.

The second half of the trip was considerably different than the earlier part. He couldn't have avoided their conversations if he'd tried. Everyone wanted him to ride next to them as he'd single-handedly slain a hellbender with a machete.

"An enchanted machete," he tried to tell them, but his deflections meant nothing.

They reached camp after traveling down another set of rivers and then climbing to a plateau that had a gorgeous view of another valley with bulbous storm clouds crackling with electricity.

A huge white tent was filled with tables and soft magelights while a team of chefs prepared a delicious smelling meal.

Damon was given a new set of clothes since his old ones were covered in ash. The hunting apparel made him look like he was a member of their club, and their promises for donations made him beam with pride.

"I don't think you could have scripted it better," said Brennan in a quiet moment near the bar.

"I'm just glad no one got hurt. I really thought you'd been severely burnt."

Brennan cocked a grin. "You can't hurt me that easily. That's one of the benefits of being extremely wealthy."

"Speaking of," said Damon.

Brennan raised his glass towards the others. "I think after today, most of the donation gap is going to be covered."

"It's not that. I mean, it's great. But our problems are more immediate."

"And that is?"

"Do you remember the ghost we told you about?"

Brennan nodded.

"It's been damaging the wards."

The wealthy benefactor made a strange face. "I didn't think it should be able to do that. Otherwise, what's the point of Veil wards if a ghost can bypass their protections?"

"Exactly what we thought, but yet we've found damage on them and Remi caught it in the act. It seems like the ghost mage is trying to break them down."

"That is concerning."

"I was wondering if the maintenance crew could get an early disbursement for upgrades. I know it's a lot, but we need it right away."

"Yes, I'm sure you do."

Brennan pumped his eyebrows.

"But I have a better idea. One that will help things right away, because even if we get you the money, it will take time to get quotes, find a vendor, etc., etc."

"I don't understand."

"Besides being a wealthy patron of the healing arts, I'm also a collector of powerful trinkets and artifacts. I have a piece in my collection that should help bolster the wards until they can be fixed permanently. And don't worry, we'll release the disbursement too, but that will take time to work through the system."

"Thank you, Brennan. I can't thank you enough."

Brennan clapped him on the shoulder. "You did it yourself with your heroics killing the hellbender."

He winked.

"Now let's get back to the others."

The rest of the event felt like a dream. They toasted him multiple times and by the end of the night, he was riding a high he'd never felt before. He felt giddy and a little bit outside himself.

They left by a portal near the tents. Regina brought a couple of drinks, as she'd been supplying him all night with libations. They were given a limousine to ride back to the hospital. Damon felt like he was floating on a cloud.

When the limo dropped them off, Regina tugged on his hand.

"You should come back to my place, babe."

Damon's hands felt like balloons and his face tingled. He let himself be tugged towards her sports car for a few steps before he dug his feet in.

"That's not—"

It was all he could get out. Words escaped him. He felt like he'd been fine a half hour ago, but maybe the alcohol had finally caught up. Every one of her touches sent chills of pleasure down his spine.

"Come on, babe. You know you want to. I felt it between us all night. Let's celebrate your success. Our success. We have a half dozen invites to other parties. This was a life-changing event. We could make a killing in these circles. Think how much money you could raise for the hospital."

While he'd never clarified his relationship with Remi, and the long hours made it impossible, he didn't want to lead Regina on.

"I have to go to bed, Regina. Tonight was...I'm not sure I have words for it, but it was great having you as my date."

"Damon..."

Before he knew it, she'd stepped close and set her hand against his cheek, pulling him into a kiss. Her lips were soft and made him forget every thought in his head.

She tried to pull him toward her sports car again, but he politely removed his hand from hers. She frowned.

"I'll see you tomorrow...babe," she said.

Heady and confused, Damon meandered back to the side entrance of the hospital. He wasn't sure why he looked up, except that he felt like he was being watched.

Standing at the cafeteria window, looking down with a great view of the parking lot, was Remi. She turned away, leaving him with a knot in his chest.

TWENTY-SEVEN

The cap on the pills wouldn't open no matter how Remi tried. The patient watched her with concern. She was so frustrated that it wouldn't open. It was a stupid pill bottle. She'd opened hundreds of them.

"Let me help with that."

Damon leaned over and tried to remove the bottle from her hands but she yanked it away.

"I can get it. I don't know what's wrong with me."

Damon stared at her with eyes rounded, but he said nothing. Finally, the bottle lid popped, releasing the medicine inside.

"I'm sorry, Mister Fallon. It's been one of those days."

The patient looked between them with wide eyes.

"Here, take two. Then we'll finish the spell and you can be rid of us."

The crackle of a television changing stations beyond the privacy curtain had them glancing in that direction. A surge of patients had forced the hospital to start room sharing, but it was nowhere near as bad as their first year.

"Do you want to go over it first?" asked Damon.

"I read through the spell. It's not that hard."

"But coordinating our movements. I know you haven't done many dual spells..."

Remi growled under her breath, bulging her eyes out in the direction of the patient.

"I'll be fine. It's not my first dual spell. I did one last week with Dr. Martinez."

His eyes glanced to the pill bottle.

"Remi..."

The patient cleared his throat. "You can practice the spell if you want. I don't mind."

"It was the plastic on the lid. There's a burr on it. That's why I couldn't open it. I'm fine."

Damon tilted his head. "Remi. I know you're mad about the charity event."

"The charity event?" she asked heatedly. "Is *that* what I'm mad about?"

"It was a rousing success. We raised almost the entire target amount."

Heat rose to her cheeks. She hated the way they were looking at her like she was faulty.

"It was the lid," she mumbled.

"Look, I don't know why I let Regina kiss me. Maybe it was the excitement of the night, or the drinks I'd had."

"I thought you've told me more than once that werewolves don't get drunk that easily."

"That's true."

"Look," said Remi. "You don't have to apologize. It's not like we've clarified our relationship. I guess I'm just the person you occasionally fuck."

"Remi..."

The patient cleared his throat louder. "Don't mind me. I'm not just lying right here. Or maybe you could turn on the TV so I could at least pretend to be doing something else?"

"We'll get to you in a moment," said Remi, holding her hand up.

Damon spread his hands. "I want a relationship with you. I do. But we're so damn busy with our work. It's like last year. The only time we could find to get together was when you had to chain me to the wall and then when you tried to ride me, I fell asleep when you were getting the condoms. If that's not emblematic of our relationship, I don't know what is."

Remi was vaguely aware that the volume of the television on the other side of the room was going up.

"I get it. You had to take Regina to the event. You couldn't take me. But it was like you purposefully kissed her in front of me."

"I didn't know you were there, I swear."

"Oh shit," said the patient, recoiling.

Remi pointed at him.

"See. He gets it. Look, if you don't want to have a relationship, fine, but just tell me. Then you can go back to fucking that Krak woman in the closet, or the lab tech girl in the bathroom, or wherever you two plan to get it on."

"I'm not fucking her!" yelled Damon with his arms high.

The curtains slammed open, revealing a family of six sitting around a bed. The mother was standing at the opening with the remote control in her fist while five young kids stared at them with eyes wide.

The mother glared at them for a long time before sliding the curtain back over, leaving their side in stunned silence.

"This is better than the television," said Mister Fallon intently.

Remi took a quivering breath.

"Maybe we should finish our spell."

"That would be good," replied Damon.

They started the spell a half second off, but Remi quickly caught up. Hearing their voices in tandem helped smooth away her anger and let her focus on the job. While they were pulling faez separately, the coordinated effort brought a warmth to her midsection as if it were intermingling. The dual spell felt like singing a song together and she felt empty when it concluded.

Silence intruded into the space with only the television on the other side providing background noise.

"I need to catch up on my rounds," said Damon.

Remi watched him leave. After he was gone, she pulled out the alcohol wipes and started cleaning the runes off the patient's thigh.

The patient stared at her the entire time, which wasn't unusual, but felt that way given the earlier conversation.

When she was finished, she pulled the blanket over his leg and asked, "Any questions?"

"Yeah. Did you really chain him up?"

TWENTY-EIGHT

The hum of equipment provided background noise in the central ward room of the basement floor. Lily stared at a chunk of obsidian contained in a glass box. Eldritch light plused from etched runes covering its surface. The space was larger than the other four rooms where the rest of the wards were kept.

"Whoa," said Remi, entering with Damon right behind. "You could have a party down here."

Her friends stood on opposite sides, which seemed purposeful—and unusual—since they were usually mooning over each other. Things hadn't been the same since the charity event.

"You have the artifact?" asked Lily.

Damon unshouldered his backpack and gently revealed a carved white rod with crimson runes etched into the surface.

Lily accepted the artifact, feeling the smoothness and light weight.

She rubbed her finger over one of the runes. It was a language she was unfamiliar with, though parts of it seemed like she should recognize them.

"That's a bone, right?" asked Remi.

"Doubtful," said Damon. "It's a creature in the Veil. They don't have bones."

"It sure looks like one," said Remi, crossing her arms.

Lily frowned. "They don't have bones, but this could be something else. Like bone, but not quite. I don't think any of us know much about the Veil."

Damon checked around. "How are we doing this? I thought the ritual took five people?"

At that moment, the door opened again, revealing Biddy and Alice both in the clothes they'd worn when they first came to Invictus.

"Thank you for helping us, sisters," said Lily tersely.

"Anything that gets you to focus on Medb again," said Biddy.

The urge to say something got caught in Lily's throat. Before she could work herself up to it, she caught Alice shaking her head from behind Biddy.

Lily sighed. "Let's get to work. I'm sure everyone would like to get this over with as soon as possible."

"I was thinking—"

Biddy started reaching for the artifact, but Lily slapped her hand away, forcing a standoff between them. She knew she shouldn't have done that, but Lily was getting tired of her older sister assuming she knew best.

"This is what we're going to do," said Lily, grabbing the bone-like object. "I'm going to stay here at the spirit ward. Damon is on earth, Remi at air, Biddy on fire, and Alice is water."

Everyone glanced between each other suspiciously but said nothing.

"Good. To your stations. I hope you all read over the spell before you got here. Unless you want to practice before we do it for real."

"Nope," said Remi, shaking her head while looking at Damon.

"I don't need it," said Biddy, then she marched out of the room.

Alice stepped near. "She's just..."

"Let's just get this over with," said Lily.

After everyone left, Lily pulled out her phone and began tracing the diagrams on the glass box. It wasn't runic magic, or any other arcane language she recognized, but it'd been supplied by Brennan so she knew it would be good.

Lily finished the magical scaffolding by the time the others reached their wards.

"Alright," said Lily into her phone. "Remember, you need to try and focus on your element. I gave everyone the one I thought best suited them. I know it's hard to isolate a single part of your faez, but do your best. Now, I'm going to give everyone a countdown of three and then we start."

"Does that mean we start when you get to one, or right after?" asked Remi.

"You can't bloody start on one," said Lily, frowning.

"Right. The beat after."

Lily stared at the phone feeling like the leader of a band that had been having problems while on tour.

"Three, two, one—"

The five-person anchoring spell started almost perfectly. A miracle as far as Lily was concerned. It wasn't particularly difficult, but coordinating the five people over the phone made it challenging.

She'd been so focused on the others, she almost forgot to isolate the spirit portion of her faez. Since the raw magic came from a place somewhere at the base of the skull, filtering for one type of element felt like putting her thumb on a garden hose to make it spray, but only to get a single stream of the water.

The flavors of the five elements each felt different as they passed through the mind. Spirit felt glossy and thick as if it were made of liquid glass.

Since she was the conduit for the spell, she felt the other elements reaching her from the wards. They hit her in the back and flowed through her, requiring Lily to twist them together and connect them to the arcane diagram. She felt like a magical electrician, wrapping wires together at a power source with golden light filtering out her fingertips.

As all five elements zipped through the lines of the protective ward, the thick smell of sulfur hit her nose. Lily glanced around looking for the ghost mage. If he chose to strike now, she'd be virtually defenseless, but she couldn't hurry for fear of ruining the spell.

As she continued weaving the elements together, the smell grew stronger. Then she saw sparks bursting at the edges. Was the ghost invisible? Trying to ruin her efforts from the edge of the Veil?

Lily continued enunciating the words of the spell while her eyes darted to the corners of the room, looking for signs of incorporeal beings.

As the spell rushed to its conclusion, Lily felt pressure on the back of her skull. Something was wrong, but she couldn't quite figure it out. Lily funneled her concern into finishing the spell.

When the last threads of elemental magic finished flowing through her and the arcane diagram lit up like a mini-supernova, Lily released the spell. She watched as the glow subsided until she no longer had to squint.

"Did it take?" asked Remi over the phone.

Lily checked the corners of the room. "Like a mutt to a mud puddle."

She watched the slow pulsing of the arcane diagram indicating that the scaffolding tying the five wards together more tightly through the artifact was working. Lily wished there was some way to test the effectiveness of their efforts, but that would come in time. If the ghost no longer bothered them, then they would know that it had worked.

"I think we're good," she said to the others. "You may return to your regularly scheduled chaos."

She was about to end the call when Biddy said, "If we're done, then I need to talk to you about your new priorities."

"Biddy..."

Lily smiled at their youngest sister's attempt to keep the peace.

"I have rounds in ten minutes. I'll let you know when I'm free. Later."

"I'll be waiting."

Lily hit the red phone icon. With the ghost problem out of the way, she was finally going to have to deal with her older sister.

TWENTY-NINE

Damon knew it was going to be a bad day when he couldn't find any clean scrubs even though he was certain he'd laid some out the night before. After borrowing some extras from a second year who was a similar size, he showed up late to rounds, receiving a disappointed frown from Dr. Martinez, who didn't seem to be her normal positive self.

"The last time I checked, you're third years, not wet-behind-the-ears first years. The charts go back on the end of the bed when you're done, not taken back to your room because you forgot. Boon."

Boon hung his head.

"And while we're at it, let me remind you that just because you're feeling horny doesn't mean you can play grab ass in front of the patients.

"And last, we've got some of the hospital board coming by this afternoon, so let's try not to look like a bunch of fuckups."

After they were dismissed, Damon mumbled to Sasha, "What's with her? And where's Dr. Decker?"

"Not a bloody clue on either account, but I had the worst dreams last night. I took my temperature, hoping I was sick so I didn't have to go to work, but just my bloody luck to be fabulously healthy."

Sasha split off towards the hex hallway, leaving Damon thinking about the bad dreams he'd had. The details were vague but he recalled being locked in one of the basement rooms of the hospital trying to get out.

He'd almost made it to his first patient's room to renew an aura enchantment when he heard Dr. Decker laying into Nurse Mandy about forgetting a check-in that morning. The normally stoic nurse had wetness around the corners of her eyes.

Damon went around the long way, reaching his patient's room a few minutes after he had originally planned.

"All ready for your renewal, Miss Tabor?" he asked the older woman in the bed.

"No, but you're going to do it anyway," she said with a smirk. "You know what I like about you, Healer Damon?"

"What's that?"

"At least I get to look at you while I'm having to go through all this crap."

He chuckled. "The price of getting—"

The lights flickered, followed by the monitoring equipment going blank and then restarting.

"That's weird..."

"Third time this morning," she said, shaking her head.

A pit formed in his stomach. "Did you have any strange dreams last night?"

"Did I..." She blew out an exaggerated breath. "I haven't had a nightmare like that since I got divorced from my second husband. Why? Is something wrong? You look like you just saw a ghost."

Right then he heard a scream from across the hall. Damon ran into the arcane imaging lab where the technician was pulling a patient out of the machine. The woman was screaming with her eyes open.

"Don't let him get me! Don't let him get me!"

Damon ran to her side, shaking her.

"You're awake. You're awake."

The woman startled before looking at Damon, face etched with lingering fear.

"I thought I—"

"What did you see?"

"I was in the machine and then I wasn't. Someone was coming to get me. I could feel their hate. They wanted me dead."

The quiver in her lower lip told Damon how real the vision had been.

"You're okay now."

"I'm not going back in the machine," said the patient.

"I'm sure it had nothing—"

The sound of metal rending like a giant had grabbed two halves of a steel girder and was tearing it in half echoed through the hallways. Damon stuck his head out the door. The noise was followed by a crash. He ran to the source, finding a woman in her patient gown stuck against the wall with her eyes rolled back in her head. The orderly that had been pushing her was staring in abject terror.

"What happened?"

"I saw… it was… I can't—"

"Help me get her down."

Damon grabbed the woman's legs, but she wouldn't budge. She was stuck fast. When he turned to yell at the orderly to help, he saw the writing on the opposite wall.

Written in scrawled blood it said: Decker Lies!

"Oh, shit."

Damon was reaching for his phone when it buzzed.

"What's going on?" asked Remi.

He snapped a picture and sent it to her.

"That's not good. Have you seen Decker?"

"No," responded Damon as he turned back to the woman on the wall. "But I have a situation here I have to take care of."

"I'll find Decker," said Remi, then she hung up.

Dr. Martinez came running around the corner. She stopped and stared at the patient.

"What are you waiting for? We have to get her down!"

"Dr. Martinez."

"What?"

He pointed at the wall.

"Oh no."

"Yeah. I'll take care of this. You find Dr. Decker."

THIRTY

Remi ran through the hospital following the signs of destruction. She asked everyone if they'd seen Dr. Decker. It wasn't until she ran past Nurse Mandy that she learned he was headed to the next floor up.

She burst up the stairwell, nearly knocking down Dr. Paddock, who screamed at her as she thundered past him, throwing herself through the door and nearly knocking over an orderly pushing a mop bucket.

"Dr. Decker?"

The orderly shook his head.

Remi started running one direction when she heard a scream. She found a woman sitting in the hallway with her eyes closed. Remi shook her awake.

"He's here. He's here."

"Who's here?" asked Remi even though she knew the answer.

The woman trembled with fear. A nurse came running up, so Remi handed over responsibility.

Around the next corner she found another scrawl of blood on the wall.

"Decker Kills!"

At the nurses station, she asked them about Decker.

"He went past a few minutes ago. He looked like he'd just gotten back from a rave with his eyes all glossy and blank."

Remi had seen him shortly after the morning meeting with Dr. Martinez, so she knew he hadn't been out the night before. But it made it more important to find him right away.

"Were any of you here when Dr. Decker worked before?"

The nurses glanced between themselves until one of them called for a nurse from in back named Hugo. He had brown skin and his jet-black hair pulled into a ponytail.

"Dr. Decker? Yeah, I worked with him before. Never did understand why he came back after everything that happened."

"Do you remember which room Martin Freely's wife died in?"

Hugo blanched at the question. "That was a long time ago."

Remi chewed on her lower lip as she ran through what she knew about the events back then.

"Is there a room that never quite feels right when you go in it? Or has a reputation for patients dying or having weird dreams?"

Hugo's eyes shot open.

"Three eighty-three."

Remi ran down the cross hall until she reached Room 383. The door wouldn't open and when she tried to pick it, the lock wouldn't budge. Lights flickered inside. She wasn't sure how she knew, but she could feel the barrier between their world and the Veil was thin. It was like a cold hand caressing her neck.

"Dr. Decker, are you in there?" she shouted.

When the interior blinds rattled and the hallway lights burst into sparks, Remi blasted the lock with a force bolt. She'd never been good at the five elements, but the adrenaline coursing through her veins supercharged the spell.

It was whirling chaos inside the room. The equipment was pressed against the wall and anything loose or light was swirling around in an unseen wind. As soon as she stepped inside, the door slammed behind her.

Dr. Decker was pressed against the far wall with his scrubs shredded and blood dripping from points along his face and arms. He held a scalpel against his inner wrist and was staring at something at the center of the chaos.

The ghostly figure looked like a smallish man with dusty brown hair in a white orderly jacket. Remi recognized him from her research.

Martin Freely.

"Dr. Decker. Oren. Put the scalpel down."

He stared past her with a blank expression. The blade slipped against his skin, opening up a thin slice.

"Martin Freely. Let him go."

The apparition turned.

He was so ordinary, yet Remi had never been so scared in her life. Behind Martin, she could see the hazy, greenish mist of the Veil—the land between the living and the dead.

She didn't understand how he could be here after they'd bolstered the wards, but that was a problem for later.

"He must pay."

The strength of Martin's voice worried Remi. He shouldn't be this real.

"He's paid enough. Whatever happened with your wife, he's spent the last ten years beating himself up for what happened. For what you did in revenge. And that's not on him. *You* did that."

"He killed her. He killed my Sarah."

The apparition of Martin Freely extended his hand toward Oren and the knife went in deeper.

"Oren! Wake up!"

Remi tried moving towards Dr. Decker, but the apparition stepped in her way.

"I'll bleed him like a pig."

"He doesn't deserve this. Nor do his patients. He's a good doctor. I've seen it myself."

"A good doctor wouldn't have let Sarah die."

Remi studied Martin Freely. His orderly whites were pristine and freshly pressed as if it was his first day on the job.

"Doctors aren't omnipotent. They can't fix everyone no matter how hard they try. They're just human with powers that don't make sense for anyone to have. But that's the way things are."

"I'll make him die slowly and in pain, just like she died."

She looked past Martin into the Veil to see a collection of junk piled on glistening rocks. Remi stepped forward to get a better look. It was a children's book. *The Happy Train.* Remi saw other detritus of Martin's life. Vials and syringes from the hospital. A model boat in a jar. Dead lilies in a pile. All things she'd learned about the man from her research.

But it was the book that struck Remi.

Then she remembered what she'd read about Sarah. She'd been a financial analyst. Why would they have a children's book?

Her parents had taught her the art of the con involved using the key points of people's lives against them. Hide the trick within their desires just like the Trojan horse. In that instance, she saw a new truth that hadn't been in any of the newspaper articles or books she'd read.

"Sarah was pregnant. Or you were trying. You both wanted kids."

The apparition of Martin Freely surged towards her, turning into a white-hot scream of hate, features unrecognizable as human. Sparks jumped from the edges of the ghost.

"You know nothing about Sarah!"

She pushed Martin backwards, which shouldn't have been possible. The shove confused the ghost too.

Remi spotted Dr. Decker slumping against the wall as he stared at the scalpel. The ghost of Martin Freely had lost its hold on him.

For now.

"What would Sarah think? Do you think she would want you to do this? What happened to her was tragic. But the reason she was in this hospital wasn't Dr. Decker's fault. Or that she died. No one can save everyone."

"He has to pay."

Remi felt a second presence in the Veil. It was scared and distant, but she felt it.

"Sarah Freely. Show yourself."

A woman's form, hazier than Martin's, appeared in the room. Her arms were blackened with poison and her eyes were cavernous. Remi hated that she was seeing two ghosts, but she didn't know any other way to save Dr. Decker.

"Sarah, please, tell Martin that it wasn't Dr. Decker's fault."

The ghostly woman stared back at Decker, who was fully conscious and staring back with the weight of the world on his shoulders.

"Sarah, please. More people are going to die on your behalf if you can't get Martin to stop."

Ghostly Sarah shook her head. Remi checked between her and Dr. Decker and then she saw it. The pain and knowledge in Oren's eyes.

"You *did* make a mistake."

Dr. Decker gave a tiny nod of the head. Barely perceptible, but acknowledgement enough.

"I treated her with the wrong antivenom spell," he said. "I fixed it shortly after, but by then the mistake had been made. I'd missed the window to save her."

The ghost of Martin Freely seethed in place. Lights flashed and the spinning papers and small items continued whirling around the room.

Remi was aware that people were banging on the closed door, but the ghost was keeping them out.

"I'm sorry, Sarah," said Dr. Decker. "I don't know how I made that mistake. But I did. It's my fault. I'm sorry for you too, Martin. That mistake changed both your lives irrevocably."

He hung his head and then added, almost as an afterthought, "And mine."

The ghost of Sarah Freely stepped forward until she was face-to-face with Oren. He looked on the verge of breaking, but lifted his chin to stare at his former patient.

"I forgive you."

A sob slipped out of Oren's lips. His knees buckled but he managed to stay partially standing against the wall.

"No!" screamed Martin.

His ghostly wife turned. "I forgave him, Martin. You should too."

"He ruined us. Ruined our lives. We were going to name her Janice."

Sarah approached Martin and grasped his hands. It looked like a wedding in the land of the dead. Remi bore witness as Sarah leaned forward, kissed Martin on the cheek, and gently led him into the Veil.

In the span of a half-minute, the ghostly pair was gone and everything in the room fell to the ground, including Dr. Decker, who collapsed into a heap, sobbing heavily.

The door burst open revealing Dr. Martinez. She stared at the destruction and then Oren against the wall. His wrists were covered in blood.

"Did he…?"

"No," said Remi. "It was the ghost of Martin Freely."

A couple of nurses ran in and with Dr. Martinez' help, they put Oren in a wheelchair. He looked like he'd aged two decades. His ex-wife spoke quietly to him for a while until he nodded and they wheeled him away.

"I had him sent to his apartment. I'll take care of him until he's better, but I have to know first. What happened?"

Remi explained everything, including the part about the mistake that had killed Sarah Freely.

"Merlin's tits. No wonder," said Dr. Martinez, shaking her head. "He'd never come to terms with that mistake. And neither had Martin. The guilt between the two helped with the conduit between here and the Veil. But he shouldn't have been able to come over. Not with the wards."

"That's what I thought too."

Dr. Martinez stood close with confusion on her brow. "And you shouldn't have been able to see into the Veil like that, or know that she was nearby."

"I don't understand it either."

"Now's not the time for discovery, but sometime later we need to talk about what happened. Not for Oren, but for you and what happened here with the Veil."

Remi was left alone in the destroyed room as Dr. Martinez took Oren back to his apartment. The weight of what had happened fell heavily on her shoulders. She felt something lodged in her throat and the sudden urge to cough. After a deep hacking, she spat out one of the dead lilies she'd seen in the Veil.

THIRTY-ONE

It had taken two construction workers and a healthy bribe to have the potted tree from the main entryway relocated to the spirit ward in the basement. The room's unusual construction with high curved ceilings and arcane sigils built into the walls made it ideal for Lily's plan, especially with Brennan's artifact providing a bulwark against the Veil's imposition.

"I don't care about your bloody hospital," said Biddy with her arms crossed after she entered.

The eldest de Meath wore her drab dress with her hair plaited into two braids that ran down her back. Lily almost expected to see a riding crop in her hand for unruly students.

"This isn't about the hospital," said Lily. "I have an idea about the corruption."

"If this is a sad attempt to keep me from dragging you back to Ireland, you can forget it now. You can't fix the kalkatai from this three-penny basement."

"I can't fix it. Not yet. But all these problems with the hospital and Veil have given me an idea."

Biddy flattened her lips.

Lily sighed and continued. "The corruption didn't happen all at once. The Oak Father's lands only had small problems at first. Trees with rot, Fae beings gone wild, overgrowth choking away the old paths. It was an insipid disease, barely noticeable at first, but eventually it broke down the Fae's defenses and then when Oberon was no longer on his throne, the rot metastasized."

"The summer lands are not a person."

"No," said Lily. "But there are similarities to what's happening in the hospital. The defenses grew worn over time..."

"Are you daring to say that the Oak Father let his guard down?" asked Biddy.

"I'm not saying it, because I don't bloody have to. It happened! The corruption exists and Oberon let it happen."

"Blasphemy. Medb should cut your tongue out and feed it to a Green Man."

Lily lifted her chin.

"It didn't happen by accident. It's not just Oberon, and I'm not saying that because of your threat. Someone or something caused the kalkatai."

"Who?"

"There are many candidates. While most of the other Fae realms have been quiet, the city Fae still war with each other in the Eternal City."

"The maetrie have never bothered with the other Fae because they only care about their broken, carnage-filled lands and they know they would be destroyed by the Fae's collective might," said Biddy.

"I'm just saying. They have the power and the motive. But I don't think it's them either. Then there's the Mara."

"The Fomorians? Ha!" Biddy spit on the ground. "Those fools destroyed their own realm and most had to escape here. Without those links, they are weak. I can't believe you'd think that Balor of the Evil Eye, or Cethlenn, or Tethra, or any of those fools could take down the Oak Father. Blasphemy, I say. Blasphemy!"

"But we don't know it's not them. And there are others too. What about the Veil? When the city of sorcery became a crossroads for the realms, it brought old conflicts closer, made it easier for old enemies to reach their foes."

"You bleat like a sheep. Get on with whatever you're doing here," said Biddy, gesturing dismissively towards the potted tree. "Because once you're done playing at being a student mage, I'm going to take you back home where I can put your feet in clover where you belong. Put you back to work for Medb."

"Biddy—"

"I've made up my mind. I've given you months to prove me wrong, that this side trip was worth the expense to our family, but I can see no benefits. And now that you fixed your little Veil problem, it's time to go."

"I'm not sure it's fixed," mumbled Lily under her breath.

"What was that?"

Lily kept her lips squeezed tight. She didn't want to give her older sister the satisfaction of saying that she might have failed.

"Come help me at the tree."

Biddy approached, but stayed at a distance. "You don't need me for a Greenwalk."

"It's easier with two."

"If you can't manage it on your own, then I don't know why everyone said you were the strongest of our clan."

Lily growled under her breath.

"You will come with me to the Eó Ruis tree?"

"I will extend my sight, but this journey is yours and yours alone."

Lily approached the tree feeling like a child on their first Greenwalk. Her traitorous hands shook, so she hid them from her sister using her body.

The potted tree was as wide as two fists. The Fae runes were already etched in the trunk. She had wood putty to cover them up afterwards.

"What are you waiting for?" asked Biddy when Lily glanced back.

At first, her tongue stumbled over the words of the ritual. She hated that Biddy had that effect on her, but once Lily got into the flow, nerves calmed and she let the magic flow through her.

When Lily opened her eyes she was no longer in the basement of Golden Willow hospital.

But nor was she at the Eó Ruis tree in Ireland.

Thick vines and overgrown foliage surrounded her. The cloying rot filled her nose, making it hard to breathe. Lily stepped forward, her foot sinking into a log covered in black bark, releasing a puff of spores.

"Where am I?"

She asked the question already knowing the answer, but she didn't want to acknowledge the truth.

The reality was she was nowhere near the Eó Ruis tree.

She was in the Fae.

Lily pushed through the twisting vines, knocking away buzzing insects from her face. She slapped one against her arm. The misshapen critter had five wings and two differently sized bulbous eyes. The change made her stomach twist in revulsion.

Fighting through the undergrowth as a partial spirit left her exhausted. While she wasn't completely in the Fae, as her body remained in the basement of Golden Willow, she wasn't incorporeal either and had to interact with overgrown plant life.

Despite her view, Lily knew that Biddy was smirking at her struggles from the hospital basement. As a child of Medb, Lily should be able to move through with the grace of a panther, but without that link she was a bumbling fool.

If it weren't for Biddy's presence, she might have cut the link and returned to try again at a later date when she understood why she wasn't at her intended destination. But she persisted for the sake of not giving her eldest sister the satisfaction of seeing her fail.

A massive log the size of a marble column had crashed through the forest, taking down vines and smaller trees in its collapse. As Lily climbed over it, she realized that it wasn't just a tree trunk. Carvings on the surface bore the shapes of stags and birds and wolves.

When her hand brushed the symbols wrapped around the circumference, she pushed away the vines to reveal the words and spoke them in English as not to give offense due to her poor mastery of the Fae.

"Here lies the kingdom of Oberon."

Fear coursed through her veins. Not only had she missed her mark, she'd somehow ended up at the Court of the Summer King. Lily glanced back through the portal, which was perpetually a few feet behind her, but she couldn't see the hospital or Biddy.

In normal times, her arrival at the court without an invitation would have been catastrophic. Without a king at the hearth, she knew not what her presence triggered.

Part of her wanted to end the Greenwalk, but she felt there was something here that she needed to see. Maybe there was a clue to the source of the kalkatai.

Lily continued pushing forward until she found herself in an enormous empty space with sunlight streaming through gaps in the canopy creating a cathedral-like space. The old flower columns, long since rotted to browns and blacks, climbed up the trees on either side. As she craned her neck, a creature bounded through the branches, leaping away from the canopy. Lily watched until she was certain it wasn't going to return.

Ahead of her, misshapen statues made from twisting vines no longer looked like their likenesses. Lily had never looked upon Oberon, but his tall form at the center of the open space appeared warped from the corruption.

If she squinted, she could imagine what the court of the Summer King might have looked like in good times with nobles in their bright colors speaking energetically with each other. She pictured the hairy wolf form of King Nuada at the foot of the throne.

Lily spun around when she smelled smoke. Fire in the summer realm, except with permission of Oberon, shouldn't have been possible. Not even with the corruption should it be possible.

The source of it remained hidden until she realized that the edges of her green portal were hazy with black fumes as if it were leaking in from another place.

"I need to leave."

But she didn't.

Even as she felt the danger condense around her, Lily continued forward, determined to discover what this vision was holding for her.

Lily ran towards the throne area.

As she passed through the wide space she had visions of dances in the Court, Fae lords and ladies spinning in bright clothes to the music of the wind. The scene was beautiful—and distracting. Lily shook off the dream.

The smoke grew thicker in her nose. The portal's edges were turning black with embers outlining the doorway. If she didn't hurry, her link back to the hospital would be cut off and she'd be stuck in the Fae.

Not watching her feet, Lily stumbled over a vine. She landed on a pile of bones and antlers, the material cracking under her knees. A tuft of white fur was stuck between the gaps.

She hurried on as the portal shrank behind her, the smoke puffing into the Fae from the edges. Lily reached the throne area, looking for something that might tell her the source of the corruption.

At the base of the wicker throne, she spotted a gap. A chaos-shaped hole that seethed like a pulsing worm wrapped around itself. Or shadowy tendrils. She thought she spied a strange crystal at the heart of the darkness, but it was hard to look at.

Lily tried to reach the dais but a vine grabbed her ankle, yanking her back. She crawled forward, but another wrapped around her thigh and another around her arm.

"Let. Me. Go."

The more she struggled the more the vines reached out to pull her back. Behind her the portal was filling with smoke, the edges burning to embers.

Lily tried a spell that would have let her pass through the vines, but her words had no effect. The vines continued to constrict her.

She was trapped.

When a leafy branch slapped against her mouth, she realized she wasn't getting out. The corruption had her. She would turn into a being like the White Worm.

Then a hand reached through the portal. Bright words sliced the vines from her body.

Biddy hauled her back.

Lily landed on the concrete next to the potted plant, the Greenwalk ended by her sister's intervention. The smell of smoke lingered for a moment in her nose before she could breathe again.

"Thank you."

Biddy was on her knees next to Lily with her face wracked with concern.

"I tried to call you back, but you wouldn't listen. Why are you always so stubborn, Lil?"

"I couldn't hear you. I swear."

Biddy frowned.

"Why did you keep going? I saw the Court. You're not supposed to be there."

Lily realized her scrubs were covered in green and brown smears from the rotting vegetation. Her neck and arms had scratches from the thorns and her hair smelled like smoke.

"I don't know why I ended up there rather than the Eó Ruis tree. But I felt like I was supposed to see something. When I was near the throne, I saw a chaos-shaped hole."

"Did you figure out a way to hold back the corruption as you promised?"

Lily's cheeks burned with embarrassment.

"No. I don't know what happened. That was nothing like I wanted."

Biddy stood tall above her.

"This just proves what I was worried about. Cutting yourself off from Medb has made you weak and mistake prone. You managed to screw up a simple Greenwalk, ended in a forbidden place rather than your intended destination."

"I didn't screw up. I did the ritual exactly as I intended. Something else happened. I don't know what, but I know it's important. Please, Biddy."

Biddy's mouth shifted to the side. "It's too late. I've made up my mind. Get your affairs in order. I'll give you a week, but then we're heading back home."

"Biddy..."

"No," she said. "I've been far too lenient with you. But now I see it. What others see as potential, I realize is arrogance. It led you to bond with a changeling despite the rules against it, to come to the Halls and join the very organization that is killing our world, and to cut yourself off from Medb, our source of power."

Her eldest sister marched out of the room, while Lily remained on her knees, feeling like the world was collapsing around her.

THIRTY-TWO

The lights flickered and the monitor restarted, ruining Damon's procedure for the fifth time in ten minutes. He stopped the timer and shoved his phone in his pocket.

"I'm sorry, Miss Donovan. We've been having a lot of electrical problems lately."

The older woman frowned, deepening the wrinkles around her mouth as she shifted in the plastic tub full of saltwater.

"I've been coming to Golden Willow once a month for the last fifteen years so I can control my urges and I've never seen so many electrical problems."

She made air quotes around *electrical.*

"I'll try again in an hour. Maybe it'll be calmed by then."

Miss Donovan started climbing out of the tub in her swimsuit, spilling water over the edge. For a woman of her advanced age, she was still as fit as an Olympic swimmer.

"I haven't tried to drown anyone in years, I think I can skip a month until you get your issues figured out."

"I'm sorry, Miss Donavan. I really am."

She cupped his cheek with her wet hand and winked. "I believe you, handsome."

Damon left the room so she could change. He was halfway to the nurses station to give them an update when Boon came flying out of a room, slamming the door behind him.

"What's wrong? You're bleeding."

Boon was breathing heavily, and blood trickled out of his ear. He stared at the wetness after he put his fingers in it.

"I thought I heard a child crying and went in to check. It was a damn wailer. Barely got my hex off in time to get out. I can't keep doing this. Every room is a potential land mine and it's only getting worse."

"At least it wasn't the, you know."

Boon rubbed his own shoulder. "Yeah. The Ghost D-Bag who shall not be named."

Damon wasn't so sure that talking about the ghost mage would summon him, but everyone was so spooked that it'd become the norm around the hospital.

"I'm going to talk to Dr. Martinez."

"Can you send the ghost team here first?"

Damon put a hand on his friend's shoulder. "I'll let them know at the nurses station."

When he got there, Nurse Mandy had a flat stare. "Another?"

"Boon's outside the room. A wailer."

She nodded and picked up the phone. Mandy was talking to the ghost team as Damon went in search of Dr. Martinez.

He found her talking to the head of maintenance about a broken water pipe in the alchemy lab. The bursting water had ruined thousands of dollars of reagents that morning.

"What is it now?" asked Dr. Martinez when she saw him standing nearby. "If it's about another event, you'll have to deal with it yourself. I'm already juggling fifteen different emergencies and without Oren I'm barely keeping up."

"How's he doing?"

Dr. Martinez massaged her forehead as she stared in the distance.

"He's better today than other days. He ate some gummy bears. Not *those* kind. And took a bath. He stunk like Old Man Herne."

Damon wrinkled his nose. "We need help, Dr. Martinez. Things are going to hell fast. All the equipment is going on the fritz and we're dealing with new apparitions every other day."

"What do you want me to do?" asked Dr. Martinez, clearly exasperated.

"I don't know. We need that charity money soon and a bigger crew to fix things faster."

"I thought the wards were supposed to be improved."

Damon scratched the back of his neck. "I thought so too. But it's only gotten worse."

"Did you install it correctly?"

"I'm certain we have. I don't understand. None of us do."

"I'll let Brennan know when he gets here," said Dr. Martinez, checking her phone, which was blowing up with messages. She looked ready to throw it through a wall.

"When?"

"A few days, this weekend I think."

"We need him now. Another disbursement could pay for some specialists from the city that can help us deal with these Veil beings. At least until the wards are fixed. Can you call him?"

She shook her head. "He's in another realm. Sorry."

"Anything you can do. We need him."

"You need his money."

Damon shrugged. "Same thing."

"I'll try."

Dr. Martinez headed the other way in a hurry, busily typing on her phone.

Damon stared down the hallway blankly, thinking about what they needed to do to fix the problem. They couldn't wait for Brennan or outside help. They needed to do something right now. He planned on meeting with his friends when they were all free later in the day.

He was about to head towards the labs when a nurse came screaming out of a doorway covered in greenish goo. She collapsed against the wall, heaving with breath.

"Coming, Nurse Tishanti!"

THIRTY-THREE

Remi was hurrying around the corner when she ran into Regina. The beautiful lab technician looked like she was ready for a photo shoot with her meticulously painted makeup and a clipboard in her hand.

"Oh, I'm sorry," said Regina as she tried to step around Remi, who moved in her way.

"I need to talk to you."

Regina slipped past despite her best effort to stay in the way.

"My shift starts soon."

Remi hurried after her. "You have twenty minutes. You're swinging by Damon's route. That's a copy of the rounds list in your hand."

Regina pulled the clipboard to her chest and spoke over her shoulder.

"Why do you care? You clearly don't want him."

Remi had to run to keep up with the long-legged Regina. Remi grabbed her arm, spinning her around.

"It's not that."

"Then what is it?"

The words died in Remi's throat. "We're both busy."

"So am I," said Regina with a light shrug.

"It's not easy, and I don't know. But it doesn't matter. You're not playing fair. In fact, I don't even think you want him. I think this is a scam. You've been playing him since you first got here."

Regina screwed up her face.

"A scam?"

"Yeah, a con. But I haven't figured it out yet."

"I don't know what you're talking about."

Remi shook her head. "It doesn't matter. There are bigger problems in the hospital and Damon can't be distracted."

"You certainly are."

"I am. Because of you."

"That's not my problem."

"I just need you to back off," said Remi.

"And I'm sure you'll do nothing while I'm doing my nails," said Regina derisively.

"There's this mage—"

"I know about the mage. Everyone knows. It's not like we haven't had to deal with problems in the lab. Why are you so worried about it?" asked Regina.

"Because it's destroying the hospital."

Regina narrowed her gaze.

"Seems like it's more than that."

Three orderlies pushing food tray carts came wheeling down towards them. Remi was distracted by their approach and then Regina touched her on the shoulder and whispered something in her ear.

The words made no sense, but she found herself frozen until the orderlies bumped her with a cart.

"Hey!"

But Regina was already at the end of the hallway in her black high heels. Remi had to dodge around the carts to follow, but by then Regina had a massive lead.

"How did she…?"

The race to catch up had her running into a sign-in area with long lines behind the tables. Remi didn't see Regina, which seemed impossible since the gorgeous woman stuck out wherever she was.

Then Remi saw the black cat slinking through the legs of the patients in line. A few years ago she wouldn't have thought anything of it, but after her time in the hospital, the sighting made her suspicious.

"Shadows below, what is going on?"

THIRTY-FOUR

Lily was returning to her room to take a ten-minute nap when she saw the ghost mage. They'd been working double shifts for the last few weeks as the constant interference from the Veil was creating chaos in the hospital. Lily had just helped with three successive exorcisms and was looking forward to closing her eyes for a short spell.

She almost didn't realize it was the ghost mage at first. He looked as tangible as the nurses chatting further down the hallway, but his clothes were from the 1800s, and she could just see through his faintly transparent midsection.

He stared back menacingly as she studied him, looking for clues to his identity. His hands were covered in arcane tattoos and he bore the glint of mental illness that one saw in those afflicted with faez madness.

"Been looking for me?" asked the ghost mage.

He raised his hand towards the lights, which made them flicker intensely before bursting, then he extended his arm towards the wall. Cracks rippled along the surface and in the room beyond, she heard a patient scream.

Lily spat a hex at the ghost.

The curse should have impacted the incorporeal being. A flinch even. But the mage stared back at her with the intensity of a supernova.

A mother and child walked up the hall oblivious to the danger. As they passed the mage, he reached out and plucked the baseball cap from the child and set it on his own head.

"Bloody hell," muttered Lily.

The power required for a ghost to physically interact with their world sent waves of concern through her.

"Excuse me," said the mother, turning on the mage. "You took my son's hat."

The mage smiled broadly and handed over the cap with a short bow. The woman seemed to recognize the malevolence and quickly snatched the hat and dragged her son past Lily. As they hurried by, Lily saw the faint marks of the Veil on their flesh—greenish lines threaded with black.

"Don't worry, little witch. It's all going to be over soon. My time has come. Who knew that dying would be the best thing that ever happened to me? When you summoned me to my Samuel's room, you introduced me to a powerful new friend and a place rich with souls for the plucking."

"I'll banish you."

He wagged a finger.

"No you won't. You don't have the power to oppose me. I can do anything I want. I could even take control of one of your friends. Which will it be? The pup or the thief?"

Lily raised her arm to blast him with spirit magic, but the ghost shifted through the wall, waving as he went.

"Fuck."

Lily punched the wall in frustration, then crouched in the middle of the hallway.

After a minute of thought, she texted her friends, telling them she needed them right away.

Lily was pacing before the whiteboard in their break area when Remi and Damon arrived.

"This can't be good," said Remi, her messy hair sticking in all directions.

Their expressions started out concerned and shifted to deeply frustrated by the end of the explanation—though Lily left out the part about the ghost mage taking control of one of them.

"What do we do? The hospital's already at the breaking point," said Damon.

"Why aren't the wards working?" asked Remi.

"Does it matter? We have to deal with this ghost right now," said Damon.

Remi grabbed her messy hair in bunches. "This feels like a con."

"Everything's a con to you."

Before Remi could spit back a response, Lily slammed her shoe onto the tiles.

"Enough. We have bigger issues than your bewildering relationship," said Lily.

Her friends stared back sheepishly.

"What should we do?" asked Damon.

"We need to banish the mage. Like I tried to do last year, but it wasn't enough. He was too prepared. He slipped past me like a fox into the chicken coop."

"Why haven't we tried this before?" asked Remi.

"Because I thought the wards, not the mage, were the problem. I'm beginning to think it's the other way around. I didn't think the ghost was actually damaging the wards."

Remi crossed her arms. "I told you he was."

"Well, the Veil isn't exactly your specialty."

"It might be," said her friend quietly.

"I also didn't know the right ritual. For your common ghost, any banishing will work, but the more powerful the being, the more specific your spell has to be."

"Then what's changed?" asked Damon.

"I think this mage suffered from faez madness when he was alive. Which would explain his willingness to do awful things to Sammie. His mind is riddled with holes, which is why he probably found a home in the hospital. Most locations don't have their very own touchstones to the five elements. Which means if we use the scaffolding of the wards, I think we might be able to get rid of him."

"Great. Let's do it," said Remi.

Damon gestured towards the hallway. "I have patients I have to see."

"Damon," said Remi as she spun on him. "Isn't this more important?"

"I… It is. You're right. My patients can wait."

"Three is the minimum for this ritual, but we could really use five, just like when we installed the artifact."

Damon pulled out his phone. "Let me check with the rest of the class."

Remi put her hand on his arm. "Be careful how you tell them. We don't want anyone to know why the mage is here, or Lily will get kicked out."

Lily knew she should have told them that Biddy was making her leave soon, but they were already at the frayed edges, she didn't want to make their morale any worse.

"I think this has become more important."

Her friends spent the next few minutes messaging the rest of their class.

"No luck," said Remi. "Everyone's slammed with hospital backup. I was just in the sign-in for the department and there were long lines. It's almost like our first year again. This couldn't have come at a worse time."

Damon held up his phone. "I got Boon!"

"Great. That's four. We could really use a fifth," said Lily.

"What about your sisters?" asked Remi.

"Not available, I already tried," lied Lily.

Remi furrowed her brow but said nothing.

"Don't get mad, but what about Regina?" asked Damon as he prepared himself for the backlash.

"I thought she was only a lab tech?" asked Lily.

"And I don't trust her," said Remi.

"She's more than that," said Damon, frowning. "What, I don't know, but she clearly knows magic."

"She did something to me in the hallway a few days ago," said Remi. "I just don't think we can risk it."

"We need a fifth," pleaded Damon.

"Remi," said Lily, "is this because you don't trust her or you don't like how she interacts with Damon?"

Remi stomped around in a little circle before answering, "Both."

"Then we'll do it with four. It's not ideal, but I think we can manage. I'll swing by my room for some materials. You two grab the ritual kit from the hex room and head down to the spirit ward room in the basement. I'll meet you there."

"Aye, aye, captain," said Remi with a salute. "Come on, wolfboy, we've got a ghost to banish."

After the two left, Lily headed to her room. She'd been squireling away some specialty items in case this happened. Lily was formulating the adjustments to the ritual when she found Biddy and Alice waiting for her in her room.

"How did you get past the locks?"

Biddy stared back ambivalently while Alice looked close to tears behind her. A duffle bag was on the bed, stuffed full with her clothes.

"As if that simple magic was enough to stop me."

"This is good, you're here. I need your help. The hospital—"

Lily never got the words out as Biddy slashed her arm downward. A glowing ball of light hit her lips, trapping the words as they tried to escape. Lily jawed at the air, but nothing came out.

"There's no more delaying, Lil. It's time to go home. Your failed Greenwalk told me how far you've fallen during your time in the Halls. We need to get you back to Medb so we can tackle this problem together. As family."

Lily tried to make a run for it, but without her voice, she had limited access to magic. Biddy captured her arms with invisible chains.

"It's time to go home, Lilith de Meath."

THIRTY-FIVE

The lines of the banishing circle were neat and without false starts. Even the runes looked like they'd been copied out of a text book. Remi stood back and admired her work.

"Never thought I'd be drawing magic symbols in the hospital basement."

She looked up to see Damon returning from relocating the strange potted tree. His forehead knotted.

"Where's Lily? I thought she'd be back by now."

"Or Boon."

Damon's lips squeezed tight.

"Dr. Paddock grabbed him for an exorcism on the fourth floor. He tried to get away, but Boon said that asshole threatened to get him expelled if he left and put the patient's life in danger."

"Fuck."

"We can't do this with two. We can barely do it with three, but we can't even do that," said Damon.

A purposeful scuff had Remi spinning around to find a strange young man standing in the doorway. There was an air of Fae to the newcomer with autumn brown hair and a smoothed face that looked both youthful and intensely wise.

Remi sensed danger, but not to her. She also felt familiarity, but not why.

"Can I help you?"

Damon spun around and immediately his claws were out. She waved him back when the young man made no motion to flee.

"Remi..."

"I don't know who this is, but he's not here to hurt us."

The young man pointed to Remi, then tapped on his chest and mimed feeding. When she didn't understand, he made wide circles around his head like a halo and demonstrated something burrowing in.

The last part put the pieces together for Remi, who exclaimed, "Neko?"

The young man nodded enthusiastically.

"You changed to human form?" asked Damon.

Neko put his hand to his temple and made a pained expression.

"It hurts?"

He nodded again.

"You're here for an important reason, or you wouldn't have used this form," said Remi.

Neko's expression broke with sadness and anger. He put a fist over his heart, then mimicked the big hair again.

"Something's happened to Lily."

Neko nodded and then made himself stiff like a soldier at attention. He jutted his hand forward as if he were hitting someone with a riding crop.

"That's Biddy," said Damon, receiving acknowledgement from Neko.

The changeling finished his charades act by holding out his wrists as if he had shackles on them, after which he made wave motions and pointed into the distance.

"Biddy's taking her back to Ireland. Blood and bone, we can't do this without her. We have to go find her," said Damon as he moved towards the exit.

"It's been over an hour since we last talked to her. Neko, can you lead us to her?"

The changeling shook his head, then mimed driving.

"Great. Biddy took her by car. Or taxi?"

Neko shook his head again.

"We can't do this without her," said Damon.

Remi paced back and forth in thought.

"Remi?"

"We can't go after her. We have to finish this and banish the mage."

"Are you serious? You're going to abandon your friend when she needs us?" asked Damon, throwing his hands in the air.

"If you have a good idea how to find her then I'm all ears. But even if you know where she's at, you know that you and I can't take Biddy alone. She outclassed Lily and she's the best of us. No, Lily came to us because this ghost mage is about to cause serious problems in the hospital. This is the bigger emergency. Just like Dr. Morrison taught us in the ER. It's simple triage, Damon."

He looked away.

"Nothing about triage is simple, but you're right. Fuck, I hate that you are, and when did you become the person who lectured *me* on hospital procedures?"

An ache formed in her chest at the realization of what she had said.

She checked back to Neko, who nodded and pointed to the circle.

"Thanks, Neko." She paused. "There isn't any way you can help us with the banishing?"

Neko tapped on his lips and shook his head. Then he held his head in his hands as if in pain.

"Got it. If you need to, change back to your regular form. Don't wait on us. You did what you needed to do in letting us know about Lily. We'll get her back once we're finished with this mage. Hopefully, it doesn't take too long."

In her heart, she knew that was unlikely, but wasn't going to let Damon know that. Besides, they had bigger problems. They needed a third to even begin the ritual, let alone finish it successfully. But there weren't many options available during the hospital crisis. It'd have to be someone not tied up with patients, or who had enough authority to make that decision.

"Damon."

"Yeah?"

"We need a third."

He tilted his head. "I know."

"Go talk to Regina. I'll see if I can get ahold of someone else. With Lily gone, I don't think it matters if we spill the beans about the mage. I'll try Dr. Martinez first."

"Are you sure?"

"Just do it."

Damon left to talk to Regina, leaving Remi alone in the ritual room. She stared at her phone, trying to formulate how she was going to ask the head of the department to set aside the hospital-wide emergency to do a banishing.

She sniffed the air when something acrid hit her nose.

"Is that brimstone?"

THIRTY-SIX

The bars of the cage shocked Lily so hard she fell on her rear. She expected scorch marks on her fingertips.

"I can't believe you're doing this to me."

Biddy glanced up from her phone as she was typing.

"You did this to yourself."

The interior of the shipping container echoed with her sister's voice.

Lily plopped down in the center of the cage and crossed her arms. Two cots, a big cooler, and other bags were nestled in the opposite corner. She assumed that the three of them were going to cross the Atlantic in the shipping container.

"Don't you get seasick, sister?" asked Lily.

Biddy put the phone in her pocket. "I would have taken you by portal, but I couldn't risk us going astray. The Greenwalk proved that something is wrong with you. We'll figure out what it is when I get you back with the clan."

A heavy screech announced Alice's arrival as she opened the container door, hauling in multiple plastic bags of groceries in both fists.

"I got the Exploding Corn Nuts that you like," said Alice without looking at Lily.

"Thank you, sister. At least I can count on one of my kin. Go ahead and put it away. We've a few hours before we get loaded onto the truck for the port. I need to talk to our logistics person to make sure everything is good for the trip."

"By talk, you mean bewitch," said Lily.

"I will do them no harm," said Biddy as she slipped out the container door.

When it slammed shut, Alice got busy with the groceries.

"I can't believe you're okay with caging your sister like an animal."

Alice's chin dipped towards her chest.

"She's made up her mind."

"Have you?"

Alice turned her head slightly.

"I hate what she's done to you."

The words Lily wanted to say about their eldest sister would have felt cathartic, but she knew that it wouldn't help convince Alice to free her. She imagined what Remi would say in this situation before choosing to speak again.

"Biddy believes she's doing the right thing, Alice. I understand that. But she's making the wrong decision."

"I don't know."

"Alice, will you look at me? I have something important to tell you. Please?"

Her sister turned around. She looked close to tears.

"Before you grabbed me in my room, the ghost mage revealed himself to me in the hallway. He was like nothing I'd seen before. He was nearly corporal. He took a hat from a passing kid and cracked the plaster on the wall. Nothing good can come of what he's planning, so I'd gathered my friends to try and banish him in the basement. I have no idea if it was going to work, but I had to try. Please, Alice. Let me go. There's too much at stake."

Alice's pained expression nearly broke.

"She said you were going to say something like that. That you'd spin a tale of green and gold. That I needed to harden myself against it. I'm sorry, Lily. She'll kill me if I let you go."

The ache and frustration in Lily's chest was like being caught in a vise. She squeezed her hands into fists as she knelt near the cage bars.

"Please, Alice. Search your heart. You know this is wrong. People are going to die because of Biddy's decision. I need to get back to the hospital right away. Remi and Damon are in grave danger. They can't manage this ritual alone. It's dangerous enough if you know what you're doing, like I do, but for amateurs, if they muck it up, they could end up in the Veil without a way back. And we both know they wouldn't last two minutes in the land between the living and the dead. Don't let that happen to my friends. Please, Alice."

For a moment, Lily thought she'd convinced her younger sister. Alice took a step towards the cage and then stiffened her spine.

"I'm sorry, Lily. I really am. But Medb is more important."

THIRTY-SEVEN

A crackling in the air like a nearby electrical fire had Damon worried even before he stepped into the ritual chamber. The acrid smell made his nose itch and his claws want to come out, but he needed his head clear for the spell.

"What is that?" he asked when he saw Remi standing near the circle muttering to herself as she studied her phone.

"Huh? Oh yeah. I'm getting hints of sulfur and other stuff."

"Hints? I was looking for the fire when I walked in. It's burning my nose. Did you start the ritual already?"

"No. Practicing the phrasing." Her mouth shifted to the side. "It's not simple. Maybe I should have reviewed it before I decided that we could do it."

A can light in the ceiling burst, sending shards of glass onto the concrete. The other bulbs increased in intensity for a few seconds along with a heavy hum.

"I guess that answers that," said Remi, glancing at the ceiling. "Did you convince Miss Laboratory to help? Or was she too busy knocking beakers off the table?"

"I'm right here," said Regina, stepping into the room, crossing her arms and glaring at Remi.

Damon took a step back to survey the both of them. They looked ready to launch themselves at each other.

"Hey, let's not..."

"Let's not what?" asked Remi, turning on him.

Damon swallowed. Maybe he shouldn't have tried to intervene.

"Regina agreed to help us with the ritual," he offered.

Remi turned back to Regina and after a moment's consideration, sighed heavily.

"We're happy to have you," said Remi.

"Under one condition," said Regina with her arms still crossed.

Damon knew what she was going to ask, because she'd said as much when he found her outside the lab. He wanted to crawl under a rock until it was over.

"What's that?"

The beautiful lab technician extended a meticulously manicured fingernail at Damon.

"I want him."

"What? I don't own him," said Remi.

"Not that. I want to have sex with him."

Damon simultaneously was aroused and embarrassed.

"Why?" asked Remi, scrunching up her face as if Regina was asking to have sex with a mole person.

"Hey," said Damon.

"I get it. He's a hunk. Not quite Dr. Hunk, but he's attractive. Why do you want *that* in return for helping us?" asked Remi, clearly suspicious.

"I have my reasons."

Remi's questions had him realizing he'd accepted her request without scrutiny.

"You're not going to suck my soul out or anything?" asked Damon.

Regina pouted. "I'm not a monster. But I have my reasons. Reasons I'd like to keep to myself, but no harm will come to Damon. And I hope he'll have a good time."

The earnestness of her answer had Damon reeling. He understood nothing.

"It's up to you. If you don't want me to do it, I won't."

"The hell it is," said Remi, crossing her arms. "This is *your* decision just like it was when you kissed her outside the cafeteria."

It was only the three of them in the basement but he felt like a thousand eyes were upon him.

"I agree," he said eventually.

Remi nodded curtly.

"Then let's get this started. Regina, how long will you need to memorize the spell?"

She strode across the room to Remi and collected the phone, quickly scrolling through the text.

"Five minutes tops."

"Are you sure?"

Regina rolled her eyes. "It's child's play."

"Great."

The beautiful technician sniffed the air. "Do you…?"

"Yeah."

Regina's forehead knotted with concern. "It smells like...never mind. I have a spell to learn."

It took her less time than he expected.

Before long, they were standing at three of the five nodes of the circle. They'd chosen spirit, fire, and air since those were the elements most associated with the Veil.

The first few stanzas of the ritual they were not quite in sync, but eventually they settled into a rhythm that felt pleasing. Damon let himself get carried away by the ritual with the two women.

The lights flickered again. No burst bulbs but the smell of sulfur grew stronger, briefly distracting him.

Damon grew more worried when the runes on the hospital wards started glowing crimson. They shouldn't be affected by the ritual as they were on a completely different magical circuit and he could feel no resistance from their spell.

But they couldn't stop and discuss it.

As they finished the last third of the ritual, which would prepare the circle to be a gateway to the Veil, a greenish mist flowed up from the edges.

It was working.

Now they had to complete the next two parts. Pulling the mage back to the circle and then banishing him to the Veil where he shouldn't be able to come back.

Tension formed in the back of Damon's head where he accessed his faez. He was standing on the air node, which wasn't his strongest, but he shouldn't have felt resistance.

The crimson lines of the hospital wards glowed brighter along with the smell of brimstone and fire. He listened to Regina to make sure she wasn't somehow sabotaging the ritual, but she looked as confused as he was.

The greenish mist rising up from the edges of the circle contained bright sparks which wasn't supposed to happen, but they couldn't stop now or risk launching themselves into the Veil.

Something was wrong.

Damon could feel it in his chest, the way he was accessing his faez, and by the activation of the hospital wards. He could only halfway turn, but he could see something was happening with the bone-like artifact that Brennan had gifted the hospital. It was levitating above the spirit ward box.

"Branch and bough."

The sudden appearance of Lily nearly threw the ritual off course. She stumbled into the room, head craning in all directions, but no one could ask the question they wanted to.

"This ain't bloody good," said Lily, examining the floating artifact and then stepping to the circle. "Something's trying to saddle your spell and ride it through. The three of you ain't enough, but I'm afraid if I join, with only the four of us, it'll throw the ritual off-balance."

The Irish witch knelt on the floor, examining the greenish mist and sniffing heavily.

"Bloody hell, I know what this is trying to come through. This is Mara. The ancient realm of Fomorians. The land of nightmares."

THIRTY-EIGHT

The ritual felt like pulling an icicle from the base of Remi's skull. It made the back of her eyes ache as if a migraine was coming on. Even Regina looked like she was straining.

"I'm so sorry, I should have been here," said Lily. "Had I been, I would have seen that you shouldn't have started the ritual."

Remi grimaced, understanding because the spell felt off, not because she knew why Lily had said that.

A second can light exploded on the far side of the room. The hospital wards pulsed expectantly like a flashing warning sign. Remi could hardly see straight, but she had to keep going. The ritual felt like being loaded into a slingshot and slowly being pulled back. One wrong word and she'd get launched somewhere else.

"Fuck me running," said Lily. "We need a fifth. I can't join the ritual without throwing everything off. This has gone pear-shaped."

"Did I hear you need a fifth?"

Remi nearly flubbed a ritual word when she saw Alice step into the room.

The sisters briefly hugged.

Alice surveyed the situation. "I smell Mara?"

"Aye," said Lily. "It's trying to hijack the ritual, but I don't know why."

The sisters approached the circle, taking position at the two empty spots. Joining a ritual mid-spell was not recommended, but the two witches stepped in barely creating a wobble.

The relief was immediate.

Tension in the back of Remi's skull and at the crown of her head reduced. Not as much as a normal spell, but her vision was no longer blurry.

They'd reached the point where they were starting to pull the ghost mage to the banishing circle. It was like a magical tug-of-war. The five separate flows of magic lit up the lines brightly, oscillating with colors.

Then Remi's vision started blurring again. But not from a migraine.

The magical weaving of five different mages was cinching them together. She could feel their breathing and heartbeats syncing as if they were her own. She'd never experienced such a thing though she was aware of the phenomenon from her studies.

The potentness of Damon's therianthropic essence was like getting high on his pheromones. She would have liked to stay in them longer, but then a wave of Regina's spirit washed through her.

Remi choked on her aura, stumbling over a word, which sent the ritual wobbling for a few seconds. She saw briefly through Regina's eyes, but not in her current form. Instead, she was weaving through many sets of legs from a position near the floor.

And even more than Damon, her soul was intoxicating. Remi could almost understand Damon getting swept up in her aura.

Before she could settle on who Regina might really be, the impact of the sisters sent Remi spinning out of consciousness.

One moment, she was in the basement of the hospital, the next she was standing in a smokey hut lit by crackling embers. A foggy window was covered on the outside by writhing vines. A gaunt woman sat on a wooden throne with a broken spear at her feet and a cracked shield leaning against her leg.

Medb.

The ancient woman leaned forward, peering into the darkness beyond the firelight.

"Who's there?"

Remi sensed her power.

And the rot.

The corruption had reached Lily's former patron. But even with her essence reduced, Remi couldn't help but feel miniscule in comparison. It was like holding up a match to a raging bonfire.

The idea that Lily had willingly given up that powerful connection was inconceivable.

Even that little taste made Remi feel like she could be the greatest thief in the world if she only had a sliver of that link.

But she wasn't able to linger on those thoughts as the world shifted again, sending up waves of vertigo.

Suddenly, she wasn't in the basement, or the Fae, but back in solitary confinement in Utica Juvenile Penitentiary. Her face and ribs hurt from the beating she'd taken from the Scythe Sisters.

Her thoughts during that time felt like she was reliving them as she lay on the thin cot, telling herself that it was all going to be over soon. That in a few weeks, she'd be let out of Utica and her parents would pick her up and everything would return to normal.

#

The ritual room faded from view as Damon fought to maintain the words of the spell, but his consciousness shifted until he was standing in his grandmother's house.

Damon recognized the row of ceramic wolves on the mantle. She would let him handle them but only with supervision as she smoked a menthol cigarette at the kitchen table, fearing that he'd drop and break one. He didn't understand why he was seeing her place until he heard the soul-rattling scream.

He ran to the window to see his cousin Lydia sprinting across the lawn with a figure in black in pursuit. The bright slash of a weapon was followed by the splatter of blood across the grass.

Damon pounded his fist against the window.

The deathless assassin paused as he stood over the headless woman, half in transformation, and looked directly at Damon. Koschei smiled briefly before loping off towards the next house.

The screams had Damon racing out of the house.

Scattered across the cul-de-sac lay motionless bodies in awkward positions as they'd fallen the moment Koschei had cut the life from them. Half had made it through transformation, which made the scene gruesome.

"No—"

Damon had never dared to look up the pictures that had circulated online after the slaughter. He'd spent the weeks afterwards lying in bed half in change and in a constant state of pain. He would watch as his fingernails turned to claws and then back again—all against his wishes.

He'd lost weight during that time. He'd been a healthy, strapping young man in the middle of puberty before but by the time he could get out of bed again he looked like he'd survived a forced starvation, with ribs poking through his skin.

The memory made him dizzy with grief. He stumbled to the house where Koschei had gone, but when he touched the handle it was burning hot.

Smoke was rising from the building.

He turned around to find himself standing in a wasteland of sulfurous fumes and charred earth.

§

The ritual flowed from Lily's lips like a bad dream.

She felt the heat and smelled the smoke long before her vision blurred. The world tried to shift, but Lily hung on. It felt like when her Greenwalk had gone sideways, depositing her in the corrupted Fae.

Lily forced herself to stay in the here and now, even as she could no longer feel her body or tell if she was still uttering the words for the ritual.

Flashes of faces rose up.

Old family members that had passed when she was younger.

Aunt Morticia's charred corpse appeared at her feet in the green grass. She'd been determined to meet the young dragon that lived on a little island to the north, but had met a fiery end.

As the world tried to shift again, she slammed her foot against the ground.

"Ancaire mo chosa!"

The sudden stop made her dizzy, but she found herself back in the basement.

The walls were hazy and transparent. Lily could see endless rolling wastelands of smoking vents and bright lava. The realm of Mara, land of the Fomorians, was leaking into their world, but she couldn't understand why.

In the center of the circle crouched a figure. At first Lily worried some hospital worker had wandered into the room and gotten caught in the center of the arcane webbing, but then she saw the old clothes and felt the malevolent presence.

The ghostly mage stood tall.

To her surprise, his body was not fully transparent. Parts of him looked whole and hale as if he were being colored in by the gods.

The spell should have been preparing him to be banished, not making him stronger, but that's what she realized was happening. The ghost mage turned and faced her with a crooked grin.

"Lilith de Meath. I would like to thank you for what you've done for me. Little did I know that you had such powerful friends."

Lily glanced around the circle at the others, but they were locked in their private hallucinations. Even the newcomer, Regina, appeared transfixed by things only she could see, her mouth wrinkled with unspoken horrors.

"After I'm finished with the lot of you, I'll be making this place my seat of power. With all the old souls lurking just beyond the Veil, I will have plenty of fuel for my conquest.

"Because I know you're painfully curious who you unleashed on this world, I'll let you know, since there's nothing you can do to stop me now. My name is Nicholas Hansen. I was born in 1803. I nearly died when I became old enough to realize I was a mage as the village thought I was a warlock. I made sure every one of them regretted their choice.

"Then I sought out others like me. It was hard in those days. You spoiled brats these days don't know what it was like to fear discovery. I was powerful, but I had to sleep sometime. It was only through whispers and forbidden books that I found what I was looking for.

"You know, Sammie wasn't the first. Nor will he be the last. Not only was he the most recent of a long line of experiments, but he was the best. And you took him from me. Ruined him for all time. And for that I will relish what I get to do to you once this is finished."

Black acrid smoke drifted past Lily, making her eyes burn. She withheld a cough as she fought to maintain the ritual, hoping that the others would be lucid when it ended.

The mage, Nicholas, cocked a grin as he looked over his shoulder at the fiery plumes in the distance.

Lily wasn't sure what she feared more, the imposition of Mara in their realm, or that the ghost mage was becoming a fully formed specter. But it probably wasn't going to matter much longer.

"Time to die, Lilith de Meath."

THIRTY-NINE

The concrete walls of solitary confinement squeezed around her like an earthen fist. Remi pounded her palm against the floor from her position on the cot, then rolled onto her back.

How long have I been here?

Remi felt like she was supposed to remember something. Be somewhere else. Something. Anything.

She approached the door and put her mouth to the food tray slot, which had been left partially open.

"When do I get to leave? Isn't it time? Hello?"

Normally, she could hear the TV at the guard station at the end of the hall. She would amuse herself by sitting against the door so she could catch snippets of the conversation and fill in the rest with her imagination.

A series of marks on the wall had her surging forward. She was supposed to be in solitary confinement for a few weeks before getting released on her eighteenth birthday, but there were dozens and dozens of marks.

Hundreds by the count. Months of time.

Did they forget me?

Remi put a hand to her stomach. She didn't feel hungry. What was going on?

She slammed her fist against the wall. It didn't hurt as much as she thought it should, so she did it again. It was like banging against a mattress. Something was wrong. She couldn't remember why she was here, but she knew she wasn't supposed to be.

She was supposed to be somewhere else.

"The ritual—"

As soon as she said the words her memory came flooding back, followed by the thick smell of burning smoke in her nose. The burning, metallic scent was choking.

"Mara. Lily said Mara, the land of nightmares."

The words banished the vision and she was no longer standing in a small cell in Utica but the basement of Golden Willow.

She looked up to see Lily get thrown across the room by a figure in olden clothes, looking like he was going to step on the stage of an old play.

Stunned by the sudden change, she stared at her friends who were locked in their own stasis, mouths agape and eyes rolled into the backs of their heads as they twitched with nightmares.

"I'll grind your bones to dust," said the figure as he held his clawed hand out.

Lily fell to her knees choking. The color in her face was bright purple.

The memories of Remi's dreams kept her from acting right away. She felt like she was still in Utica.

As she looked around the room, she realized that the ritual had been broken, but the walls were still changing along with the ghost, who looked more physically present by the second. She knew a con when she saw one.

They'd somehow been tricked into helping the ghost return.

But why the link to Mara? Why was that long-destroyed realm opening into the basement of Golden Willow?

Her gaze fell upon the bone-like artifact upon the spirit ward as it levitated above the glass.

"No!"

Remi broke from her immobility and sprinted towards the mage. She kicked him in the ribs, which were surprisingly solid.

The impact interrupted his hold on Lily. She dropped to the ground.

But the mage slowly turned towards Remi.

She slammed him with earth magic, but he knocked it away easily. She followed up with fire and then water, but those barely made him flinch.

"A sleeper has awoken. But to no avail, little thief. Oh yes, I see you. I see you more than the others. You stink of divided loyalties. The Fae. The Veil. What did you do to have such strong scents?"

Lily was still recovering from her asphyxiation, so Remi thought to give her more time to intervene.

"Mortui mortui manebunt," she said, repeating the hospice ward's warning sign.

The mage flinched.

"How dare you?"

"Mortui mortui manebunt!"

The second time she infused it with faez, which made the mage's form ripple with uncertainty.

He stalked towards her. She opened her mouth for a third time and he snapped his hands together, silencing her. She moved her mouth but no sound would come out.

Remi bumped into an unconscious, but open-eyed Damon, moaning in fear with his claws extended.

She shook his arm but nothing happened.

"The sleeper will not awake. *You* should not be awake, but it's clear you're not quite what you seem."

The mage had almost reached her when a knot of vines burst from the concrete and wrapped around him. Lily had her hands out, controlling the plant life.

"Do you really think you can stop me?"

The mage sliced his arm downward and the vines turned to ash. Before he could return fire on Lily, a booming voice startled them.

"What is the meaning of this?"

The wealthy donor Brennan stood in the doorway, jaw rippling with anger. His eyes flamed with intensity. Remi sensed uncorked power coming to the surface.

"It's the mage. The one we told you about. We tried to banish it but it resisted us somehow," said Remi, suddenly able to speak again.

Brennan's gaze shifted over the scene from the unconscious ritualists to the mage and finally the transparent walls with the broken and fiery realm of Mara leaking through.

"I didn't think this could happen," he said, shaking his head. "I worried you wouldn't be strong enough, but clearly there is something about you all that rose to meet the challenge."

"The challenge?" asked Remi.

But as she looked across the room at Lily, she saw recognition and horror in her friend's expression. The Irish witch was already muttering under her breath, preparing a spell that looked like it was intended for Brennan.

"To open a portal to my ancestral home."

Remi's gut twisted at his answer. She looked into the burning landscape to see a wave of misshapen figures hurrying their way.

When she looked back to Brennan, his back was arched in agony. She didn't understand until his head snapped downward. A burning dot at the center of his forehead was growing in size, spreading out like a fiery eye with drips of lava at the corners.

"Balor of the Evil Eye, I banish you!"

The ripple of power that extended from Lily's hands cracked the concrete as it shot towards Brennan. Remi was expecting the once-handsome figure to get thrown out of the room, or turned to ash where they stood.

The wave barely knocked his hair out of place as he withstood the impact, followed by a burgeoning grin that seemed big enough to swallow the entire room.

"We finally meet, Lilith de Meath."

FORTY

The sulfurous fumes leaking into the basement made Lily's eyes burn as she watched the eye unfold on Brennan's forehead. As soon as he'd stepped into the room, she'd realized who he was, and why everything was happening.

Brennan Boleros was a Fomorian in disguise, and not just any being from the land of nightmares, but Balor of the Evil Eye. She'd rarely interacted with the wealthy donor, but now that she knew who he was, she realized that when she'd smelled sulfur or brimstone in the hospital, it was because of him.

Damn her Irish luck that she'd never had the chance to figure out who he was before now.

"Begone—"

The words died on her lips when he pointed his third eye at her. She dove to the side as a fiery conflagration of spewed lava annihilated the concrete where she'd been standing, landing hard on her shoulder which brought tears to her eyes, but she quickly found her feet.

To her left, Nicholas was laughing hysterically. Balor barely acknowledged the specter except for a twitch at the corner of his lips.

"Wake the others!"

Lily grew a shield of vines in time to stop the next blast from Brennan's third eye. The plant growth turned to char and fell away, but it gave her enough time to skitter to the opposite side of the basement.

The person that had been Brennan Boleros shed his human form. His already towering frame grew over a foot and his shoulders and chest expanded, shredding his expensive fitted suit, until he was rippling with gray muscles.

Lily didn't know how they were going to beat Balor if even half the legends were true.

She prepared a shield of force as Balor focused his eye upon her. The jet of lava splattered against the shimmering buffer, but sparks exploded through, charring her clothes and hair with puffs of flame. She put them out with a spell as soon as the onslaught was over.

A scream pulled her attention away for a moment to see Remi being held in the air by Nicholas.

But it wasn't Remi that had cried out.

It was her sister Alice.

A splatter of lava had splashed across her shoulder, burning away clothes and flesh.

"You bloody bastard."

She held her hands out expecting a flow of power from Medb, but remembered she was no longer connected to the ancient Fae. So she reached inside and summoned faez. Lily found depths to her magic that she didn't realize she had as her hands glowed with golden light as she shaped the magic into a shimmering spear.

"What's that going to do, little witch?"

The words had barely left Brennan's lips when she launched the weapon at his chest. The tip slammed into his breastbone, staggering him backwards, but it barely penetrated his flesh.

"You'll have to do better than that."

Brennan glanced over his shoulder at the hordes approaching from across the cracked and barren plain. If they were able to enter the hospital through the portal they'd unintentionally created, it would be a bloodbath.

The burning eye at the center of his forehead spread wider like the gates of hell opening. Lily prepared to defend herself, but the more it grew in size, the less of a chance she knew she had to survive.

FORTY-ONE

Damon was busy battering the door to his cousin Tyler's house down when something burned his arm. The smell of burning hair, followed by the searing of flesh, had him shaking off the nightmare.

He found himself in the basement of Golden Willow with a battle raging around him. A towering figure of muscle and flame was stalking after Lily, firing balls of flame at her from a spot at the center of his forehead, while Remi was being choked by a gentleman in a dusty old coat.

Two steps later, he lowered his shoulder into the man's dusty back—

But flew through him to tumble onto the concrete.

"How are you doing that?"

"It's all possible thanks to you," said the mage.

Damon leapt to his feet and sliced through the mage with his claws, but they flowed through his briefly transparent body before snapping back to bright colors.

"What the…?"

Before Damon could move, the mage put his ghostly hand into his chest. A cold fist squeezed Damon's heart, making him freeze in agony.

"Does it feel like you're having a heart attack? Because you are."

The mage squeezed and Damon nearly blacked out. As his vision wavered he saw Remi struggling against the mage, but he was too strong and the mix of corporeal and incorporeal was making it impossible to interact.

Unless...

Using his last bit of consciousness, Damon swiped through the arm that was holding up Remi.

As his fist went through the elbow, Remi fell to the ground, released by the ghostly nature of his arm.

From her knees, Remi punched the mage between the legs, which made him release Damon's heart.

"Mortui mortui manebunt!"

The words from Remi knocked the mage backwards and made his flesh flash between the physical and the Veil.

Damon had no idea how Remi was affecting him like that, but it didn't matter as long as it was working.

He tried to regain his feet, but the stress on his heart had taken the wind out of him. He struggled to even stay on his knees.

To his right, Alice was sobbing and holding her charred shoulder, and further across the circle Regina was becoming aware. She glanced towards the exit as if she were going to run.

Then he followed her vision to see Dr. Martinez stumble into the room.

"What in the infernal hells? Brennan?"

The towering figure of muscle half-turned as lava spewed from his forehead in fits.

"You shouldn't have come here and seen me like this. When all this is over, I would make you my queen."

Dr. Martinez pulled the sleeves of her white coat back to her elbows.

"You can eat a bag of dicks," she said as she thrust her hands forward with a potent force blast that knocked him back two steps.

Brennan cracked his neck. "You shouldn't have done that, Christina."

He opened his arms wide and the eye burned bright, sending a geyser of flame directly at her. She threw up a force shield, but the impact was burning through. In a few seconds, she would be turned to char.

Damon tried to climb to his feet, but he stumbled back to his knees from the painful effort.

As much as he didn't want to see it, they were losing.

The ghostly mage was calling spirits from the Veil to attack Remi, who was valiantly defending herself, but their numbers were growing and she was only one person.

Towards the back of the basement, Lily was lying in a heap with her clothes half-burned off with her equally injured younger sister limping over to help.

The only person unhurt and unengaged was Regina, but she looked like she was trying to slip away.

Then he made the mistake of checking back to the transparent wall where the hundreds of Fomorians were streaming towards the portal. Soon enough, they'd be overrun and there'd be nothing they could do to stop Brennan or the mage from destroying the hospital.

The torrent of flame was overwhelming Dr. Martinez's force shield. In a few seconds she'd be obliterated and turned to dust. Damon tried one last time to regain his feet, but it was like his legs had been turned to water.

The world flashed bright as if the flame had finally broken through her shield.

Damon opened his eyes to find that not only was her shield still in place, but it was stronger. He didn't understand until he saw Dr. Decker at her side.

But Brennan was keeping up the flame and Damon saw that they didn't have much longer.

Damon fought to his knees and despite the feeling that his heart was going to explode, he launched an ice ball from his fist. The crusty object slammed against the side of Brennan's head, interrupting the flow of flame.

"I knew I didn't like you," said Dr. Decker, heaving from effort.

He was wearing a pair of unicorn pajamas and looked like he'd just woken up from a two-day bender with his hair going in all directions.

"It's not going to matter," said Brennan, smirking from his position near the shimmering wall. "You're not strong enough to stop me *and* close the portal. If you leave now, maybe you can evacuate your patients in time before the killing starts. It's your choice. Leave now and you can save lives."

FORTY-TWO

After Remi kicked the ghost mage in the groin which distracted him to release Damon's heart, she tried to hit the incorporeal being with a sputtering flame bolt, but the conflagration flared and sparks barely impacted her target.

Nicholas glanced to the battle between Dr. Martinez and Brennan. A grin hitched itself to his lips.

"You're losing."

Remi found it hard to disagree. Both de Meath sisters were injured, Damon could barely stand, and a murderous horde of Fomorians were about to breach the portal.

And she still hadn't figured out a way to get rid of the ghost mage.

"Mortui mortui manebunt," she spat for a third time, but Nicholas barely flinched.

"Oh, the things I could do with your flesh. Maybe I was wrong to choose Sammie, but little did I know that my dying would bring me my biggest opportunity."

"You're a sick fuck, you know that."

Nicholas lunged forward and shoved his hand into her chest, but she knocked it away before he could reach her heart.

"You shouldn't be able to do that," said Nicholas.

"And you shouldn't be here."

The battle was raging behind her but she knew the best she could do was to distract the mage so the others could deal with Brennan. Remi looked for a clue to his ability to affect their world so easily. It shouldn't have been possible.

She saw past him into the Veil to see other creatures lurking right behind him, looking for a way in, which didn't make sense since they'd only summoned Nicholas. The transparent wall leading to Mara was also strange.

It wasn't until she checked back to the bone-like artifact hovering over the glass case for the spirit ward that she realized why it was happening.

Before they'd thought the artifact a boon because it'd come from their wealthy benefactor, but now she saw the con in its entirety. Brennan had given them the magical item knowing that it would break down the barriers between realms. She had no idea what it was but it was clearly making it easier for the mage and the Fomorians to reach their world.

The ghost mage saw the direction of her gaze and his jaw stiffened, which only confirmed her suspicions.

Before she could shout or move towards the artifact, Nicholas surged forward, reaching into her chest.

But she grabbed his arm before he could reach her heart.

"You...shouldn't...be able to...do that."

"And you look like you're trying to cosplay as a hobo," she said, kicking his shin as a distraction.

Right behind him in the Veil were figures cloaked in greenish mist, looking like they were trying to come through. When she looked directly at the mage, she could see a shimmering field around him like a doorway, but when she turned her head it was gone.

Remi had no idea what kind of beings lurked in the Veil, but they had to be better than the asshole she was battling with.

"Hey, you with the black eyes."

She didn't think it was going to work, but then the figure shifted forward until he was lurking on Nicholas' shoulder.

"If you drag him back to the Veil, I'll let you come through."

Black eyes shined bright for a few seconds and then it shifted away and out of sight.

"Damnit."

The mage doubled his efforts and his hand went further into Remi's chest. She felt his cold hands brush her heart, giving her a burst of energy to push him back.

All the while, the rest of the basement was in full battle. Flame and sparks were exploding everywhere from the impact of Brennan's lava eye against the force shield. Sometime during her interaction with the mage, Dr. Decker had entered, but Remi was too busy fighting for her life to watch what he was doing.

As Nicholas' hand collapsed around her heart, she knew exactly what it was like to know she was going to die. Remi wondered if that's how Odette had felt on those last days, experiencing the final moments of existence. Did she wish for more? Or for it to be over quicker?

"Take him back," she said, hoping the Veil beings could hear her. "Take him. He's not supposed to be here."

Her vision faltered as his hand squeezed around her heart. The end was coming quick. She could feel the warm embrace of death rising up to meet her. Soon she would be in the Veil, maybe briefly, then to the endless void.

When sight started to come back, she didn't understand. Had she died and returned for vengeance already? No. That didn't make sense.

Then she saw hands reaching out of the greenish mist, pulling Nicholas backwards as he fought to stay in the Golden Willow basement.

His hand was no longer in her chest. She could hardly stand. She'd been on the precipice of death and had returned.

But she watched as the other beings in the Veil, jealous of Nicholas, or at her suggestion—she was certain she would never know the truth—dragged him back into the place between the living and the dead.

FORTY-THREE

"You're hurt," Alice told Lily near the back of the basement where she'd been forced to retreat from Balor's attacks.

"I'm fine," said Lily, trying to regain her feet, but she'd been badly burned across her shoulder and thigh. The meat of her leg looked like BBQ and she couldn't get the smell of it out of her nose.

"You can't even stand."

"If we can't stop him, then we're all going to be dead. There's no time for healing."

Alice's eyes rounded.

"Is there anything we can even do right now?"

Lily grimaced as she made it back to one leg, balancing as she watched Dr. Martinez and Dr. Decker barely survive the onslaught from the Fomorian king. The continuous jet of fiery lava blasted the force shield the two doctors had put up.

Then Lily saw the bone-like artifact hovering over the spirit ward.

"We have to close the portal."

She took a step on her bad leg and nearly fell. Alice caught her but Lily cried out.

"You can't walk."

Lily gritted her teeth. "Hold me up while I cast this spell."

Alice grabbed her around the waist as Lily started working through the gestures required to apply a pain blocker. It was a really bad idea to ignore the pain from a gruesome injury. She was only going to make her wounds worse, but if she didn't they were all going to die.

When the spell took hold it was as if a breeze wafted through her carrying all the pain away.

"Bloody hell, that's better."

"What do we do now?"

"We have to destroy that artifact. It's making the barrier between realms thin."

Lily hobbled over to the glass box with the spirit ward inside. The eldritch runes were pulsing erratically, flashing with sparks, while the artifact vibrated above like water on a hot surface.

As she reached out to brush the wards to get an idea of their condition, she received a painful shock.

"Bollocks."

"It's been electrified," said Alice.

"Not quite. The misaligned magical fields are causing friction like rubbing your socks on the carpet."

Lily tried again, except she reached for the artifact, but received the same painful shock that felt like getting punched in the arm.

"We need to unwind the spell," said Lily.

"Can we do that?"

Lily saw the battle between Balor and the doctors was getting worse.

If they didn't do something soon, he'd be free to interfere again.

"It won't be easy, but follow my lead."

Normally ending an enchantment that she'd help create would be much simpler but they'd tied the artifact into the hospital's wards, which gave it extra protection. It was like a second generator, except this one was breaking down the barrier between realms as a bonus.

It took two more tries to find a way in without getting shocked. She had to find a loose thread to tug on like unraveling a difficult knot.

Lily tried not to get distracted by the state of the battle, but she could hear Dr. Decker screaming over the din. It was taking everything they had to keep Balor from annihilating them.

The knot proved resilient, even with Alice's help. Lily realized that not only was she not strong enough, but it would need a third person. But as she checked around the room, she no longer saw Regina, and Remi was entangled with the ghost mage Nicholas.

"We can't do it, can we?" asked Alice.

Lily looked to the transparent wall. The Fomorian horde was almost to the gate. They carried barbed spears and other gruesome weapons with far too many hooks. If they got loose in the hospital, it'd be a bloodbath.

"We can try."

Lily refocused on the knot, but every time she tried to pull apart the threads they snapped back together. She needed to be stronger, or they needed a third person.

They had time enough for one last try.

As Lily teased the threads apart, searching for the end which she could unravel, she felt them straining to close. The magical energies flowing through the wards and the artifact were making them resistant to being modified. It was like trying to rewire an active generator.

Then miraculously, the threads spread apart.

Lily didn't understand until she checked to her right to see Biddy weaving golden faez into a potent hook.

She almost faltered in surprise, but caught herself, briefly giving her eldest sister a grin before returning to the magical knot.

With Biddy's help, Lily was able to dive into the center and grab the thread she'd been searching for. Once she yanked it from the interior, Lily cut the line and the artifact clattered onto the glass.

Every light in the basement exploded.

The walls flashed from transparent to solid and back before settling on the dull gray concrete with warding runes.

"No!"

Balor sent a geyser of lava into the ceiling as he leaned back in rage. His eye opened wider and Lily sensed a great destruction was going to be unleashed.

"Shall we, sisters?" asked Biddy.

"It would be my pleasure."

Lily stood with Alice and Biddy on either side.

They didn't even have to rehearse as they'd grown up being taught the danger of the Fomorians. Every de Meath child knew the words to a banishing.

The words came like hammer blows, slamming into Balor as he tried to refocus his fiery eye. Each syllable, reinforced thrice, pushed the Fomorian king backwards until his back was against the wall.

In the nearly three years since she'd given up her connection to Medb, Lily hadn't realized how much she longed for that link to her sisters. It wasn't the power she missed, but the familiar bond, and hearing her voice repeated twice more was like hearing the winds of Ireland whisper through the trees.

"Dúisigh ó do thromluí!"

The wall around Balor briefly turned transparent and the Fomorian king was sucked back through the barrier to the realm of Mara.

#

For the first few minutes after the battle, Lily was barely conscious. After Balor had been banished, the injuries she'd been suppressing caught up to her and she collapsed on the concrete.

But luckily for her, she was in a room full of healers.

She became aware that she was being held up by Biddy as Dr. Martinez and Dr. Decker finished the final touches of the flesh-repairing spell.

"It's going to hurt like hell for the next week, but I think we got to it quick enough to keep the scarring down," said Dr. Martinez, patting her leg.

The room looked like it'd been through a major fire with scorch marks along the walls. Black smoke lingered near the ceiling.

"It could have been worse."

Alice was kneeling on the opposite side, holding Lily's hand, but her focus was on their eldest sister. Her lips were squeezed white.

"Biddy?" asked Alice.

"Aye?"

"Are you mad at me?"

The two doctors glanced at each other and then quickly stepped away to where Damon and Regina were in full discussion.

"Yes. You betrayed my trust and freed your sister."

Lily's spine stiffened. She'd hoped their battle might have released the tension between them.

Biddy's mouth twitched as she tried to start the words. After a few tries, she eventually spoke in a low, quivering voice.

"But I'm also extremely proud of you, because I was being a right eejit. I thought I knew what was best for everyone, but I was wrong," said Biddy with her head bowed.

Lily squeezed her sister's hand.

"I know you mean well."

"Aye, but I nearly let our enemies poke a hole in the realms because of my arrogance. Maybe there is a reason you're here at Aura Healers."

Biddy leaned over and kissed Lily on the forehead.

"I'm sorry, Lily. I truly am."

"Apology accepted."

Lily glanced past her sister to see Remi speaking with a trio of ghostly figures shrouded in green mist.

"What's going on there?" she asked in alarm.

Alice cracked a smile.

"I don't know, but it doesn't seem bad. They came through right after she banished the mage back to the Veil. She's been talking to them for the last few minutes while we worked on you."

To Lily's surprise, the three shrouded figures bowed to Remi and then walked through the spirit ward and disappeared, presumably to the Veil.

"Someone help me up. I'm tired of sitting."

Between her two sisters, she was lifted easily. There was a slight ache as she put weight on her recently burned leg, but it wasn't bad enough that she couldn't stand on her own.

"What was that?" she asked Remi.

"We had a little conversation. I asked them nicely if they could return to their home. They seemed okay with the request."

"Talking with ghosts?"

Remi shifted her mouth to the side. "I don't think they were ghosts."

"Then what?"

Her friend's forehead knitted at the center.

"I don't know."

Remi jutted her chin to the two doctors across the room. They were huddled close with their arms around each other, whispering quietly.

"That's good to see," said Lily.

"But not that," said Remi, frowning after Regina, who stalked out of the room in a huff.

Damon approached, scratching the back of his neck.

"Problems?" asked Lily.

"She wants her payment. I promised I'd have sex with her if she would help with the ritual. I tried to convince her not to accept, but she's adamant about it."

"Remi?"

She gave a weak shrug.

"It was the only way."

Biddy touched her on the arm.

"What about...?"

"I was thinking the same thing," said Lily.

"What are you two talking about?" asked Damon.

Lily let a smile bloom on her lips.

"I have a plan."

FORTY-FOUR

The empty dorm room had been converted into an exquisite bedroom. Two bunks had been shoved together to create a king-sized bed, covered in silk sheets, and a dozen fluffy pillows. The walls had been hung with colorful tapestries, while candles flickered on the end tables to the scents of vanilla and lavender. Light meandering mood music set the scene.

"It looks really good," said Remi, scratching the back of her neck.

"It was the best I could do with short notice," said Alice, kneading her hands in front of her.

"It'll be perfect," said Lily, putting a hand on Alice's shoulder.

Remi saw the way Lily was still favoring one leg and wearing a slight grimace. "Are you okay?"

"It'll get better. The skin is healing and pulling taut. Dr. Martinez ordered a salve of camazotz glands to rub on the wound, which should help it relax enough to heal correctly."

"Oh, speaking of salves," said Alice, pulling a jar of lubricant out of her backpack along with some other toys.

She set them on the table and quickly returned to the hallway as if she wasn't allowed to be in the room too long.

"I think that's everything," said Alice.

"Where's the happy couple?" asked Remi.

As if summoned by the question, she heard Regina's voice coming from around the corner.

"...and then she mixed the base wrong, which was *such* a surprise," said Regina, her voice oozing with sarcasm.

Damon appeared with Regina on his arm. She was wearing a slinky black dress that looked like a few strips of black fabric had been glued on while her date was wearing scrubs.

"Oh," said Regina, stopping short and staring directly at Remi. "I didn't think *you'd* be here."

The lab technician pulled Damon tighter while he was looking in all directions rather than make eye contact.

"We were just finishing up preparations," said Alice with a curtsey.

Regina poked her head into the room and cooed with surprise. "It's wonderful. I mean, for an Aura Healer dorm room. I still don't know why I couldn't take him back to my place."

"I put a sound blocker on the window and door so you won't hear any sirens, nor will anything going on in the room make it to the hallway," said Alice.

Regina squinted at Remi.

"I don't know what to say. I half expected you to back out on the agreement."

"You helped us save the hospital, and maybe the city. You deserve your reward," said Remi tightly.

Regina looked between her and Damon while squeezing him even tighter to her side.

"I guess it's a good thing he lost his voice in the battle, so he doesn't have to make this any more awkward than it is," said Regina, staring back.

"Right," said Remi, adding a two-fingered salute. "We'll be taking our leave."

She turned and hooked her arm with Lily's as they went the opposite direction.

Alice waved cheerily and said, "Have a good time!"

Lily elbowed Alice in the ribs.

"Sorry. I couldn't help it," said Alice with a grin between her teeth.

Regina stared down the hallway suspiciously before disappearing with Damon into the room.

"Do you think she knows?" asked Remi.

Lily shifted her mouth to the side. "Doubtful."

"What I want to know is, what is she? I caught a hint of Fae when we were in the basement," asked Alice.

"Aye," said Lily with a nod. "She's either an old witch, a cat Sith, or another shapeshifter. But does it really matter as long as she feels she got what she wanted?"

"No, I guess it doesn't," said Alice.

Remi screwed up her face. "What did she want? You know, besides the obvious."

"Damon comes from a powerful lineage, all the way back to King Nuada. It might be that she wanted a piece of that. Or she just wanted the hot guy in the scrubs."

Remi cocked a smile. "Both are equally valid, though I prefer the latter." She checked her phone. "I have to go. Thanks for the help with Regina."

FORTY-FIVE

The student common area was packed with the rest of Damon's class. He sat on the lime green couch with his arm around Remi, who was studying a spell on her phone while they waited for their instructor to arrive.

"I thought you were all caught up on the reading?" he asked, giving her a soft elbow.

She surfaced from her study. "Not for Decker."

"Who's it for?"

The answer never came because Lily arrived and threw herself onto the couch next to them. She had a wild grin on her lips which matched her unruly rainbow-colored hair.

"What's with you?" asked Damon.

"Guess who I just saw in the parking lot," said Lily, pumping her eyebrows.

"The White Worm?" asked Remi playfully.

"Be serious."

"The Oak Father," said Damon, receiving another elbow to the ribs.

"Not either of those, you ninnies. It was Regina. She was packing up her work gear. After I saw her, I ran down to talk to Morehouse. He said she put in her resignation."

"Really?" asked Damon, scrunching up his forehead. "I thought she really wanted her reward?"

Remi punched him in the ribs. "Why? Did you *really* want to give it to her?"

He shook his head, realizing his mistake. "No. I was just curious. Neither of you idiots would tell me what you had planned and then I got so busy, I sort of forgot it."

"A likely story," said Remi, patting his thigh.

Damon checked between the two women. "So is anyone going to tell me?"

"She got her reward," said Lily.

"She did?"

A tiny squeak issued from Lily's mess of hair.

"More than once, actually," said Lily.

The realization sunk into Damon as he leaned back into the uncomfortable couch.

"Oh."

A hush came over the room. Damon spotted Dr. Decker and Dr. Martinez in the hallway huddled intimately together. The two doctors entered holding hands, which prompted whistles and applause.

Dr. Martinez suddenly realized that she was in front of her students and released Decker's hand. He gave the class a wink which received a bout of laughter.

"Alright, you maniacs, settle down," said Dr. Martinez, rolling her eyes at Oren. "I have some news."

"Does it involve bells and something blue?" asked Boon. "Dibs on maid of honor."

Her cheeks flushed crimson as she glanced at her left hand before shoving it behind her back.

"We're here to talk about the hospital. I wanted to let you all know that despite the interruption to our normal smooth working operations in Golden Willow..."

She paused, which elicited a round of chuckles.

"We managed to confiscate a large portion of Mr. Boleros' funds, which will be applied immediately to the renovations."

They broke into applause.

After it was over, Sasha raised her hand.

"Are we going to get to learn what happened a few weeks ago?"

She shot the residents of the lime green couch a look. All three of them gave her a shoulder shrug.

"While we'd love to talk about the events of that day," said Dr. Martinez, "if it got out, it would do great harm to the hospital's reputation, so we ask that you keep your curiosity sated with funds that we recovered."

Damon whispered into Remi's ear.

"Recovered? Is that why you were gone last week with Decker?"

Remi mimed zipping her mouth closed.

Dr. Decker stepped forward. "While we're here, I thought I would announce where everyone will be studying the next two years."

Boon held up both arms. "Sex clinic!"

"We don't have a sex clinic," said Bryan, tilting his head.

"We could," replied Boon.

"Alright children, settle down," said Dr. Martinez while trying not to break into a grin.

Remi's knee was bouncing. He leaned into her ear.

"I thought you hadn't picked yet?"

She swallowed and bit her lower lip. Damon had never seen her so nervous. She tapped him on the thigh and pointed to the two doctors at the front of the room.

"…Boon will be in the ER, good luck."

"It's the closest I can get to the sex clinic. Am I right, Half-Pint?" asked Boon, half-turning.

Remi extended a middle finger.

"Ethan in Supernaturals. Sasha in Maternity. Bryan in Supernaturals. Damon in Children's Ward. Lily in Curses. And last but not least, Remi in—"

Remi sat tall.

"I haven't finalized it yet."

"Really?" asked Dr. Martinez with her head tilted.

"I was busy, but I'd like to confirm before we announce it," said Remi.

"Fair enough. I'll let you tell everyone on your own time. Oren?"

Dr. Decker stepped forward with his hands behind his back. He looked strangely subdued compared to the wild vagabond that had appeared their first day.

"I, or we, have one final announcement. I will be taking a leave of absence from the hospital. I think it would be appropriate for me to work on some personal issues before I can be an effective instructor or doctor again."

The entire class shifted forward while Damon felt a pit open in his stomach. While the eccentric doctor had taken getting used to, Damon had no doubt that he'd been an effective teacher, especially with the strangeness of their days.

"I'm very sorry to leave you after three years, but I think it's for the best."

"Where are you going?" asked Sasha.

He reached over and grabbed Dr. Martinez's hand. "We're heading to Krakatow first. I have some friends who could use a couple of medics during the faez storm season, and then after that, I don't know. We're going to take some time to relax. There are some beaches there without another soul within a hundred miles. Or maybe we'll head to another realm entirely."

"One with a good rave scene?" asked Boon, smirking.

Dr. Decker sighed heavily.

"No rave scenes. I think it's time I dealt with some things I've been putting off for a long, long time."

"But don't worry," said Dr. Martinez, holding back tears. "You're not rid of us yet. We'll be with you until the end of July."

"And then?" asked Ethan.

"We don't know who Dr. Fairlight will choose as our replacements, but I'm sure they'll be top notch. You deserve as much."

The meeting ended and the rest of the class swarmed the two doctors to give them hugs and tell them how much they were going to miss them. Damon would have joined, but Remi grabbed his hand.

"Children's Ward?" asked Remi. "I figured you for Supernaturals with your background."

Damon bit his lower lip and nodded. A little knot in his chest loosened slightly with the knowledge of his choice in the open.

"I know what it's like to go through trauma at that age. I think I'd be best suited to help Dr. Lara."

"You'd be great anywhere," said Remi. "I'm glad you were able to make your choice."

"What about yours?"

Remi leaned her head back and groaned. "I hate making decisions like this."

"It's not forever. Just a couple of years. You don't have to make it your specialty."

Remi squeezed her lips together. "But ninety percent of students do."

Damon chuckled. "Which probably means that it doesn't really matter where you go. We'll do the best we can in any department."

The fear in her eyes was palpable.

"Or once we make that decision, we're stuck because we never want to go back and have to relearn a whole new ward."

He cocked his mouth to the side. "Yeah, you're probably right. Stuck forever. Maybe you let them pick for you."

"And chance getting stuck with Dr. Paddock for the next two years? No thanks."

A round of buzzers had the entire class checking their phones.

"Excellent! A four-beller in the ER," said Boon with his eyes alight. "I'm free. Anyone else to join us?"

Most of the class had other duties, but Damon raised his hand.

"I can join. What about you, Remi?"

She closed her eyes briefly.

"I have to go talk to someone."

"Good luck," said Damon as he rose to his feet.

"I wish luck mattered."

FORTY-SIX

Stepping into the hospice ward left Remi feeling subdued as if there were the beginnings of a funeral. There were no beeps or other monitoring equipment like the other areas of the hospital and the staff talked in hushed tones.

Remi touched the plaque near the swinging doors.

"Mortui mortui manebunt," she said softly, appreciating the power in the words that had helped her with the ghost, Nicholas.

She turned around, only to find the skeletal doctor standing only a few feet away. Remi let out an exclamation of surprise.

"My apologies," said Dr. Stéphane Morsdux. "You seem quite intrigued by the plaque."

Remi smiled wistfully.

"They're very powerful words."

"Are they?" he asked with his head tilted.

Remi swallowed and stared at her feet. She didn't know how to begin.

"Would you like to walk with me? I have rounds," said Dr. Morsdux.

"That would be nice."

She rolled her eyes at herself for the use of the word, but Dr. Morsdux had already headed down the hallway. He moved like an apparition, his feet barely leaving the tiles, making it appear he was floating.

When they entered a familiar room, Remi was expecting to see Miss Donal in the bed, but it was an older, unconscious man on a breathing apparatus. He wore no gown on his upper body and a set of glowing runes had been drawn on his chest.

"Where is the previous...?"

"Miss Donal? Her disease finally claimed her."

"Oh," said Remi, feeling a heaviness in her chest.

She helped Dr. Morsdux renew the spells that were keeping a parasite in the patient's chest from growing larger. They were preserving his life for a few more days so his family could say their final goodbyes.

"Does it get any easier?" she asked outside. "Dealing with death all the time?"

"Do you want it to?"

The question knocked her back. She jawed at the air.

"I...I don't know. Maybe?"

"We are merely custodians in this life. Even the most powerful mages succumb eventually," said Dr. Morsdux.

After having spent a few years dealing with insane, supernatural threats, Remi wasn't sure she agreed. There were a lot of very old beings with too much power lurking around the realms.

In the next few rooms, Remi watched as Dr. Morsdux chatted with the dying patients. Despite his haunting looks, the patients seemed warm to his interactions. Maybe they saw him as a visage of death and his kindness made their passing easier?

"You strangely have a knack with them," said Remi.

"You seem surprised," said Dr. Morsdux.

"I'm sorry it came out like that."

He turned and faced her with cavernous eyes. "You're worried that you won't be able to do the same."

She groaned internally at how easily he pierced her exterior.

"Is it really just this? Walking around and checking on dying patients? Trying to give them a semblance of peace before they go?"

Dr. Morsdux glanced away. He stared into the distance for a time.

"I think you know the answer already. Mortui mortui manebunt. The dead shall remain dead."

Remi didn't know if he knew about what had happened in the basement with Nicholas, or the other beings from the Veil.

"What if I'm not a good fit?"

Dr. Morsdux raised a fuzzy white eyebrow.

"I don't think you would be here if you didn't believe that it could be possible. Some students refuse to meet me because they're only concerned about saving people."

"Like Dr. Decker."

"In his younger days, he called my department the Ward of Bones."

"You were around when he was here before?"

"Not many doctors want to take my place," said Dr. Morsdux.

She realized that he might be much older than she originally thought.

"I never expected to be in Aura Healers," said Remi.

Dr. Morsdux put his hands behind his back.

"If you join my ward, I cannot promise you fame and fortune. There will be no charity events, no hobnobbing with donors, or conferences paid for by D'Agastine Industries so you can sit on a beach for a week. You won't save any patients. Without question, they're all going to die.

"In the hospice ward, or the death ward, if you prefer, the best we can do is to help them travel over the horizon with peace and dignity. And help make sure they do *not come back*."

The weight of his final words hit her firmly in the chest as she thought about the beings from the Veil. Remi was sure she wouldn't be standing in Dr. Morsdux's ward had she not had that experience. The day after, Lily confessed to her that it shouldn't have been possible, which made her question herself. Remi wondered if it was lingering guilt from when she was in Utica and severely injured the Scythe sister. While she'd never heard the fate of the girl, Remi had always feared the worst.

"Is there something you want to tell me?" asked Dr. Morsdux.

The urge to reveal what had happened in the basement was strong, but she'd promised not to tell anyone else, and she feared that it would sound like bragging, or exaggeration.

"Before I give you my answer, can I ask how many Aura Healer students you have each year?"

"Each year?" he repeated, chuckling, which made his bony shoulders bounce up and down. "My dear Remington, excuse me, Remi. But I haven't had a student choose my ward in thirteen years. Very few choose to work here for many reasons, many of them I completely understand and agree with. But that does not make what we do here any less important. If you don't, I understand, but in this case I think it would be a mistake. There's something about you that tells me this is the right place for you."

"Why's that?"

He squeezed his lips tight.

"I wish I could tell you. Maybe it's an old man's fantasies about finding someone to replace him, or maybe after dealing with death and the Veil for this long, I can see when someone has a gift. Either way, I cannot make the decision for you."

When she opened her mouth, she thought it would feel weighty, but it was the exact opposite. Remi felt a weight lift from her shoulders as she gave him an answer.

“My parents named me Remington because they lost a bet.”

Dr. Morsdux raised an eyebrow.

“Interesting. Is there a reason you’ve chosen to tell me?”

“See you in a few months.”

FORTY-SEVEN

Lily was standing outside of a patient's room reading their chart when she saw her sisters standing at the corner. Alice was wearing a bright pink backpack over a Hundred Halls hoodie while Biddy was wearing her normal drab dress.

"I'll be with you in a minute, Miss Abel."

She hung the chart on the hook and headed to her sisters.

"You look like one of them," said Biddy tightly.

Lily checked herself to see what her sister was talking about. She was wearing a white jacket over scrubs with three pens sticking out the pocket and a matching fanny pack filled with alchemical reagents.

"One of them?"

Biddy's mouth screwed up as her eyes uncharacteristically rounded. Her eldest sister seemed to be working through her thoughts, which only made it look like she was in pain.

"I'll always be a de Meath," said Lily.

Biddy hung her head.

"Mother will think I failed."

"You know, everyone always said you look like her, but I think that's bollocks."

Biddy's head snapped up.

"You remind me of Medb more than anything. You've always been a warrior for this family," said Lily.

The glistening in Biddy's eyes forced her to look away as she squeezed back her emotions.

"I'll tell them it's best that you stay in the city of sorcery. We can't miss any chance to fix Medb."

"I didn't want to come here either," said Lily. "But once I did, I realized it was the right choice. The battle is not going to be in the Old Country. I don't know if it's going to be here, but I know this is where I need to be. I wish you were staying. We wouldn't have beat Balor without you both."

"I'm not going back," said Alice suddenly, catching them both by surprise.

"You're not?"

Alice couldn't take Biddy's heavy gaze.

"I'm not joining the Halls or anything crazy like that." Her eyes widened. "Sorry, Lily."

"I understand, little sister."

"But I can't go back, not after seeing this place, experiencing what the city has to offer."

"What are you going to do?" asked Biddy.

Alice lowered her chin. "I'm going to work for Lady Nimueh."

"What?" asked Biddy, her voice echoing in the hallway.

"Not like that, sister. Not that there's anything wrong with it. She wants me to work with her staff. Healing their aches, making sure none of the clients get out of hand. I know, I know, it's not what you expected of me, and Mother will be cross, but I couldn't go back. Not after seeing what I've seen here. And I know it would be good to have another de Meath in town."

"I don't know what to say," said Biddy.

Alice grabbed Biddy's hands. "I know this is going to make it harder to go back. But I swear this is the right choice for me."

Biddy's mouth shifted to the side, before wrinkling with emotion. She stared into the distance.

"It's not that."

"Then what is it?" asked Alice.

The ache in Biddy's gaze was almost unrecognizable. Lily had rarely seen anything but stern disapproval in her sister's eyes in the last decade. But there was a time she remembered her sister's laughter, when she was a young witch still learning the arts. Biddy wanted to stay too. But her responsibilities had tied her to the family, to Mother, and most importantly to Medb.

"Oh, Bridget."

Lily pulled Biddy into her arms, squeezing her tight and feeling a gentle release in her sister's chest.

"Don't worry, sister," Lily whispered in her ear. "I've got you. I came to the Halls for a reason. And that's to fix Medb. I swear to you that I will find a way. I know it doesn't seem like it's possible right now, but I've already had to deal with a Green Man, King Nuada's heir, and now Balor of the Evil Eye. If that doesn't tell you that I'm not in the right place, then I don't know what would."

Biddy pulled away. "King Nuada's heir?"

"Oh, did I not tell you that part?"

Biddy's lips squeezed to a knife-like line and Lily thought she was going to get yelled at, when her sister broke with an exhausted smile.

"I'm sure you have your reasons. And you're right. This place seems to be the center of things. Maybe you'll find the answer here. And thank you. It's nice knowing that I'm not the only one carrying the load."

"If you want to go fast, go alone, if you want to go far, go together," said Lily.

Biddy nodded.

"You have two great friends."

"I have two great sisters, too."

"What are you going to do now?" asked Biddy.

"We still know so little. Where did the corruption come from? Where is the Oak Father? How to fix it? But I feel it in my bones that we're circling around the truth, as if it's right under our bloody noses."

"I see that too," said Biddy, nodding, then after glancing at a clock on the wall sighing heavily. "I need to get to the airport."

Lily threw her arms around Biddy, hugging her tight until her older sister forced her to let go. Then Alice did the same, which brought wetness to both their eyes.

"Give everyone my love. Evangel, Nyx, Zella, Kerensa...tell them I miss them madly and wouldn't be sad if they came to visit, or at least wrote me a letter."

"Evangel and Nyx would have to stop torturing them boys to do that," said Biddy with a smirk. "But I'll tell them."

"Tell Mother too."

A tightness formed at Biddy's eyes. "I will."

"I'll walk you out," said Alice as she grabbed Biddy's duffle bag. "And see you around, sister."

Lily stayed in the middle of the hallway, watching them disappear around the corner, and wondered if that proclamation about nearing the answer had been wishful thinking or the gut-honest truth.

A tiny squeak issued from her hair. Lily reached up to touch a wet nose.

"You're going to miss her?"

A second squeak had Lily chuckling with understanding.

"That's not a very nice thing to say, Little One. But maybe one day you'll learn to love Biddy as much as I do. She means well, even if she's as bloody headstrong as a mule."

A third squeak had her tilting her head.

"Me? Well that's it. No fresh cookies from the bakery for you," said Lily, laughing as she returned to her patient's room, grabbing the chart on the way in.

"How are you today, Miss Abel? Ready for that aura cleansing? Good. Let me grab the divining rod and get things started."

§ § §

This ends the third book of the Aura Healers Hall series. Stayed tuned for the fourth book:

TWILIGHT HORN

Special Thanks

From the ashes of failure, new growth can form.

As my newsletter readers know, this series started off as something entirely different. I wrote a book that once I got to the end I realized was neither a Hundred Halls story, nor was good enough to publish. Yet, without it, this series wouldn't exist in the wonderful form that it does. For that I have to thank my best friend and wife of twenty-seven years, Rachel, for her excellent advice as we discusssed what I should do with that failed book on the way to see Phish in Denver for four days. That conversation helped me find clarity of where I'd gone wrong as well as how to start over with fresh eyes.

I must also thank my team who help make each novel as best as it can be: Sasha Almazan & Gene Mollica from GS Covers, Tamara Blain from A Closer Look Editing, the beta reader team (Tina Rak, Andie Alessandra Cáomhanach, Lana Turner, Phyllis Simpson, and Melanie Coupland), as well as my writing group that we affectionately call the Murder Cabin (Andrea Stewart, Anthea Lawson/Sharp, Annie Bellet, Megan O'Keefe, Marina J. Lostetter, Jamie Thornton, and Tina Gower). Additionally, the Vanguard plays defense for little errors that sneak through the cracks, and for this book, I have Leslie King, Debbie Davis, Phyllis Simpson, and Brian Busby to thank!

ABOUT THE AUTHOR

Thomas K. Carpenter resides in Colorado with his wife Rachel. When he's not busy writing his next book, he's hiking, skiing, and getting beat by his wife at cards. He keeps a regular blog at www.thomaskcarpenter.com and you can follow him on twitter @thomaskcarpente. If you want to learn when his next novel will be hitting the shelves and get free stories and occasional other goodies, please sign up for his mailing list by going to: http://tinyurl.com/thomaskcarpenter. Your email address will never be shared and you can unsubscribe at any time.

www.ingramcontent.com/pod-product-compliance
Lightning Source LLC
Chambersburg PA
CBHW030423310726
48979CB00009B/1593/J

* 9 7 8 1 9 5 8 4 9 8 2 5 5 *